# ESCAPE
## FROM
# FRED

# BRAD WHITTINGTON

# ESCAPE FROM FRED

BROADMAN
& HOLMAN
PUBLISHERS

NASHVILLE, TENNESSEE

13-digit ISBN: 978-0-8054-3159-9
10-digit ISBN: 0-8054-3159-4

Published by Broadman & Holman Publishers,
Nashville, Tennessee

Dewey Decimal Classification: F
Subject Heading:  CHRISTIAN LIFE–FICTION
                  DISCIPLESHIP–FICTION

Scripture citation is from the King James Version of the Bible
and the Holy Bible, New International Version, © 1973, 1978,
1984 by International Bible Society.

Quoted material on page 56, chapter 7, in Jack Kerouac, *On the
Road* (New York: Penguin Books, 1999); first published by Viking
Press, 1957.

06  07  08  09  10    15  14  13  12  11  10  9  8  7  6  5  4  3  2  1

**To The Woman:**
There are many stars
And a handful of planets
But there is only one sun
Which outshines them all

Faith is measured breathing in the face of uncertainty.
Faith is turning your heart to faithful living
when your mind has reached the end of its rope.
Faith is the choice you make when you face the darkness.

– Gordon Atkinson,
"Turtles All the Way Down,"
www.reallivepreacher.com

# CHAPTER ONE

I awoke in the dark, unsure where I was. The pain in my back indicated that wherever I was, it wasn't at home in bed.

I pulled myself up by what appeared to be the arms of a chair. My fingers settled into the smooth grooves of wooden hand rests. I swung my right arm around and banged against the vertical shaft of a floor lamp and followed it up to the switch.

I was sitting in an armchair with brown upholstery, matching ottoman at my feet. A bed lay to my right, unmolested, made with military corners. Against the far wall, a roll-top desk with swivel chair, IBM Selectric blocking the pigeonholes, a gray wooden file cabinet to the right. To the other side of the bed—a door, shower and toilet visible within.

I exhaled and settled back into my grandmother's chair. I was in Dad's study in Fred, Texas. I checked my watch. Three A.M. The midnight of the soul as Bradbury called it. A fading echo of images from my dreams swirled in my brain—a pale woman clothed like Godiva, hand outstretched, a red dirt hill, a white steeple against a cobalt sky, the ferric taste of blood, the musty scent of pine pitch, the sensation of pine needles pressed into my cheek. My hand reflexively stroked the pale scars on my face.

"The mark," I heard myself whisper into the thickness of the silence.

The patches of vapor cleared, and I recalled why I was here. The phone call from Heidi, the rushed arrangement of flights, arriving in Houston, driving to Fred.

He was already gone by the time I arrived. The next morning Heidi, Hannah, and I drove to Farmer Funeral Home in Silsbee for the viewing. Then we spent the day going through the house. I took the study, a job worth several other rooms for the filing cabinet alone. I remembered cleaning the desk and looked around. The small black three-ring binder I found lay on the floor next to me, one tab for each letter.

I picked it up and flipped through it. The first entry for the letter *F* leapt out at me.

> **Faith, *n*:**
>
> —Ambrose Bierce's definition: Belief without evidence in what is told by one who speaks without knowledge, of things without parallel.
>
> —Paul's definition: The substance of things hoped for, the evidence of things not seen.
>
> —Matthew Cloud Lexicon definition: The determination to believe that which resonates in the soul, particularly when it ceases to resonate. **See:** life.

I fell back and wondered what had awakened me. I felt the suggestion of a door snapping closed. No telling who looked in. I was glad whoever it was saw fit to leave me alone. I didn't need anyone telling me to go to bed.

Dad. Faith. My mind worked back to the time when the entry was likely written. The year Patty Hearst was convicted, Apple Computer was formed, Son of Sam began shooting people, and Viking 1 landed on Mars. The year of the bicentennial.

It was the year that changed my life. The watershed year that divided all that came before from all that came after. The time leading up to that year began innocently enough. It wasn't until much later that the wheels came off.

# CHAPTER TWO

"Feagin Hall? They named the guy's dorm Feagin Hall?" I looked back at Bubba.

He set his suitcase on the sidewalk and examined his fingernails. A semicircle of stairs led to thirty-foot white columns along the outer edge of a half-moon porch. The gabled roof three stories up was labeled in Roman letters.

I was undeterred by his studied disinterest. "It's not spelled the same, but I bet it's pronounced the same."

Bubba scuffed the taps on his cowboy boots against the sidewalk.

"Do you know who Fagin was?"

"Can't say I've had the pleasure."

"He took in young boys and trained them to be pickpockets and sneak thieves. *Oliver Twist.*" Silence from Bubba. "Charles Dickens."

"Never met him either."

Bubba ranked fourth in our graduating class, a fact he kept hidden from the gang like a shameful secret. He knew Charles Dickens. But during the drive from Fred to Marshall, a strained formality developed between us. Perhaps I was too vocal about his pigheaded obsession with the welfare of his Corvair convertible. He doubled our travel time to five hours by driving 30 mph the entire trip. Before we left, Darnell Ray told him the head gasket was very iffy. I scoffed at the diagnosis, a fatal mistake that destroyed my credibility. We both knew it was more likely that Donny and Marie would marry each other than Darnell would be wrong about an engine.

But few things are more unnerving than creeping along a two-lane farm-to-market road while pickups and LTDs pulling bass boats stack up behind. On the straightaways they screamed past en masse, hurling obscene words, gestures, and fast food containers. I didn't endure it gracefully. My reflections on Feagin Hall were the first words uttered in thirty miles.

"If the guy behind the desk introduces himself as the Artful Dodger, don't say anything. Just follow me back out."

Bubba snorted. I walked up the steps. He picked up his suitcase and followed. The lobby was littered with easy chairs and couches facing an old console television. The ceiling was two stories up. A balcony overlooked a grand piano and a set of more delicate-looking chairs. To the right, a half-door revealed a guy with blond hair that swept down across one eye and flipped up at his collar. Much like mine.

I walked to the door and dropped my suitcase. The guy didn't even look up.

"Name?"

"Twist. Oliver Twist. This here's Bill Sykes." I nodded at Bubba. He rolled his eyes.

The guy flipped through a roster on a clipboard.

"Don't see no Twist. Or Sykes. How do you spell that?" He glanced up for a second and flipped a few more pages.

Bubba pushed me aside and leaned on the counter. "I'm Bubba Culpepper. C-U-L pepper."

The guy flipped back to the first page. "Culpepper, B. Got it." He looked at me. "But we ain't got no Twist."

"He's Mark Cloud. Probably right above my name."

"Here it is." He eyed me. "Wise guy, huh?" I batted my eyes sweetly. His eyes narrowed. "Hmm. I think we have a room for you on the third floor." He consulted a floor plan. "Yes, Room 320. You'll love it." He turned to the wall and grabbed a key and a piece of paper. "Here, sign this."

"Sure." I stepped to the window. "Where's the elevator?"

"Right there." He pointed to the stairs.

"Great." I signed my name and grabbed the key.

He went back to the clipboard. "Let's see. Culpepper. Looks like . . . looks like you're roommates with Oliver Twist." He winced. "Sorry about that."

"Is it too late to change?" Bubba asked.

He gave Bubba a sympathetic look. "Yep, 'fraid so. We got a full house."

Thirty minutes later the Corvair was empty and Room 320 was full. Such as it was.

From the door, a narrow hallway opened into a small rectangle of floor space. At each end, a writing desk with chair sat below a bookcase hanging on the wall. Two beds were end-to-end under the windows on the far wall. Actually, the term *bed* was too generous for what we beheld. In reality, a plywood platform three feet deep and two feet high ran the length of the room. A two-by-six split the platform in the middle. On each half lay an institutional pinstripe mattress with the density of a collapsed star.

We made the beds, placing the pillows at opposite ends. I plopped on my bed, the one that allowed me to look down the short passage to the room across the hall, adjusted the pillow, and leaned against the wall. Bubba took the bed by the door to the bathroom that was shared by the adjoining room.

I looked at Bubba, who was arranging the reference books Dad gave him as a graduation present, and then out the window to the porch three floors below. "Hey, you need the exercise anyway."

His lack of response was relieved by the bathroom door opening. A light-brown Brillo-head poked into the room. A tall, slender body followed.

"Hey, you must be our suite-mates."

Bubba whirled around, knocking a Strong's Concordance to the floor. "Sweet mates?"

"Yeah." Brillo Head stepped into the room and held out his hand. "Phil Moore."

"Bubba." He looked at the hand, evidently reluctant to shake hands with a sweet mate.

"Bubba what?"

"Bubba Culpepper."

"Hey, Bubba Culpepper."

I waved from the corner. "I'm Mark."

"Mark what?" he said, crossing the room in two strides.

"Mark Cloud."

"Hey, Mark Cloud. Phil Moore."

"Fillmore what?" I asked, shaking hands.

"That's it. Just Phil Moore."

"Just Fillmore?"

"Yep, no middle name."

"What about a last name?"

"Last name is Moore," he said, puzzled.

"Fillmore Moore?"

"No, just Phil Moore."

We were interrupted by a short dark-haired guy entering from the bathroom door. "Hey, just checking to see who's here. I'm in the next room."

Phil was next to him in an instant. "Then we must be roommates." He grabbed the dark guy's hand, towering over him. "Phil Moore."

The dark guy looked puzzled, his arm going up and down like a pump handle. "No, Phil Lancaster."

"Nope, I'm definitely Phil Moore."

"You're Phil Moore?"

"Yep."

"I'm Phil Lancaster."

Bubba's laughter startled everyone. "Phil and Phil."

"This could be a problem," Phil said.

"Yep," Phil said.

"Looks like we have our fill of Phils," I said. Bubba smiled. The Phils didn't.

"We could go by our last names," Phil said.

"Moore and Lancaster?" Phil asked.

"Or Lancaster and Moore," Phil answered.

"Too long," Phil said. "I don't want to have to say 'Lancaster' every time I call you."

"Then don't call me."

"Might I make a suggestion?" The Phils turned to me. "How about Thing One and Thing Two?" Blank stares. "Theodore Geisel." Blank stares. "Dr. Seuss. *Cat in the Hat.*"

"How about Phil One and Phil Two?" Phil suggested.

"Which one is One?" Phil challenged.

Then it hit me. I leapt from my bed to the center of the room and held one finger aloft. "Since there is more to Phil Moore, we call him Phil-more. And, as there is less to Phil Lancaster, we call him Phil-less."

"Phyllis?" Phil roared. The short one.

"Fillmore. I like it," Phil said. The tall one.

"No way," Phil said.

"Let's vote," Phil said. "All in favor." Bubba and I held up our hands. So did Phil. The tall one. "All opposed." Phil scowled. The short one. "Abstaining? Looks like it passes. Fillmore and Phyllis it is."

Phyllis muttered a curse and disappeared into Room 322. Fillmore shrugged.

Monday night a group of sophomore sadists rounded up the freshman guys, known as Fish, for a forced march to the freshman girls' dorm where we were obliged to serenade the inmates. The next night we were lounging in Room 320 when the door slammed open and Captain Kangaroo burst in.

It wasn't actually Captain Kangaroo, but the guy could have been his kid brother. He had the same blond Dutch Boy haircut and bristle brush mustache. Before we could protest, he raced to the windows.

"This will hardly do. The screens are still on." He leaned over my legs as I lay on the bed, punched the screen out of the window, caught it just before it fell, and hauled it into the room. "Here." He dropped it in my lap and did the same to Bubba's screen.

"What are you doing?" I demanded.

"I understand your alarm, but expedience must take precedence over propriety," The Captain boomed. "Take these and fill them with water from the sink." He dropped a bag of twenty-five party balloons on the screen. He pointed at Bubba. "You, sir. Clear the immediate vicinity of all screens and mattresses."

I knocked the screen off my lap. "What are you talking about? And who are you?"

"Allow me to lay the essential facts before you. In a mere three minutes that porch will be teeming with freshman girls singing the school song in dulcet tones. Doubtless they will have an encore planned, perhaps 'Bicycle Built for Two' or 'Purple Polka Dot Bikini.' In anticipation of their arrival, I propose that we prepare a minimum of one hundred water balloons." He began dragging the mattress off my bed with me on it. "So let us now secure these mattresses in the shower and fill the balloons."

Bubba leaped from his bed and wrestled his mattress to the shower.

"I approve of your prompt response," The Captain called over his shoulder to Bubba as he dumped me on the floor and shoved my mattress toward the bathroom. The Phils appeared in the bathroom, demanding an explanation.

I finally grasped the plan. I grabbed the pack of balloons. "Do you have more of these?" I asked The Captain.

"Indubitably." He pulled out a handful.

I grabbed two bags and cornered the Phils. "Remember our serenade last night?" They nodded. "The girls are coming here to return the favor. They will be crammed onto the porch." I pointed to the windows. "Before they get here, we need lots of water balloons."

I tossed a package to Bubba. He tore it open and wrapped a balloon over the bathroom faucet. "One person fills, the other ties. I'll help Bubba." I shoved a package into Fillmore's hands. "Take these across the hall and get whoever is there to help you." I turned to The Captain. "Next door, 324. Phyllis, you take 318."

By the time we heard the sounds of a crowd gathering below the windows, Bubba and I had twenty balloons stacked on the plywood. I left Bubba to fill the last five. I dragged the mattresses off the Phils' beds, removed their screens, and took a pillowcase to the neighboring rooms to harvest the crop.

As the girls began warming up with the school song, The Captain slapped the light switch and marshaled our forces in the gloom. Bubba and I, the two Phils, and three accomplices from the other rooms lined up along the beds.

"First, I want everyone to wave to the ladies." We leaned over the balloons and looked out. More than a hundred girls were packed into the half-circle of the porch twenty-five feet below us like cattle at the stockyards in Ft. Worth. More pressed in from the steps. We smiled and waved. The ones who could wrest an arm free waved back, oblivious to their fate.

"I shall now reveal the plan. Four to a room, two to a window. Starting from this end you shall consider yourself numbered 1, 2, 1, 2, 1, 2, 1, 2. Do you apprehend me?" We all nodded. "In front of you find two rows of six balloons, one row for each hand. When I call out your number, eject two balloons through the window and acquire another set. They will emerge eight at a time. Before the first set reaches its intended victims, there will be a dozen more in the air. When the little dears realize their predicament, a hundred water balloons will be descending upon them."

The light spilling through the windows from the porch cast upside-down shadows on our faces, transforming our smiles into macabre leers.

"Gentlemen, to your positions." When all was ready, he began repeating "one, two" in a steady rhythm and it was just as he said. Before the first squeals broke through the melody of "I'm Looking Over a Four-Leaf Clover," a third of the balloons were airborne. We unloaded the whole nine yards on them, poked our heads out, and waved again. Some girls returned fire with the handful of balloons that didn't break, but we easily fended off the few that made it to the window. The rest assaulted us with unmaidenly verbal abuse, hair plastered to their Fish heads. We smiled and waved before tumbling back into the room in an orgy of laughter.

I looked around the room. The Captain had disappeared.

———

After the soggy girls departed, I put "Dark Side of the Moon" in the tape deck and leaned back against my pillow, watching Bubba put his mattress back in place and fuss over the arrangement of his shaving mug and aftershave collection.

It would be interesting rooming with the twin brother of Jolene Culpepper, the beautiful but incurable practical joker who humiliated every eligible male in a thirty-mile radius of Fred. One might think that Bubba would have partnered with his evil twin at an early age and shared in a reign of hilarity and terror. One would be wrong. Jolene used Bubba as a target for many years before dating widened her scope. By the time I met him in 1968, he was reduced to a cautious misogynist who flinched at loud noises like a Weight Watcher on a midnight refrigerator raid. It was a wonder he was still sane.

Then in 1972, a white-shoed, saliva-spewing evangelist swept through Fred like a wildfire, burning away the chaff. Bubba was set ablaze, to the astonishment of many. His photographic memory and voracious reading gained him a reputation for having a ready Scripture for any occasion. His popcorn delivery of verses startled many of his old friends, but after awhile, no one flinched.

Unbeknownst to the gang, the following year he pounced on Dad at frequent intervals and quizzed him about all manner of doctrinal and theological issues, often trapping him in his study at the church on Saturdays. Had we known, it might not have come as such a shock when he announced after graduation that he was going to college to become a preacher.

Bubba arrived on campus with the fire still burning, although perhaps not at the white-hot intensity that characterized the early days. The coals were banked, prepared to burn through the night.

By contrast, I traveled a more rocky terrain. As a preacher's kid I was inoculated with the virus of faith at an early age, and as often happens in such cases, it served as a vaccination, sufficient to safeguard against any serious case of religion, even when most of my classmates succumbed to the epidemic of revival that claimed Bubba.

However, the Hound of Heaven stalked and eventually overwhelmed me in the California desert. I attempted a practical implementation of the gospel with the bumbling intensity of adolescence. In the process, I formed an unlikely bond with a WWII vet and caused the deacon board to demand Dad's resignation.

Graduation and a summer job at the lumberyard in Silsbee tempered my passion. By the time I arrived on campus, spiritual matters were of less consequence to me than starting a fresh era with a clean slate. I wanted the chance to live outside the PK straightjacket, to be taken for who I was and not what people thought I should be. I asked only for anonymity and the chance to experience life. Bubba and Heidi knew I was a PK. I saw no need to publicize it to a larger audience.

# CHAPTER THREE
After a week of orientation, it was a relief to be initiated into the mystical rites of registration. Heidi provided the instruction with the double whammy of the condescension of a junior lecturing lowly freshman and the mother-hen played as only a big sister can. She took Bubba and me aside at dinner and briefed us on the arcane mysteries of bureaucracy, the triplicate form, the #2 pencil, and filling in the oval completely without stray marks.

She asked me about orientation week. I told her of carpet-bombing the serenading female Fish, which she found amusing until she heard that The Captain instigated it.

"You shouldn't hang around that guy," she said.

"Why?"

"He's a drama major, for one thing."

"And?"

"They're just weird. And they end up on academic probation a lot. Ernest was on probation last spring. I guess he came back a week early from Florida."

"Ernest?"

"That's his name. He's not a captain, you know."

"Yes, I know; he just plays one on TV."

"What?"

"I can take care of myself."

"Just be careful, is all I'm saying. Nobody knows you up here, so you'll be judged by who you hang out with. Drama majors are weird. You'll get a reputation."

"Yeah, yeah."

"I'm just trying to help. Here." She shoved a parcel into my hands. "Mom sent you a care package."

"Cool." I ignored the advice but accepted the loot. We had chocolate chip cookies in Room 320 that night.

━━━━━

The next day Bubba and I occasionally crossed paths in the maze of lines for financial aid, counseling, degree plans, parking stickers, meal tickets, and scheduling. I was in the line for people not sure of which line to stand in next when I saw a notice for a photographer for the school newspaper, *The Compass.*

Several lines and hours later I had a decent schedule and some spare time. I left Bubba discussing the merits of hermeneutics and exegesis with a skinny cowboy and located the office on the flier. It was on the second floor at the end of an empty hallway. A wooden door with a frosted glass pane stood ajar. I pushed it open tentatively. An empty reception area lay beyond.

"Hello?" I crept across the room to the next doorway and peeked in. A short man in a tweed jacket and a fringe of unruly hair stood with his hands clasped behind his back, staring out the window. "Dr. Fulton?"

He turned his thousand-yard stare on me without speaking. I held up the notice. "You looking for a photographer?"

"Ah," he said, slowly emerging from reverie. "Ah, yes. *The Compass.*" He took the flier and reviewed it as if it were my resumé. "You want the job, then?"

"Sure."

"You have a camera, I take it."

"Yes. An Argus C-3."

"A C-3. Yes, then. An Argus C-3. I expect it will do. It's three hundred dollars a semester against tuition. Any surplus can be drawn from the registrar's office." He turned back to the window, rolling up the flier as if to swat flies.

"Uh, do I need to sign anything?" Dr. Fulton looked back as if surprised to see me still there. "I mean, don't you need my name at least? For the paycheck? And who do I talk to about what pictures to take and what to do with them?"

"Ah, yes. I suspect you're right. Write your name on the pad on the receptionist's desk. I'll have it taken care of."

I doubtfully took my leave and wrote my name, room number, and "*Compass* Photographer" on the pad.

A few days later I was at my writing desk, attempting to wrap my brain around a calculus problem. Bubba was reclining on his bed, working through a sizable *Survey of Civilization* text. Phyllis was crossways on my bed, leaning against the window and flicking the ashes from his cigarette onto the porch. Fillmore was sitting in the other chair, playing chromatic scales at a blinding speed on an Alvarez acoustic guitar.

Phyllis pulled his hand to his mouth as if it took all his strength, took a long drag on the cigarette, and blew the smoke out slowly while draping his arm back out the window.

"The cafeteria menu tonight is sauerkraut and weenies," he said for the second time. Nobody responded. "And Reuben sandwiches."

Bubba looked over his book. "A what sandwich?"

"Reuben."

"What's that?"

"Beats me."

I slammed my pencil down on the desk and protested the difficulty of doing calculus under such oppressive conditions when The Captain strolled through the open hallway door.

"Gentlemen, I fear we failed to make proper introductions last week. I have come to rectify that omission and further your education on the revered traditions of this esteemed institution of higher learning." He held his hand out to me. "Ernest Lee Franks at your service."

I shook his hand. "Mark Cloud. That's my roommate Bubba."

Bubba said, "Howdy, Captain." The Captain nodded.

"And these guys have the other room. Fillmore and Phyllis."

The Captain narrowed his eyes at Phyllis. "Phyllis?"

"Don't listen to that dingleberry. I'm Phil Lancaster."

The Captain looked at me. "Phyllis?"

"We have two Phils and need to distinguish them. Hence Phil-more and Phil-less."

"A most excellent resolution." The Captain's eyes twinkled. "Now, to the issue at hand. Doubtlessly you have seen tonight's dinner menu."

Phyllis snapped his fingers. "Just what I was saying."

The Captain regarded him with a doubtful eye. "A degree of refinement unexpected in one of your lowly aspect."

"What is that supposed to mean?" Phyllis bristled.

"And what is a Reuben sandwich, anyway?" Bubba asked.

"A monstrosity constructed with sauerkraut, corned beef, rye bread, and Swiss cheese." The Captain shuddered, pulled a cigarette from the pack of Marlboros laying on the edge of the bed, and lighted it.

"Hey, those are mine," Phyllis said, starting up from the windowsill.

"Very gracious of you, sir. Most gracious." He blew out a stream of smoke with satisfaction.

Phyllis looked around to see if we noticed this bold-faced act of larceny. "Just who do you think you—" he began, but was drowned out by The Captain's stentorian voice.

"Let us not dwell on the Reuben sandwich. We shall be delivered from it by the tradition of which I previously spoke."

"I wasn't dwelling on the sandwich," Phyllis said.

"It is the tradition during the first week of classes that the Fish shall treat an upperclassman to dinner. Rather than see my comrades in combat suffer by being paired with a beneficiary of lesser eminence, I have come here to grant you that special honor."

Phyllis broke the stunned silence. "You're going to let us buy you dinner?"

"You apprehend me precisely, sir. There is a charming little establishment on Grand known by the habitués as Neely's Sandwich Shop. There we may find a repast to charm the most discriminating palate. I can personally recommend the premier item on the menu, the Brown Pig. Most delectable."

"Do you get this guy?" Phyllis asked.

The Captain smoked, unperturbed, as we sat speechless, staring at each other. Even Fillmore looked around with a half-smile, his scales forgotten. The Captain flicked his ash into Bubba's shaving mug.

"All that remains is to determine the mode of transportation. I assume one of you is in possession of an automobile. There are only five of us; one vehicle will do."

"Bubba's got a car," Fillmore blurted out.

"Excellent. By tradition, one who contributes transportation is excused from providing cash."

"It's a Corvair," Phyllis said, with evident satisfaction.

"Hmmm. Most unfortunate." He regarded Bubba through a rising ribbon of cigarette smoke. "And most unexpected, I might add."

The silence was broken by a soft rap on the open door. A stocky guy in a flannel shirt and jeans stepped into the room. He looked old for a college student, with short black hair and a goatee streaked with gray. "Mark Cloud?" He looked around, uncertain in the unnatural silence. He nodded at The Captain. "'Lo, Franks. Fleecing the lambs?"

The Captain shifted uncomfortably and moved his cigarette to the other hand. "What brings you here, Wise Guy?"

I raised my hand. "I'm Mark."

"Henry Weissman, *Compass* editor. I'd like to get started planning the first edition. We can talk over a Reuben sandwich."

"What exactly is a Reuben sandwich?" Bubba asked.

Weissman glanced around. "Corned beef, sauerkraut, Swiss on rye. Toasted. The food service guy does them right. He's from New York."

I grabbed a notebook. As I left with Weissman, I heard The Captain's voice. "The Corvair will accommodate our needs after all. Shall we, gentlemen?"

---

One tentative bite of Reuben confirmed Weissman's evaluation. He nodded at my appreciative grunt.

"So, Cloud, how long've you been shooting?"

"Shooting?"

"Pictures."

"Oh. A couple of years."

"Darkroom?"

"A little, for the annual."

"It's a start. We have a small darkroom in the basement of the admin building. The school has a deal with the local paper. We use the *News-Messenger* facilities after hours to do headlines and layout. If we leave copy in the basket, they'll set it for the next night."

"OK," I said, letting him assume I knew what he was talking about. I flipped open the notebook I had brought along. It was a portfolio of sorts, a collection of things I thought were good. "Here's some of my stuff."

He glanced at a few pages. "You know we're not doing an art magazine. We're doing a newspaper. Headshots and sports pictures. Nothing fancy."

"Yes, sir."

"Sir? What do you think this is, a military academy?"

"No, sir."

"Then drop the 'sir' stuff."

"Yes, sir. I mean, OK."

"Only thing you need to know is F8 and be there." No doubt my blank look failed to instill confidence. "Set the F-stop on the camera at F8 for plenty of depth of field and get the picture."

"Ah." I took another bite of Reuben in self-defense. Weissman did likewise and flipped through the book, occasionally stopping.

"Where was this taken?" he asked through a mouthful of chips. Light streaming through the framework of a window created an angular cross of shadow on a warped wooden floor littered with detritus.

"An abandoned shack I found in the woods."

He flipped a few more pages. "What about this?" It was a shot of a gas pump.

"Fred Grocery."

"Fred's Grocery?"

"No. Fred Grocery. In Fred, Texas."

"That sounds familiar." He took a reflective sip of water. "Is that down by Beaumont?"

"Pretty close. On 92."

"Yes, yes. I hitched through there. There's a lake near there, right? A dam and everything."

"Right. Dam B."

"Dam B. Yes, yes. About ten years ago a very uptight Johnny Law in Jasper made it clear that I should keep moving. Made his point with the help of a rifle butt. Completely unnecessary. I was moving through as fast as I could. Then a cat in a Vette took me up next to Texarkana."

"A cat and a vet?"

"A guy in a Corvette."

"You hitchhiked through Fred? Where were you going?"

"I was getting out of Mexico."

"Mexico? Where are you from?"

"All over."

I wanted to tell him to cut to the chase, but I wasn't sure how he fit in. He was an upperclassman at the least. He looked old enough to be my dad. I didn't want to make the mistake of insulting a member of the faculty.

"So, are you a professor?"

Weissman choked. "A professor? Do I look like a professor?"

"Not really, but you look a lot older than the other students."

"That's because I am older. Thirty-three."

"So, you're a student?"

"Bingo. Got it in one."

"What year?"

"Third."

"What's your major?"

"Religion."

"You're a preacher boy? I mean . . . uh . . ." This was the less-than-flattering term used to identify religion majors, those studying to be preachers, like Bubba.

"You're two for two. No need to apologize. I'm not ashamed of it."

"How did you end up here?"

"It's a long story."

"Maybe you should start at the beginning."

"I grew up in Baltimore, left home when I was sixteen. Hit just about every major city in the U.S., Mexico, Canada, and Europe."

"What did you do, join the Navy?"

He laughed. "No, I joined the Beats."

"The beats?"

"The Beat Generation. Jack Kerouac." He looked at me. I shrugged. "William Burroughs?"

"Didn't he write *Tarzan?*"

"That was Edgar Rice Burroughs. Allen Ginsberg?"

I snapped and pointed at him. "The Watergate hearings!"

Weissman shook his head. "Give up. I read *On the Road* and decided that was the life for me. I went to New York and found the other Beats and from there it was all over the world. I even ran into Jack in Mexico City in '61."

"Jack?"

"Kerouac. *On the Road.* You're not paying attention."

"How do you spell that?"

"J-A-C-K."

"How do you spell Kerouac?"

"Just like it sounds."

The next morning Bubba told me about dinner at Neely's. As the evening wore on, Phyllis took greater umbrage to The Captain's condescending manner, the brunt of which seemed to be focused on Phyllis. By the end of the meal, he was a mound of fuming silence. Then a strange thing happened, Bubba told me. Phyllis suddenly looked at The Captain and smiled. He said it wasn't a very nice smile. In fact, it was on the scary side. Didn't say anything, just smiled.

After breakfast I was crossing the Quad when I saw what seemed to be a huddle of girls stumbling drunkenly by the fountain. A closer look revealed three girls attempting to edge a fourth girl into the fountain. The victim was smaller than the other three, but they still had difficulty moving her even a foot. I also noticed that she was as cute as a bug's ear, if not twice as cute.

"Hey," I hollered. "What's going on?"

The cute girl called out through teeth clenched with effort. "Please help me. These mean girls want to throw me in the fountain."

"Stay out of it," one of the other girls yelled. She was tall and wiry and had buckteeth. "It's none of your business."

"Please, kind sir. Save me from these mean girls!"

"If you come over here, you're next," another girl called. She was very wide, and I had no doubt that she could single-handedly make good on her threat. The fourth girl appeared to be her twin.

I opted for Plan B. I set the camera to F8 and proceeded to take pictures of the crime in progress. I began with a long shot that took in a good portion of the Quad and the fountain. Then I stepped in closer and got tighter shots of the struggle with the edge of the fountain in the background.

The quartet neared the fountain in stumbling lurches punctuated by moments of stasis. Finally they tumbled to the edge in a rush and the short girl toppled in, dragging the tall girl halfway in after her. The twins jumped back as the short girl splashed water in their direction.

I continued to take pictures, but backed to a safe distance after she soaked my legs. I inspected her through the viewfinder. Her shoulder-length blonde hair hung in wet clumps. Her jeans and softball jersey clung to her body, revealing an athletic build–broad shoulders, muscular legs. I found myself being drawn through the viewfinder, out of my comfortable and accustomed role as observer, desiring to become a participant, especially in whatever she might be doing. I lowered the camera and gestured.

"OK, everybody together for a group shot."

They didn't rush together. "Group shot?" the tall girl asked. "What for?"

"The school paper. This is the biggest thing that has happened all week. It'll probably make the front page."

They immediately lined up. The short girl climbed from the fountain and slogged over to the group, pushing into the middle and hugging two girls close to her. They protested and struggled to escape.

I moved with my back to the sun, counted to three, and took a few pictures. Then I pulled out a notebook. "I'll need all your names for the caption." I wrote them all down, but I underlined "Lori Street."

I pointed to Lori. "You're in Merle Bruce Hall, right?" She nodded. "You know, there's a play tonight over there in the theater. *Barefoot in the Park*. Starts at eight. I can get tickets. Wanna go?"

"Sure," Lori said.

"Yeah," the tall skinny girl said.

"Oh, yes," the twins said together.

"Uh," I said. Then they all ran off to Merle Bruce Hall.

# CHAPTER FOUR

I finished off the roll on an archery class and sprinted to the basement of the admin building. I locked the door to the darkroom behind me; set the film, a spool, a developing tank, a bottle opener, and a pair of scissors on the counter; and turned off the light.

In total darkness I cracked open the film canister and rolled the film onto the spool, cutting the end from the spindle with the scissors. Then I dropped it into the tank, secured the lid, and turned the light back on. From here on it was just chemicals. An hour later I hung the negatives up to dry and ran upstairs to my calculus class a few minutes late.

After lunch I returned to the darkroom. In a few minutes I had a contact sheet and selected several frames to print. I used the enlarger to crop one detail from the first frame. In the glow of the red light, I watched Lori's features burn onto an eight-by-ten-inch sheet of white paper. When the timer went off, I pulled the picture from the bed and dropped it into the developer.

I tapped the edges until her face began materializing like a ghost seeping through a wall. When I thought she couldn't get anymore perfect, I moved the print to the stop and then to the fixer. I flipped on the light, squeegeed the print, hung it on the line above the sink, and stared at it.

This shot caught her just before she tumbled into the fountain. She was leaning backward, her face visible between the shoulder of the skinny girl and the head of one of the twins. I caught her as she was turning her head to look behind her. Her hair was in motion, swinging halfway across her mouth, a smile failing to mask the determined set of her jaw. Her eyes were squinting. They looked like the eyes of an old man looking into the sun. Her eyebrows were raised.

I wanted to smooth out the wrinkles in her forehead. I wanted to brush her hair back from the corner of her mouth. I wanted to push her into the fountain myself, and then follow her in. I turned from the print and flipped the light off.

I skipped U.S. History and spent the rest of the afternoon making prints. I made a few that could be used for the paper, but mainly I made prints of Lori. Wrestling against the twins, the big splash as she fell in, climbing to her knees, water streaming from her hair, splashing water at me and laughing. And the group shot, a tight crop showing only Lori and the shoulders and arms of the girls on either side.

The longer I looked, the more lost I became. I felt like I was wandering deeper into a strange wood, telling myself I should turn back before I completely lost my way. But the path was so easy and the wood so enchanting.

*It's beautiful, but it's not safe,* the little voice said. The voice of reason or perhaps the voice of fear. *Remember what happened with Jolene,* it said. *Turn around before the birds eat the breadcrumbs. Remember Becky. Girls are friends with guys like you. That's all. Enjoy the pictures, but don't take any chances,* it said.

A dull ache pulsed in my chest, and my arms felt the emptiness of not holding her. I felt a yearning, a raw thirst in the back of my throat that crawled down to my gut. I had to quit looking at the pictures.

---

After dinner Bubba was polishing up his notes for the week. Fillmore was leaning against the wall playing along with *Led Zeppelin II*. They were waiting for Phyllis to finish his shower so they could go see *Godfather II*. I had just settled on a chambray work shirt for my upcoming date when a guy in a long-sleeved white shirt, thin black tie, and crew cut walked into the room. This in itself wasn't surprising. The door was usually open, and all kinds of people walked in.

He strode across the room, jabbed his finger at the eject button in the middle of "The Lemon Song," and snatched the tape out of the player. He turned to us and held the tape up like it was Exhibit A.

"This will be perfect."

"It was perfect 'til you stopped it," Fillmore said. "In case you didn't notice, I was practicing with it."

"Perfect for what?" I asked. I had a special interest, since it was my tape.

"For the bonfire tonight."

"Bonfire?" Fillmore and I said together. He leaned the chair forward, front legs clumping against the floor. I stopped buttoning my shirt.

Crew Cut turned and looked through the stack of cassettes on the bookshelf. I seemed to remember his name was Morris or Horace or Doris or something along those lines. He pulled a tape from the middle of the stack, toppling the rest onto Bubba's writing desk. Yes's *Fragile* fell to the floor. The case popped apart and the cassette skidded against my foot.

"This is even better." He held up Alice Cooper's *Killer* album.

I stepped across the room and jerked it from his hand. "What do you think you're doing?"

"Tonight is the last night of the revival at Longview Temple. We're burning devil music and occult stuff."

I lunged at him and wrestled the Led Zeppelin tape from his grasp. "Then go burn your own devil music. This is mine."

"I don't have any," he said, trying to get the tape back from me.

I pushed him away. He turned and started rummaging through the pile of tapes on Bubba's desk.

"And you have plenty." He held up *Shotgun Willie*.

Bubba jumped from his bed, slipped between Morris and the desk, and grabbed it. "Since when is Willie Nelson devil music?"

Morris grabbed the tape from his hand. "Just look at the songs." He read from the back of the case. "Whiskey River," "Bubbles in my Beer," "Devil in a Sleeping Bag," "You Look Like the Devil."

Bubba grabbed it back. I jerked on Morris's shirt.

"You ever heard of the concept of private property? I think it's in the Bible somewhere, probably around that troublesome verse that says 'Thou shalt not steal.' You should check it out sometime."

"I'm doing you a favor. You need to be delivered from this devil music. These guys are nothing but a bunch of revelers, and the Word says that those who commit revelries are evil and will be killed by the Destroying Angel." His eyes narrowed. "In fact, if you listen to this music, you might be a bunch of revelers."

"What's going on?" Phyllis stood in the doorway to the shower, dripping.

"Phyllis. Towel," I said.

"Oh." He fumbled for his towel and wrapped it around his waist.

"Doris here is recruiting members for a new club, Petty Thieves for Jesus."

"I'm trying to warn you before the Judgment of Almighty God falls on you and Consumes you like a Fire. Such as these will not Partake of the Kingdom of Heaven. And it's Morris, not Doris."

"What?"

"He wants to confiscate our tapes and burn them in a bonfire."

"Oh. One of those." Phyllis stepped into the room menacingly. "Why don't you just take your little petty tyrant god and get out of here before we throw you in a bonfire?"

Morris stood his ground. "I'm not scared of you. You can kill my body like they killed the Prophets but I will enter into my Reward. But you are a Mocker. You will not stand in the Judgment, but be thrown into the Lake of Fire. God is not mocked."

"My God doesn't torture people for listening to certain kinds of music. Your God is small and mean, just like you, and deserves to be mocked." Phyllis shook his finger in Morris's face, but the effect was diminished by having to grab at the towel before it fell.

"My God? Your God? There is only one God, the God of the Bible, and the fire of His Anger burns to the lowest Hell to consume the Wicked." Morris looked around the room. "Will you keep company with this Mocker and burn in Hell with him? Or will you Repent of your revelries and burn this evil music?"

I returned Alice and Zeppelin to the bookshelf. "Doris, I think you can't see the forest for the trees you cut down to make your bonfire. If God really is as mean as you say He is, I don't want any part of it." I put the rest of the tapes back on the shelf.

Bubba put Willie back. "And for the record, Jesus told the hyperreligious people that it was their forefathers who killed the prophets. Not the revelers."

Fillmore set his guitar aside and stood up, towering over Morris. "Yeah, what they said."

Morris looked at each of us in turn, then pushed his way through and stormed out the door, stepping squarely on Yes as he left.

---

A few minutes before eight, I approached the reception counter in the lobby of Merle Bruce Hall.

"I'm here to see Lori Street."

The girl behind the desk appeared to be young, but she was dressed like a spinster librarian from the '50s, including a shapeless gray sweater and a chain holding a pair of cat-eye glasses. She slid on the glasses and inspected me closely.

"Your name?"

"Mark Cloud."

She picked up a slip of paper and pressed the button on the microphone in front of her.

"Lori Street, Myrna Floy, Karen Small, and Kathy Small," she said, reading from the paper. I could hear her voice echoing over loudspeakers through the halls and down the stairs. She looked up at me. "Mark Cloud is here to see you."

She released the button. A chorus of voices answered back through the speaker. "We're coming, Mark sweetie."

I smiled nervously at the spinster. She looked at me severely. "They are coming."

"Thanks." She continued to look at me. "Uh, I'll just wait over there." I backed to a couch and sat down.

In less than a minute, the girls came rushing down the stairs. I stood up as they swarmed me. I was engulfed in a cloud of conflicting perfume, which set me to sneezing. As I recovered, to my dismay, the twins slid their arms through mine on either side. The other two took the flank positions. We proceeded five abreast to the door, where they were forced to break formation while I opened the door for them. They resumed ranks as we crossed the Quad to the Playhouse.

I led them down the steps to the ticket booth, where I presented the five tickets I picked up earlier that afternoon. As the usher led us through a black curtain to the aisle, I stepped aside and let Myrna and Lori pass. I cut in front of the twins and let them follow me in. I might have to endure a group date with the ugly stepsisters, but I fully intended to sit next to Cinderella.

The place looked as if it could seat 150 and it was more than half full, people talking in subdued voices in the dim light. The girls whispered to each other behind their programs.

The lights flashed the one-minute warning. I skimmed the program, glancing nervously at Lori. Myrna said something and laughed. Lori smiled and the three rows in front of us lit up. The hollowness in my chest returned, accompanied by the voice. Sitting that close and not touching her was torture. How would I stand two hours of it?

As I was agonizing on these thoughts, the house lights went down. In the total darkness I heard loud kissing sounds on either side of me and a voice said, "Mark! Stop!"

"Stop it," I hissed in the dark. "Quit that." Beyond the embarrassment of the false impression they were creating, the breach of theater etiquette horrified me. The sound continued a few seconds until the stage lights came up. I glared at Lori and Myrna, who dropped their hands down to their laps and smiled at me. They had been kissing the backs of their hands. Lori batted her eyes at me. I glared at the twins but had to start shushing again when they started laughing.

Hoping they would behave themselves, I leaned back in my seat and focused my attention on the stage. Due to the bulk of the twins, I leaned away. My arm pressed against Lori. She didn't draw away, so we sat leaning against each other. It was small compensation for the embarrassment I had suffered.

Other than being startled when The Captain came onstage in the part of Victor Velasco, the play proceeded without further incident. After the last curtain call, I took the girls to the green room and introduced them to The Captain. I thought they were impressed that I was on first-name terms with a member of the cast. The Captain basked in their attention, but when he began leering at Lori, I herded them out.

We returned to the dorm in the same fashion as we left it. On the porch, the four of them crowded around and kissed me on the cheeks simultaneously. The spot where Lori's lips touched my cheek tingled all the way back to Feagin Hall.

**CHAPTER FIVE** The next evening I met Weissman in the cafeteria for dinner before my first session at the *News-Messenger*. We were bravely working through an institutional chicken parmesanga when I saw Weissman's jaw drop. I turned to see The Captain looking like a Pict who left off in preparation for battle to drop by for dinner. There were bold blue jagged stripes running down his face, extending into his mustache.

"Franks, has the theater changed plays? I thought you were doing *Barefoot in the Park,*" Weissman said.

The Captain reluctantly stopped at our table. "We are, Wise Guy."

"Is this some new interpretation of Victor Velasco?"

"No, my dear fellow. I have been the victim of a vicious but anonymous prank. When I went to the bathroom for my morning ablutions, I discovered this in the mirror." He gestured to his face. "As if that weren't horror enough, the screams emanating from my roommate who unexpectedly emerged from the shower were enough to put me off my feed for a month."

"It didn't wash off?"

"Don't be a ninny. I am not a complete mental defective. I tried soap, rubbing alcohol, cold cream, and naphtha. All equally ineffective."

"How will you work this into your part for the play?"

"I expect the makeup to cover it. I would wear it all day but it causes me to break out."

"No idea how it happened?" I asked.

"Someone evidently compromised the lock and administered the pigment in the deep watches of the night. I am a particularly heavy sleeper. I found the door ajar this morning, although I locked it myself last night."

"Bummer."

"It is indeed, as you say, a bummer." He released a heavy sigh and continued to the door to prepare for the evening's performance.

Weissman and I finished our meal and rode his motorcycle to the paper offices. We entered through a steel door by the loading docks, past conveyors loaded with folded papers, and through a second door. Chest-high workbenches lined the walls and ran down the center of a large room. Stools were scattered throughout. Strips of paper hung like laundry on the far end in front of a glass wall that looked out on a larger room full of desks.

"The layout editor is supposed to do this, but nobody has applied for the position. So we get to do it." Weissman dropped his helmet and leather jacket in a corner. I dropped my jacket on his. "Let's see if our copy is ready."

He walked to the laundry and skimmed through a strip of paper a few inches wide and a few feet long. "Here's one." He handed it to me and went to the next strip. Soon I was holding a dozen strips varying in length from a few inches to a few feet. He walked to a cabinet with shallow drawers, opened one marked "The Compass," and pulled out a large sheet of paper. It was marked in a grid.

"Page one. That's the flag." He pointed to the words "The Compass" running across the top in large letters. "We take these," he pointed to the strips I was holding in my hand, "and put them on there. Like this."

"Measure." He selected a story and measured it. "Cut." He cut it into three sections of approximate equal length with an Xacto knife and a straightedge. "Wax." He fed them through what looked like a wringer from an old-fashioned washing machine. "Layout." He placed them on the page, leaving a gap below the flag. "Now we need a headline. Let's see, something like 'Missionaries visit campus'."

He sat down at a keyboard and typed it up. A strip of paper with the headline slid out of the machine. He waxed it and placed it above the story. "There. One down, a bunch to go."

For the next hour we prepared a few more pages, leaving space for the pictures I would take that week. As we were putting everything away, I looked out the glass wall.

"Who's that guy?"

All of the desks were empty but one. A guy sat with his back to us, hunched over a stack of papers, a pen in his left hand. His forehead was leaning into the palm of his right hand, fingers clenched in his thinning hair. He slashed at the papers with the pen.

"Oh, him. Don't know his name. I call him The Rack."

"The Rack?"

"He always looks like that, like he's being tortured on a rack."

I shrugged and grabbed my jacket. Calculus awaited me.

---

At 11:05 P.M. I felt like The Rack looked. I was pulling my hair out over a nasty set of integrals in Room 320. Bubba had just returned from a study session with some other preacher boys. He put on Willie Nelson and propped himself in the corner on his bed with a cup of coffee. I was about to complain about having to do higher math while listening to Shotgun Willie when Fillmore entered through the bathroom door, followed by Phyllis dragging two chairs.

Fillmore cleared Bubba's desk, throwing all the stuff on my bed, and dragged it to the center of the room. "All right, boys, it's time for the Mandatory Annual Monday Night 42 Game." He dropped a box of double-six dominoes on the table and sat in the chair Phyllis dragged behind him.

Phyllis sat down and set a cigar box on the table. Bubba crawled over to a chair and pulled it up to the table. They looked at me.

"Annual Monday Night Game?"

"Yep."

"How does that work? Is it once a week or once a year?"

"Pull your chair over here and find out."

"I have calculus homework."

"Don't matter," Fillmore said. "It's mandatory; don't you know what mandatory means?" He pulled the lid from the domino box and flipped it over onto the desk with a loud crack.

"By whose authority is this mandatory?"

"The Society."

"The Society?"

"The Suite 320/322 Society," he said, shuffling the dominoes.

"Suite 32 Society. Shorter," Bubba said.

Phyllis shook his head. "You boys got no style. No resonance." I snorted. "Suite 32 Society don't scan. We need something with style. Like . . ." He flipped open the box and pulled out a slender cigar with a wooden mouthpiece. "Like the Hava Tampa Society."

Fillmore grabbed one. Phyllis pushed the box to Bubba. It said "Hava Tampa Jewels" on the top. I noticed a blue stain on the middle finger of his right hand.

"Hey, what happened to your hand?" I pointed.

"What?" Phyllis held his hands out like Madge in the Palmolive commercial.

"The blue stain. Where did that come from?"

"Oh, that. The pen I was using leaked." He lighted his cigar and passed the matches to Fillmore.

"Pen, huh? You're lucky you didn't get it all over you. That's what usually happens to me."

"Yeah, just lucky, I guess."

"Did you get it on your shirt? I've ruined more shirts that way."

"Nope."

"Strange."

"Are we going to talk about my pen or are we going to play 42?"

"I have homework."

"Boys," Fillmore said, lighting his cigar and passing the matches to Bubba, "I get the feeling somebody here ain't a team player." He looked at me. "It's not every man for himself. We're a team. It's after curfew. The girls are tucked safely in their beds in Merle Bruce. And now the men gather, free from the distraction of the weaker vessels, to do manly things that men do."

"Like play dominoes?"

"Exactly. Now enough of this me, me, me stuff. You're letting the team down. We have to stick together."

"Do nothing from selfishness or empty conceit, but with humility of mind regard one another as more important than yourselves," Bubba said.

Fillmore nodded. "Yeah, what he said."

"I can see I'm not going to get any studying done, no matter what." I closed my book. "But I don't know how to play 42."

Fillmore squinted at me. "Are you a Texan?"

"Yes."

"Where were you born?"

"Ft. Worth. St. Joseph Hospital."

"You're telling me you're a Texan and you don't know how to play 42?"

I looked at Bubba. "Didn't I just say that? Can you hear me? 'Cause I can hear me." I dragged my chair to the table and leaned to Fillmore. "I'm telling you I don't know how to play 42."

"Then it's about time you learned. It's a good Baptist game, very spiritual. Invented in Weatherford by two teenagers when their parents burned their cards."

"Look, are we going to sit here yakking all night or are we going to play 42?" Phyllis grumbled. He shoved the cigar box in front of me.

"I have to smoke a cigar too?"

"Mandatory," Phyllis said.

"Team player," Fillmore said.

I looked at Bubba. "You got a verse for this one?"

"There went up a smoke out of his nostrils. Psalm 18:8."

"Unbelievable." I peeled a cigar and struck a match. The next thing I knew I was coughing.

"Don't inhale the thing," Fillmore said. "Just puff on it."

"Then what's the point?" Phyllis asked.

"These things'll kill you," Fillmore said.

"Chemistry 2 will kill me quicker," Phyllis said.

I puffed on the cigar between coughs. My mouth felt like I had eaten dinner in the fireplace, and my head was spinning like a 16-rpm record. Phyllis grabbed Bubba's shaving mug and flipped ash into it.

"Hey," Bubba said. "Get an ash tray."

"Thanks, already got one," Phyllis said.

"Observe and learn," Fillmore said and began turning over the dominoes.

———

At dinner, Phyllis, a chemistry major with no knowledge of theology, was arguing some arcane point of doctrine with Bubba.

Fillmore and some other guy were arguing over whether John McLaughlin's work with Mahavishnu Orchestra was better than his solo work on *My Goal's Beyond*. I was mechanically shoveling beef tips over rice into my mouth and silently contemplating Lori Street, who sat halfway across the room in a cluster of girls.

My few forays into romance during high school had been disasters. After several abortive attempts to declare my intent with minimum risk to my self-esteem, Becky quashed my frontal assault with the declaration of how she valued me as a friend. But at least it was a private debacle.

My ill-advised date with Jolene resulted in humiliation of epic proportions, recorded for all posterity in the school annual by a gleeful student photographer. The next year I got a camera. The same photographer trained me in the darkroom by making prints of me accepting the Lil' Abner crown at the Sadie Hawkins dance with my shirttail jutting out of my fly.

Since third grade, when I penned my first multiple-choice love note and had it delivered via trusted emissary, the longing was my constant companion. All my failures and humiliations did not inure me to its call. I knew I could not live with it forever; it must be satiated. My torment was further exacerbated by the fact that the object of my longing was constantly thrust before me. Lori shared two classes with me: history and tennis.

The tennis class was a horrible mistake. I signed up for badminton, but it was full. Tennis afforded a rare opportunity for me to humiliate myself in front of Lori. The regulation blue and gold gym shorts ballooned around my pale skeletal thighs like a lampshade. And my wrist was so weak, I couldn't return a serve if it was offered with return postage guaranteed. Lori, on the other hand, blasted her shots with such ferocity that the stripes had to be repainted where the ball struck them.

All of this I acknowledged as gravy dripped from my fork. The voice, my constant companion in matters romantic, rehearsed the facts without referring to notes. I had no answer except the hollowness in my chest.

*What of that?* I asked the voice.

*What of it?* it asked back.

*Well, it must count for something.*

*That and a quarter can get you a cup of coffee. It's just hormones. It's nothing twenty-five cents worth of chemicals couldn't fix.*

*You're saying I should walk away from the girl that could change my life?*

*Change it into what? Another lingering humiliation recorded by the school photographer?*

*I'm the school photographer.*

*For the paper. Not the annual.*

*Touché.*

I watched Lori and her friends walk out, frozen into inaction by a sarcastic inner voice.

---

That evening I put the final picture in place on the first edition of *The Compass* and set the straightedge down. It was time to take a break. Weissman was stumped on a headline.

"Where's the john?"

"Beats me." He jerked his head at The Rack. "Ask him."

I slipped out the door and approached The Rack, who was in the same pose as before: hunched over, forehead in hand, fingers clenched in hair.

"Excuse me."

The pen slashed a red gash across the paper and his hand jerked back from his head so violently I expected to see hair between his fingers. He turned to me with an oath. His bushy eyebrows jutted in all directions over two eyes, black and smoldering. His 5 o'clock shadow was working on 8:30.

"Who are you?"

"I'm working on *The Compass*. In there." I nodded back to where Weissman labored on the headline. "I'm looking for the bathroom."

He glared at me. "Over there."

As I walked past his desk on the return trip, The Rack stopped me.

"You working on that rag for the college?"

"Yes, sir."

"What kind of propaganda are you printing up this time?"

"Propaganda?"

"Declaring the Pope the Antichrist and the Catholic Church the whore of Babylon? Advocating pogroms on Wiley College across town?"

"I'm afraid I don't follow you."

"Unfortunately too many people follow you."

"What?"

"You fundamentalists would force the rest of the world to bow to your little tin god if you had your way. Sending your interfering missionaries all over the world to disrupt indigenous cultures."

"Uh . . ."

"I don't know why they let you work in there. If I was made king for a day, I'd surround that little Nazi campus of yours with razor wire and Dobermans."

"Uh . . . OK. Look, I'm just the photographer working on the paper."

"Photographer, huh? What kind of camera do you have?"

"Argus C-3."

"And you call yourself a photographer? Why not just get a Polaroid and be done with it?"

He had cut me to the quick. I struck back. "What kind of camera do you have?"

"Don't have one. I'm an editor."

"Must not be much of one if it takes you 'til after eight to get your work done."

His eyebrows bristled and his nostrils flared. "You hold down a job for twenty years in journalism. Take pictures of a black boy no more than fifteen dragged behind a car and strung up by a lynch mob. Take a few shots of a kid who starved to death in her own bedroom 'cause her parents handcuffed her to the bed and were so drunk they forgot to feed her. Bring me your prints of the rabbi with a swastika burned in his forehead with cigarettes.

"Then you can come back and tell me how I should do my job. 'Til then, you should just shut up and go back to your nice little white-bread campus and take pictures of the class president who thinks that Darwin was born with a tail and horns and the cheerleaders riding in the convertible Daddy bought and the preacher-boy club smiling for the camera and holding their Bibles to cover the lusting for those cheerleaders."

His speech left me breathless. My pulse beat like the lifters in Darnell's truck. I had lobbed a rock at him and he had hit me with a nuclear arsenal. All I had was more rocks. I tried to select one small smooth stone for my sling, but he had already turned back to his papers, marking them viciously.

I went back through the door without a word.

**CHAPTER SIX** The first edition of *The Compass* hit the stands. I secured a lunch table for the gang and was peppering the green beans and bacon when Heidi dropped her tray across from mine. Her companions surrounded me.

"My kid brother didn't bother to tell me he was the photographer for the school paper," she scolded with obvious pride.

I was about to tell her the seats were taken when I saw the other girls. I held my tongue and looked back at Heidi with a smile.

"Sorry. I was so busy working on the paper, I didn't have time to tell you." I looked to either side and back to her.

"Have y'all met Mark? Mark, this is my roommate, Lani. She's from Hawaii."

I turned to Lani expecting a handshake. Instead she hugged me, pressing her cheek to mine and making a kissing noise. She was the island beauty of my high school dreams that disappeared every time I opened my eyes. Long dark hair, dark eyes, dark skin, and a smile that made me want to explore all the meanings of the word *aloha*.

"And this is Olga. She's from Sweden." I turned to Olga with arms out for a hug, but she just grabbed my right hand and shook it awkwardly. She looked like the heavenly twin sister of Lani. Blonde, fair skin, blue eyes, and a smile that hinted of saunas and frisky tumbles in the snow afterward. I couldn't think of a more unlikely pair to encounter in East Texas.

In the past, Heidi's tendency to hang with the foreign students failed to render such positive results. While they were fascinating, they weren't particularly attractive. But this year it appeared she won the daily double. I recalled the offer she made the year before to hook me up with her friends when I got to college. I was game, but I wasn't as confident of the willingness of Lani and Olga.

Heidi broke in on my fantasies. "Now I know why you were eating with that Henry guy the other night. He's a little weird, isn't he?"

"Weird? Why do you say that?"

"For one, he's like twice our age. Then he used to be a drug addict or something and hung out with beatniks and stuff."

"Maybe, but he's a preacher boy now."

"I think he's cute," Olga said.

"Yuk." Heidi shuddered. "He's forty or something."

I shook my head. "Thirty-three."

"He looks older."

"True. Must be the mileage." I looked up and saw Lori alone with her tray, scanning the crowd. Our eyes met. She smiled and started to our table. She saw who was on either side of me, froze, then turned and took a small table by the door, alone.

I had never seen her eat alone before. It was the perfect chance for me to make a move. And she smiled at me. What more did I want? But this was the first time Heidi had visited with me since registration, and I was in the company of two beautiful women. It would be rude to abandon them. I stayed where I was and wondered if Lani liked younger men.

———

It wasn't until Halloween that things began to deteriorate.

Although he wouldn't admit it later, I'm sure it was The Captain's idea. It had his fingerprints all over it. It was a simple plan: Put the campus up for sale. The womenfolk were safely sequestered in their respective dorms. It was the time for manly men to do manly-men-type things. We were ulcerating in our room, which had been dubbed Cragmont's Corner Mead Hall and Delicatessen.

The name was the product of an Annual Monday Night 42 Game back in September. As we sat around the table puffing on Hava Tampa Jewels, listening to Jerry Jeff Walker, and forbidding Fillmore to go nello yet one more time, Bubba remarked that our suite served us a similar purpose as the mead halls in Beowulf's day–a place to gather, drink, carouse, and fall asleep.

"It's sort of like a corner bar nowadays," Bubba said, after losing the bid to me.

"You're saying this is like Joe's Corner Mead Hall and Grill?" I asked, causing my partner, Phyllis, a heart attack by leading with a six-five. I wasn't concerned since I had the double six in my hand, but I liked to keep him guessing.

"Who's Joe?" Fillmore asked, playing a six-one.

"You guys got no class. Should be a delicatessen, not a grill." Phyllis played his six-four and glared at me. "I hope you're satisfied."

"He probably is," Bubba said, playing a six-blank.

I gave Phyllis further heartburn by leading with my six-three next. In the end, we used the name Cragmont in the title, the name of the bargain soda we bought at Safeway.

Now it was Halloween and we sat around Cragmont's Corner Mead Hall and Delicatessen, lusting for manly deeds to distinguish ourselves. Had it been a Monday, our default 42 game would have occupied us. But it was Thursday, approaching midnight, and there was a nice nip in the air. Hog-killing weather. It seemed a shame to waste such a night sitting around the dorm swapping lies. Bubba resisted the idea at first, but I reminded him of the joys of orientation week and he relented.

We formed two teams because we had two vehicles. The Captain and Fillmore rode with Phyllis in his olive Chrysler Newport. I rode shotgun with Bubba in the eggbeater. Each team was assigned the task of gathering six For Sale signs and returning to the rendezvous point at 1:00 A.M.

We began trolling through the nicer neighborhoods on the theory that rich people don't hang out in the yard in the middle of the night. It didn't take us long to develop a system. We spotted a sign and drove past it, casing the street for observers. Bubba dropped me at the corner and made the block. I walked back down the street, nonchalantly jerked up the sign and continued walking. Bubba was waiting a few houses down. I tossed the sign in the backseat and jumped into the front.

In no time we had our quota. We covered the signs with an old horse blanket Bubba kept in the back for people who got cold with the top down. We were twenty minutes early to the rendezvous point, which was out by the softball field, the traditional location of the submarine races. We didn't have to worry about being surrounded by groping couples since it was almost three hours past curfew, but we thought we might attract attention if we sat there for twenty minutes, so we made a few passes down the drag on Grand.

I used the time to plan the insertion and extraction strategy for the second half of the mission. I pulled out the campus map I had retrieved from my registration packet and divided the campus into two zones to minimize our exposure. When we returned to the rendezvous point, the guys were waiting. Bubba pulled up next to the Newport, and Phyllis rolled down his window.

"About time you got here," he said. "We got interrogated by a cop."

"A completely avoidable experience," The Captain interjected from the backseat. "Had you but followed my advice, he would not have stopped."

"Einstein back there wanted me and Fillmore to make out."

"A reprehensible misrepresentation of the case, Phyllis. I merely suggested that you appear to the officer like a couple making out. This is exactly what he would expect to see and therefore would leave us unmolested."

"And who were you supposed to be, our chaperone?"

"As you may recall, I made the suggestion while supine, so my presence was not known to the officer until he probed the vehicle with his flashlight."

"What did you tell the cop?" I asked.

"I regret to inform you that your companions merely gazed into the flashlight like the proverbial deer. I was forced to take matters into my own hands and provide the officer with a plausible story to satisfy his curiosity."

"Which was . . ."

Phyllis snorted. "He told the cop his wife kicked him out, and we were trying to talk him out of a divorce so we wouldn't have to put him up for the night."

"You scoff, but the officer was satisfied, and here we remain."

"He even gave The Captain some marital advice," Fillmore said.

"Very sound advice, I might add. I have an increased respect for the men in blue."

"Fellers, I'd love to sit around chattin'," Bubba said, "but I have a half-dozen stolen signs in my backseat, and I'd like to get rid of 'em."

I handed the map to Phyllis. "You guys do the buildings marked with the yellow highlighter. We'll take the others. See you back at the mead hall."

The next day we all made it to breakfast to behold the fruit of our handiwork and hear the buzz. As relative unknowns, we escaped suspicion. Speculation centered primarily on the Payne Street Gang, a group of rambunctious preacher boys who lived in the clapboard houses back on Payne Street. They vigorously protested their innocence, which confirmed their guilt in the collective mind.

I spent the morning photographing the signs and their removal. The impunity with which the deed was executed emboldened us.

The next prank was high visibility and more expensive, but less effort and risk. Several packages of red dye and a small box of laundry detergent were all it took to turn the fountain on the Quad into a cauldron of pink frosting. Once again the Payne Street Gang received the credit.

For our next escapade we decided to fall back on the old reliable—papering the trees around the Quad. This would have been more expensive still, but Phyllis discovered that his access to the science building as a lab assistant also gave him access to the utility closet and the building's stash of toilet paper. This was good news in more ways than one. Not only did it reduce the expense of the prank, it also gave us a supply of TP for our personal use. The dorm was outfitted with chrome boxes that dispensed little squares of what appeared to be wax paper.

The week before the Thanksgiving break we took a stroll across campus around 1:00 A.M., armed with a supply of TP rolls under our coats. The Captain was on the verge of giving the signal when Bubba cleared his throat.

"Fellers," he called out. "I don't know whose idea this was, but I still say yer crazy to go out fer ice cream at this time of night, especially seein' as how cold it is." We all turned to look at him. "I say we forget it."

He walked off toward the dorm. We converged on him.

"What gives?" Phyllis asked.

"Somebody is hidin' over in the bushes. Looked like Morris. I think they're layin' for us. It might be a good idea if somebody argued with me about not gettin' ice cream. For looks."

"Most disappointing." The Captain's stage voice projected across the hill. "I had my heart set on a nice bit of Rocky Road. But if you insist, I must defer."

"Don't overdo it, Einstein," Phyllis said. He angled away from the dorm. "I'm going for a drive. Anybody else coming?"

"Where to?" I asked.

"Destination as yet undetermined."

"Might as well. I won't be able to get to sleep for an hour anyway."

The others continued to the dorm. Before he got into the Newport, Phyllis opened the trunk, tossed a bottle to me, and took one for himself. I peered at it in the streetlight. It was a Bartles and James wine cooler.

Inside the car he fired up a cigar, took a swig, and backed out of the parking place. I took an exploratory sip and was surprised. My previous experience with alcohol was limited to beer. The wine cooler was a refreshing change. Despite the cold, Phyllis drove with the window down. He took a slow meandering tour through low-rent neighborhoods, Queen blaring from the 8-track. I sat back, smoking a cigar and chasing it with the wine cooler.

We glided through the night for an hour without comment or destination. Phyllis either knew the area or was an intuitive navigator. I watched the scenery go by like a silent movie, rendered black and white by the streetlights. We drove downtown, crept through residential districts, and slithered through the streets around Wiley College, the black college across town. I thought about M and wondered what he was doing. Perhaps he had gone south for college and was in a dorm room somewhere on the Wiley campus. I thought about Lori and wondered if I should risk it.

We stopped for a fresh set of coolers and breezed out into the country. I blew cigar smoke out the window and smiled. This was my new life. Doing as I pleased, smoking cigars, and drinking

46

wine coolers and driving around in the winter with the windows down at 2:00 A.M. No Deacon Fry surveillance, no reports back to Dad. No invisible wall separating me from the gang.

The PK was erased from my forehead. The future stretched before me as a featureless plain of endless possibility. I would choose the direction; I would create my own road. I looked at Phyllis. His left elbow rested on the door, the left hand gripping the steering wheel, a cigar jutting from between his fingers. His right hand held the wine cooler on the seat next to him. He looked at the road through half-closed eyes, nodding his head to *Stone Cold Crazy*. I smiled and held my bottle up to him. He looked over, nodded, clinked his bottle against mine, and we both drank. Then we rolled back to the dorm.

**CHAPTER SEVEN** The following Friday afternoon I was lounging in the Mead Hall waiting for Bubba to get out of class so we could head home for the Thanksgiving break. I heard a noise out front and looked out the window. The green Chrysler was pulled up to the curb in front of the dorm. I caught a glimpse of Phyllis dashing into the building for another load. I listened at the bathroom door as he rushed into his room, grabbed something, and ran back out. It was but the work of a moment for me to retrieve a water balloon from the cache in the shower and return to the window.

Phyllis emerged onto the porch carrying a laundry basket full of dirty clothes. With accuracy born of frequent practice, I launched the balloon. It hit him squarely, or should I say roundly, on the head. To my dismay, it bounced off and burst harmlessly in the bushes.

He looked up, saw me leaning from the window, and did the thing that filled me with dread. He smiled.

He hastily tossed his laundry into the Chrysler. The smile reminded me of The Captain's blue visage and the blue stain on Phyllis's middle finger. He was not a man to stand by when affronted. He was a man of terrible, baleful action.

With horror, I leapt from the bed to the middle of the room and hopped from one foot to another, desperate to avoid my impending doom. What would he do?

I ran to the bathroom door and locked it. I ran to the hall door and locked it. Then I ran back and forth between the doors. What would he do?

Listening at the hall door, I heard him crash up the stairs, slam into his room, emerge, and race down the hall to mine. He stopped in front of the door. I recalled that he somehow gained access to The Captain's room in the middle of the night. I braced one foot against the bottom of the door and held the doorknob with both hands.

I searched in my mind for some clue to predict the manner of his attack and counter it. Rubbing alcohol under the door and a match? I looked at my feet, but no alcohol appeared. Shaving cream in a milk carton, stomped to spray into the room? What on earth was he doing out there?

Immediately I received my answer. With a gut-wrenching, splintering crash, a bayonet blade plunged through the door, not four inches from my ear. It receded with a grating growl and reappeared a fraction of an inch lower. It had a saw blade on it that he was using to extend the gash. I ran to my bed and grabbed the pillow, planning to wedge the blade in the gash so he couldn't remove it. Before I made it back, he withdrew the bayonet. I heard it clatter into his room and the door slam shut. His feet pounded down the stairs. I tore to the window in time to see him run to his car, wave good-bye, and go speeding away, leaving me grinding my teeth impotently.

I contemplated myriad retributions, but declined them all for fear of what new atrocity would befall me. I stood in front of the door, contemplating the half-inch wide, three-inch-long gash that afforded a view of the hall and the stairs. One thing I was sure of, I wasn't going to lose my deposit. I'd find a way to make him pay it.

I taped cardboard over the hole and headed out to the Quad with my hands jammed in my jacket pockets. It would be awhile before Bubba finished his test. As I topped the hill, I saw Lori sitting on the edge of the fountain. Alone. A suitcase and a laundry bag were on a nearby bench.

I waved. She smiled and waved back. I stopped in front of her.

"Waiting for a victim?" I nodded at the fountain.

"Nah, just waiting for my ride home."

I sat next to her. The sun was slipping behind Lineberry Hall, limning her profile in yellow light. I could see the delicate layer of miniscule fuzz on her cheek, the individual hairs of her eyebrow. She turned and caught me staring. Her blonde hair was backlit, edged in a halo of gold by the weak November sun. On the breeze I caught the scent of herbal shampoo.

"Where's home?" I blurted out and looked away.

"Stanley."

"Stanley? Texas?"

"Louisiana. How about you?"

"Fred. Texas."

She laughed and my heart stopped. "We'd make a pair. Stanley and Fred."

Was she suggesting that she would find that agreeable? I resumed breathing and broke the silence of my speculations.

"Or Fred and Stanley," I said. She frowned. "Hey, Fred always comes first. Fred and Barney. Fred and Ethel. Fred and Ginger."

"What about Stanley and Livingston? Stan and Ollie?"

"I'll give you the Stan and Ollie, but the Livingston is questionable. So I still have you three to one."

"It's not my fault there are more Freds than Stanleys."

"Life isn't fair."

"Tell me about it."

We sat in silence for awhile. I racked my mind for a topic. "So, that was a good play."

"Yeah." She laughed. "Sorry about the kissing sounds."

"Oh, that's OK. Caught me by surprise is all." We sat in silence for awhile, and I grasped for something to say. "Hey, want a Coke? I got a couple of quarters."

"Sure. But I have to stay here with my stuff."

I stood up and dug in my pocket. "No problem. I'll go get them. What kind?"

"Dr Pepper."

"Coming right up."

I raced across the street to the student center, bought two Dr Peppers, and raced back. My path was blocked by a vintage LTD in the middle of the street, doors open. Myrna was opening the trunk. Lori was picking up her bags.

"Hey, I'll get those," I hollered, handed the drinks to Myrna, and ran over to Lori.

She smirked. "Working on your next merit badge?"

"Yes, I'm working on my Beagle Scout. An obscure but prestigious decoration." I grunted as I hefted the laundry bag. "What kind of laundry do you have in here? A suit of armor?"

"Yes. Dad said he would put on another coat of Rustoleum if I brought it home."

"Decent of him." We approached the car. Myrna was in the driver seat. I wrestled the bag and suitcase into the trunk and slammed it shut.

"Thanks," Lori said.

"Sure," I answered. Lori turned to get in the car. "Hey, uh . . ." She stopped and turned. "I, uh . . . I hear they're doing some one-act plays next week. Final for some drama class. You want to go?"

She smiled. "Yeah, sounds fun."

"Just you and me, I mean. Not the whole harem." I nodded at Myrna in the car.

"Of course."

I walked her to the door. She got in and rolled down the window. Myrna handed her a Dr Pepper. Lori popped the top and held it up. "Thanks for the Dr Pepper."

"Yeah," Myrna hollered from the driver's side. "Thanks." She toasted me with the other can and took a big swig.

"Oh, yeah. Anytime." Lori looked at me and shrugged, and the LTD roared off to Stanley.

Mom threw my laundry in the washer and started on dinner. Heidi looked up from cutting onions. She nodded at the washer and leveled a look pregnant with significance at Olga, who was spending the holiday with us since she was so far from home. It was an exquisite torture for me, so near in proximity yet so far out of my league.

"You see what I mean? She never does my laundry when I come home," Heidi said.

Mom got out the big pot for the traditional Thanksgiving-week chili. "I'd do your laundry, but you never bring any."

Olga smiled. Heidi sniffed. Perhaps it was the onions. One big night of cooking created enough leftovers to allow Mom to prepare for Turkey Day itself without having to worry about menus in between. During that week, if someone walked into the kitchen and even looked as if he might ask a question, she would say "Chili" and go back to her preparations.

Hannah was at Scooter and Brenda's for a hayride. I was flipping through the encyclopedia for the letter *K*. Dad was sipping coffee with his Buddy Holly glasses propped up in front of the receding hairline. He was flipping through back issues of *The Compass,* critiquing the photographs.

"Hmm. Shadow running across this shot of the basketball team. Looks like a telephone pole." He turned the page. "Too much contrast here. Makes the guy look like Al Jolson."

I glanced up. "That is Al Jolson."

He dropped his glasses down and looked again. "Can't be. He died before you were born."

"It's a talent show. He's our resident ham. He sang 'Mammy'."

"Arthur's not a ham," Heidi said. "He's talented. I thought he did a good job."

Mom began humming "Mammy" as she browned the meat.

"Right." I flipped the pages hopelessly. "How do you spell Kerouac?"

"As in Jack?" Dad asked.

"Yes, sir. Do you know anything about him?"

He looked up from the paper. "Not much. Enough. More than I want to know. Why?"

"The editor," I pointed to his name on the masthead, "says he spent some time with Jack Kerouac in Mexico."

"How old is this guy?"

"Thirty-three."

Heidi felt compelled to contribute to the body of knowledge on Weissman. "And he's weird. Has a pointy little beard. Always wearing lumberjack shirts and jeans. And not very friendly. Arthur is a lot nicer."

"He's cute," Olga said.

"He's ancient," Heidi said.

Mom smiled. "Practically dead, wouldn't you say, Matt?"

"No question."

"You know what I mean," Heidi said.

"Thanks for sharing." I turned back to Dad. "So, Weissman said he was one of the Beats."

"And he's going to ETBC?"

"Evidently, like Huck Finn, he was one of the gang, but got religion and wished to quit it and lead an honest life. He's a preacher boy. Third year."

"That's unusual."

"So what exactly are the Beats?"

"Beatniks."

"Oh," Mom said, "like that cute little Dobie Gillis before he became Gilligan."

Dad refilled his coffee cup. "It was Maynard G. Krebs who was the beatnik and who later played Gilligan."

Mom started humming the theme to "Gilligan's Island." I attempted to bring the conversation back to the point.

"So the Beats and beatniks are the same thing?"

"Sort of. Don't take Maynard as the image of the Beats. He's about as representative of beatniks as the Clampetts are of people from Arkansas." He blew on his coffee and took a tentative sip. "Basically, the Beats were the predecessors to the hippies. Some of them, the ones that lived long enough, became hippies, staging sit-ins and love-ins and be-ins and so on. Like Allen Ginsberg."

Mom turned to the table, ladle dripping into the pot. "Weren't they the ones who started all that free-love and drugs that the hippies like to do?"

"They were instrumental in popularizing it, but I don't think anyone in this millennium can claim to have started it. The New Morality is just the Old Immorality. It's been around since the beginning."

"So, how do you spell Kerouac?" I asked in an attempt to deflect the sermon.

Dad grabbed the encyclopedia. "He was French Canadian. Here he is." He turned the book back to me.

———

Later in the week Heidi, Hannah, Olga, and I went to Beaumont. The girls wanted to cruise the mall. I took the opportunity to glean the bargain racks at the record store, picking up Bruce Cockburn's *Salt, Sun and Time*. Then I forced them to drop me off at the used bookstore where I began my research on the Beats.

I found a book titled *The Beat Generation* and skimmed through it. The Beats seemed to be deadbeats, guys who couldn't or wouldn't hold a regular job, who went on party binges lasting days, or even weeks. They attended colleges I couldn't afford, even if I would have qualified, but they dropped out or were kicked out. I couldn't figure out where they got the money to be constantly traveling—East Coast, West Coast, Mexico, Paris, Tangiers. And they appeared to be writers.

I began looking for books by the Beat troika: Burroughs, Ginsberg, and Kerouac. I found a book by Ginsberg, *Howl* written in large letters on the cover. It was so slender I figured I could read it right there. I opened it and discovered it was poetry. I hated poetry. I tried reading a few pages, but it was almost incomprehensible. It turned weird, then obscene. I put it back on the shelf and hoped nobody saw me reading it.

Not far away, a copy of Burroughs' *Naked Lunch* got my attention. In thirty seconds it was back on the shelf and I was walking away fast toward the middle of the alphabet.

I found a tattered copy of *On the Road* for twenty-five cents. Gun shy, I skimmed through the first few chapters. It didn't appear to be pornographic. I bought it.

Between church harvest services and trips to relatives in Port Arthur for the traditional Thanksgiving shrimp gumbo (such things happen when you have Cajun relatives), I didn't get much time to visit the old gang. I saw Jolene at church. And Ralph, who got on at the refinery as a welder. Didn't catch the rest of the gang.

I read on the drive and during long afternoons when the aunts and uncles lay around like a python digesting a goat.

I had a hard time at first. I couldn't relate to the characters: Sal, a guy who had just split up with his wife, and Dean, a crazy delinquent fresh out of reform school who talked like a maniac. But halfway through the first chapter when I read "The only people for me are the mad ones," I thought, *Yeah, I know just what he means*. I was hooked.

It was a crazy quilt of hitchhiking, riding buses, driving cars into the ground, abandoning wives, and drinking—peopled with writers, posers, ex-cons, junkies, drunks, and clueless relatives. It bore no relation to the world in which I had lived for almost two decades. But it was overflowing with an infectious passion and a seductive naiveté.

It was true what Dad said. There was a connection to the hippies. The Beats were enshrouded with the same aura of mystery and danger that I sensed in the '60s, my nose pressed to the glass of the Counter Culture. What was it that caused these people to throw life as we know it out with the bathwater and live only for the next hour, the next dollar, the next jug of wine, the next joint? Was it really better to burn out than to fade away?

And while I didn't envy Kerouac dying of internal bleeding in the Summer of Love—the summer of Woodstock and Neil Armstrong's one giant leap for mankind—due to his excesses, I did envy him the passion with which he flung himself at life with no apparent self-doubt or self-consciousness. I couldn't even smoke a cigar during the Annual Monday Night 42 Game without great internal debate and recrimination.

In some ways, the book seemed to attain a spiritual transcendence. About halfway through, Dean tells Sal about the people driving the car that is taking them to Denver.

"Now you just dig them in front. They have worries, they're counting the miles, they're thinking about where to sleep tonight, how much money for gas, the weather, how they'll get there—all the time they'll get there anyway, you see. But they need to worry and betray time with urgencies false and otherwise, purely anxious and whiny, their souls really won't be at peace unless they can latch on to an established and proven worry and having once found it they assume facial expressions to fit and go with it, which is, you see, unhappiness, and all the time it all flies by them and they know it and that too worries them to no end."

I heard echoes of the Sermon on the Mount. And echoes of my complaints on the drive to college three months before. "Purely anxious and whiny" was an accurate description of my part on the program. I could no more have been a Beat than a hippopotamus.

When I rode back with Bubba, the book was in my bags. I had some questions for Weissman.

# CHAPTER EIGHT
I called for Lori an hour before the play started. A cold snap had hit right after Thanksgiving. We were past hog-killing weather. It was deer-hunting weather now.

The spinster-in-training looked with disdain at my letter jacket, gloves, knit hat, and muffler. Or perhaps it was the laundry bag slung over my back. I smiled and batted my eyes. She didn't.

I heard a voice from behind me. "Look, if you're here an hour early because you want me to do your laundry, you should re-think your plan."

I turned around and gave Lori a puzzled look. "But Mom told me that the only girls worth dating are the ones that will do my laundry."

"Funny, my mom told me the same about guys." She was bundled in an ankle-length coat, mittens, and muffler. Blonde hair peeked out under the edges of a fuzzy hat with a ball on the top.

"Must be a mom thing." I opened the door for her.

She stopped on the porch. "Where are we going?"

"Patience. All shall be revealed." I stepped off the porch, stopped, and turned around. "And follow me."

She saluted. I lugged the bag around the admin building to the front, stopping in the patch of grass between the two sets of wide concrete steps that met at the front door.

I pulled a blanket from the laundry bag and spread it on the grass. I set a cafeteria tray in the middle of the blanket. On the tray I placed a candle, a thermos, a sugar bowl, and two mugs. Finally, I placed a pillow on either side of the tray and gestured for Lori to sit down. I lighted the candle and poured hot chocolate into the mugs.

"One lump or two?" I opened the sugar bowl to reveal marshmallows.

"Yes, please." Her words came out in small clouds. I pulled a set of tongs from my pocket and dropped three marshmallows into her hot chocolate. "Thank you."

"You're welcome, Stanley." I dropped marshmallows into my own cup. "You don't mind if I call you Stanley, do you?"

"Yes, I do," she said, smiling.

"I thought so. Too bad. I was hoping you would call me Fred."

"I could call you a taxi."

"Just don't call me late for dinner."

"Cheers." She clinked her mug against mine, and we both drank. She looked around. "Nice place. Did you have to make reservations?" Her hot-chocolate mustache glistened in the candlelight.

"No, it's very exclusive. Nobody comes here. Plus, the steps shelter it from the wind, so it's not even cold."

"Oh, really? I hadn't noticed."

"Are you cold? I have an extra blanket." I pulled it out. She covered her legs with it.

Once past the preliminaries, there didn't seem to be anything left to say. The comfortable silence of sipping hot chocolate threatened to grow into an ominous silence of nothing in common. I cleared my throat, opened my mouth, realized my mind was a complete blank, and took another sip of hot chocolate.

Lori broke the silence. "So, what shall we talk about?"

"How 'bout dem Cowboys?"

"Oh, could you believe that fifty-yard pass with thirty seconds to go? And with a rookie quarterback! Dad was sure when Staubach was injured in the third quarter and down thirteen points that his bet on Washington was safe. He even called Uncle Earl and talked him into doubling the bet. He lost fifty bucks on that game!"

"Yes, that was amazing," I said, even though I had been in a back bedroom of my aunt's house reading Kerouac and hadn't known until now what all the hollering was about. "Who woulda thunk it?"

"I know! Cowboys 24, Redskins 23." She took a slow sip. "Who do you like for the Superbowl?"

"Uh, I like the . . . Celtics."

"That's a basketball team."

"Oh, the Superbowl. You said the Superbowl, didn't you? Right. The, uh, the Giants."

"The Giants? They're two and ten!"

"I always root for the underdog."

"You don't know anything about football, do you?"

"Perhaps not football qua football, per se. But I feel I'm in touch with football on a more metaphysical level."

"You don't know anything about football."

"No."

"Did you tell me you were from Texas?"

"Born in Ft. Worth."

"Have you seen the birth certificate? Maybe you were adopted."

"The thought has crossed my mind. Have you met my sister?"

She laughed. "No, tell me about her."

I told her about Heidi. I told her about Hannah. I told her about Bubba, Jolene, Darnell. I even told her about M and The Creature. She told me about her six brothers—two older, four younger—and about her best friend who got married the day after graduation and already had a kid, and her cousins from Alabama with the coon dogs and her other cousins who lived in the bayou and hunted alligator.

I told her about the Phils and The Captain and Weissman and the newspaper. She told me about her roommate, Samantha and their suitemates, the twins, and the softball team and the Saturday morning missions she did with the Baptist Student Union. I told her I had no idea what I was going to major in. She told me she was majoring in Education and planned to be a coach.

Then I noticed some people walking by and checked my watch. It was ten forty-five. We had missed the play and Lori was in danger of missing her curfew. We threw everything in the laundry bag and rushed back to the dorm. The porch and sidewalk were crowded with couples saying goodnight. We threaded our way through the huggers and kissers.

"Thanks for the hot chocolate," Lori said. "It was nice."

"Sure. Thanks for missing the play with me."

She giggled. "Sure. Maybe we could miss another play sometime."

"It might be awhile before they have another play we could miss."

"Then maybe we can miss something else."

"I'll check the schedule of activities. Surely there's something we could miss. Maybe even this weekend."

"OK," she said. Before I could agonize over whether to try for a kiss, she disappeared through the door with a wave and a smile.

---

I don't remember walking back to the dorm, but I must have because I was thumping cigar ashes into Bubba's shaving mug and going two marks while Shuggie Otis played on the tape deck. It was Thursday, not Monday, but we were playing 42, killing time until 2:00 A.M., our appointed time to execute the toilet paper scheme we were forced to abandon in November.

Bubba was shuffling, and Filmore was marking down the score. Phyllis was digging the tobacco out of a cigarette with a paper clip onto a piece of typing paper.

"What are you doing?"

Phyllis stopped and looked at me. "I'm tired of The Captain bumming my cigarettes." He opened a pencil sharpener and poured shavings onto a second piece of paper. "And he doesn't even ask. He just takes them."

"And so you are . . ."

"And so I'm preparing a special gift, just for him." He formed the paper into a funnel and poured the pencil shavings into the hollow tube where the tobacco had been. He filled the last half-inch with tobacco, tamping it in with a pencil. Then he discarded the evidence and set the doctored cigarette on top of the pack of Marlboros.

The Captain showed up around midnight, and I offered him my seat in the game. As he sat down he reached across the table, grabbed the cigarette from atop the pack, and fired it up. Phyllis looked around to make sure we saw this brazen act. The Captain puffed as he pulled his hand, rearranged the dominoes, and bid. Halfway through the hand, wood smoke cut through the cigar haze. The Captain took a drag and stopped with domino in mid-air. He took the cigarette from his mouth with his other hand, looked at the burning end, shrugged, and put it back in his mouth. Phyllis smirked but said nothing. Several times during the game, The Captain inspected the cigarette, but he smoked it to the end.

As he dropped the butt into Bubba's shaving mug, he said, "That cigarette tasted funny."

The room erupted in laughter. The Captain demanded an explanation, and as Phyllis supplied it, I went to liberate the Cragmont cola I had consumed during the game. When I emerged from the bathroom, The Captain waved a dollar bill at me.

"There seems to be a shortage of libations. Phyllis has taken the last of the root beer. I will gladly pay for a round if you will find change and retrieve it."

"Sure." I grabbed the dollar and headed downstairs. The Coke machine was in the basement. I wandered the halls until I found life, got change, and bought four Dr Peppers.

I dropped on my bed, leaned into the corner, opened the Dr Pepper, revived the Hava Tampa, and reflected on the evening.

Four hours and we had been stopped by the curfew, not boredom or awkwardness. I picked up the notebook and turned slowly through the prints of Lori and the fountain. Why would a girl like that spend four hours with a guy like me? It defied everything I knew about myself, every previous experience with girls.

But she was the one to suggest we do it again. Against all odds, against all logic and reason, she wanted to do it again. I dared to hope. I looked at the picture of Lori in the fountain, water streaming from her hair.

The voice whispered to me. *Remember Jolene. She even asked you out. Remember how that ended.*

*Don't you ever take a day off?*

*Sure. I left you alone yesterday.*

I pointed to the photo. *Look at this face. See that smile? That's how she looked at me tonight.*

*I'm just saying, is all. I'm looking out for you.*

*You're all heart.*

*I try. Better safe than sorry, I always say.*

*Have you ever said, "Better to have loved and lost"?*

*Nope. But I did say, "A rock feels no pain, and an island never cries."*

*Then you should sue Paul Simon.*

*I am Paul Simon.*

*Then I just have one thing to say.*

*What's that?*

*She loves me like a rock.*

The Captain's stage whisper jolted me from my internal debate.

"Cloud, rouse yourself from your nocturnal reflections. The witching hour is upon us."

I slammed the notebook shut and dropped it on the bed. We each packed four rolls of toilet paper under our jackets and filed silently down the fire escape and into the night. We split up, taking separate routes and re-convening on the Quad, each under his appointed tree. The Captain grabbed the back of his pant leg with his left hand, pointed to the sky with his right, and said "Hark." I did the same. When all five of us completed this ludicrous all-clear signal, the festivities began.

It was like a silent ballet. White ribbons undulated in the mercury-vapor lamplight and settled on skeletal trees. Back and forth the strands crisscrossed in the night; clouds of moisture wreathed our heads as we panted with the exertion. When the rolls got too light to throw, we wrapped the trunks in barber pole fashion.

After each roll we scouted the perimeter before resuming our labors. I paired up with Bubba. We took opposite sides of a tree and threw to each other, moving a step clockwise after each volley. It took half an hour to exhaust our resources. After a last reconnaissance we stood back and admired our handiwork. The Quad looked wrapped for Christmas by a drunken tailor.

The Captain shook hands with each of us, and we returned to the dorm for a well-deserved sleep. On the way back Phyllis fell in step next to me.

"Let's go celebrate."

"Sure."

At the car Phyllis handed me a cooler. "Hey, you know how The Captain bought the round of Cokes?"

I twisted off the top and tossed it in the trunk. "Yeah, that was nice of him."

He slammed the trunk and looked at me. "He got the dollar out of your billfold while you were in the bathroom."

"What?"

He flinched and looked around. "Hey, keep it down, will you? We're holding."

I lowered my voice to a fierce whisper. "And you let him do it? Why didn't you say something?"

He got in the car. "I'm saying something now."

I slammed the door. "Yeah, now that I've already spent the dollar."

He shrugged as he backed out. "I was thirsty. Consider it a trade for the cooler."

I grunted. Phyllis began his stochastic tour of the sleeping town. After a quarter of an hour, he turned off a back road into an overgrown cemetery, parked in a copse of hardwood infested with underbrush, and turned off the engine. I looked at him but didn't say anything. He pulled the ashtray out of its slot, reached into the bowels of the dash, and pulled out a pack of Winstons. He shook one out. It wasn't a Winston. It was a hand-rolled cigarette, pointed on the ends.

He fired it up without comment, took a deep draw, held his breath, and handed it to me. I shook my head and got a cigar from the glove compartment.

He blew out a cloud of smoke and said, "Suit yourself. This is good stuff."

"I'll stick with the legal stuff," I said, holding up the wine cooler.

"You don't know what you're missing." He took another hit.

"I can live with that."

We sat in the cemetery for half an hour, listening to Queen's second album while each smoked our weed of choice. Then we drove around with the windows open for another half-hour, drinking wine coolers. I felt like I had achieved a new level in my independence. I was no longer living the protected life of a PK. I was in the real world with real people making my own choices. It felt good. I smiled at the scenery that flitted past my half-mast eyes. I was blurry around the edges, but content. In the embrace of the wine I felt confident that it was only a matter of time before I embraced Lori as well. I invited the voice to debate the issue, but it declined, so I replayed the evening in my mind and sipped my drink as Phyllis guided us through the night.

# CHAPTER NINE

There were only a few weeks left in the semester. Monday I was at dinner with the gang when Lori appeared next to the table, holding a tray and accompanied by her roommate.

"Shove over, boys. We lost a bet, and the punishment is to sit at your table." She shrugged her shoulders. "I'm Lori. This is my roommate, Sam."

Sam was only slightly taller than Lori, but there the similarities ended. She had jet-black hair that hung to her jaw line and was as wispy as a spring twig.

"Hi," she said as she set down her tray and took a seat next to Phyllis. Lori sat down next to me.

"I'm Mark," I said, nodding to Sam. "This is my roommate, Bubba."

Bubba leaned to look around me. "Howdy, ladies."

"And our suite-mates, Fillmore and Phyllis."

Sam started. "Did you say Phyllis?" She looked the Phils over. "Which one is Phyllis?"

"Neither," Phyllis said. "I'm Phil Lancaster. This is Phil Moore. Hi." He held out his hand. "I assume Sam is short for Samantha."

"Actually, it's short for Samuela," Lori said. "Her parents wanted a boy."

"Don't listen to her," Sam said. "You're right, it's Samantha. But everybody calls me Sam."

"And everybody calls him Phyllis," Fillmore said.

"No they don't," Phyllis said, looking at Sam. "Only these mental defectives call me that. The rest of the civilized world calls me Phil. So, Samantha, why haven't we seen you around before?"

"She's pre-med," Lori said. "Never leaves the books. We have to hook her up to machines to keep her alive."

During dinner, Lori and I compared schedules and looked over the activities for the week. There was a Saturday afternoon lecture in Scarborough Chapel by a missionary on furlough from Ecuador, a former stockbroker who had forsaken the concrete jungle for a real jungle. It sounded like a good thing to miss.

Across the table, an amazing transformation had taken place. Phyllis, voted by his graduating class as "Most Likely to Have His Picture in the Dictionary Next to the Word *Curmudgeon,*" was chatting Sam up in a manner most unexpected. He smiled, and not the deadly smile of doom that struck terror into the souls of all right-thinking citizens. It was an open and almost charming smile. Not completely charming, of course, since it was forced to work with the raw elements of his physiognomy.

As Lori and I watched the rehearsals for Beauty and the Beast across the table, Weissman appeared and drummed his fingers on his motorcycle helmet.

───

At the *News-Messenger,* Weissman keyed in headlines and I pasted them up.

"So you were in Mexico with Jack Kerouac?"

"I was there at the same time. I wasn't with him, but we did cross paths a few times."

"I read *On the Road* over the break."

"Oh?"

"Yeah. Those guys seemed pretty wild."

"Oh they were. Some still are."

"Were you like them?"

"In what way?"

"The week-long binges, drugs, women, no steady job. That stuff."

"Oh yeah. Nothing to be proud of. I don't talk about the details of that time of my life. In fact, God has mercifully erased most of those memories, so I don't have to try to forget them anymore."

"How does that work?"

"Beats me. I'm just glad it does."

We worked in silence for awhile.

"So, how did you go from Beat to Baptist?"

"I had a Damascus road experience. Literally. Here ya go." He handed me a stack of headlines. "For page three." I went back to work on page two.

"I was hitching to Damascus, Arkansas, back in '61, the time I went through Fred. A guy I met in Brownsville had a cousin up there. He said he could rent me a room for awhile, let me recover from Mexico, maybe get some work. I made it as far as Atlanta, up by Texarkana, when I saw a great light."

I turned around. "A great light? And a voice that said, 'Weissman, Weissman, why persecutest thou me,' right?"

"No, the voice said, 'Don't let the sun set on you in this town, you Commie hippie.' I heard it just before I saw the great light." He paused for my reaction, but I had none. "The great light was from the brick that hit me in the back of the head. Couple of local rednecks in a pickup. My hair was a little longer in those days. Think Timothy Schmidt."

"Poco? That's some long hair."

"Yes, yes, but I had to get it cut for the stitches. Never grew it back. An old black preacher found me in the ditch and took me to the hospital, then home."

"You're just a mess of Bible stories, aren't you? Ever been eaten by a big fish?"

"Not recently, but I was bitten by an alligator once. That was the last time I hitched through Louisiana. Went north after that."

"So, you're laid up in this black preacher's house . . ."

"Yes, yes, and he nursed me back to health. I was Buddhist, following the Lotus Sutra. I thought I was in harmony with the universe. That old man preached at me 'til he ran out of things to say. I would get up in the middle of a sentence and go out back and meditate, chanting my mantra.

"But no matter how long I meditated, I could not subdue my desire for revenge on those rednecks. First the cop in Jasper, then the hicks in Atlanta. I'd had enough. One day when the old man was out, I got so worked up I packed my backpack and went out with a rubber hose wrapped around a pipe, looking for that truck. Yes, yes, I was going to give them as good as I got and leave town.

"I was sitting on the side of the road where 59 and 77 come together, watching and waiting with the pipe up the sleeve of my jacket, when the old man found me. He pulled his truck on the side of the road and rolled down the window.

"He said, 'Vengeance is mine; I will repay, saith the Lord.' I ignored him. He said, 'Son, vengeance is too strong to hold in a clay vessel. It's like bringing a lion into a cage of straw. You take vengeance into yourself, you can't control it. It'll destroy you and the life of everyone you come near.' I looked him in the eye. 'Is that what you want?' he asked. 'You want to become The Destroyer?'

"I wanted to hit him with the pipe. I was disgusted with myself. It was a showdown, his philosophy against mine. I looked into his watery brown-and-yellow eyes and the desolation of wrinkles of his face. I could see the decades and decades of abuse he had suffered, probably worse than what I had been through. Things he didn't say a word about.

"I knew I had lost. I threw the pipe into the woods, tossed my pack into the back of his truck, and got in."

"Wow," I said, then realized I was still holding the headlines for page three. I waxed them and started pasting them up. "So that was it?"

"Yes, yes, I went back and lived with the old man, and he brought me to the Lord. I worked with him for ten years until he died. It was time to start something new, so I came here. Decided to get a little knowledge to go with the wisdom I got from the old man."

"How's that working out for you?"

"Not bad. Not many of my professors have been beaten with a rifle butt or whacked with a brickbat, but they have had other experiences I can learn from."

I pondered that as I pasted up the headlines. Why exactly was I here? Did I view my college career as a chance to learn from my professors? No, I had to admit I didn't think about it that way. Classes were just something I did because I was supposed to, the content something I memorized because there would be a test. I didn't really care how much pressure was focused on a dam of a certain size at a certain point, but I could calculate it.

Weissman, on the other hand, had a reason to be here. He was focused, even passionate. I could see the Beat soul under the preacher-boy degree plan. He was following the Beat road, the road Thoreau took, to live deep and suck out all the marrow of life. But it took him to a strange crossroad, one I hadn't read about in my Beat researches.

Could you be a Beat and a Baptist preacher at the same time? Maybe you could. Maybe that's what the Jesus People in California were doing. Like the Beats, they rejected the system that hollowed out men's souls and turned them into mindless consumers, but they focused it on the empty rituals of the Pharisees that shut men out of the kingdom.

Maybe what it really meant to be Beat was to throw caution and security to the wind and to live with abandon and total trust, like Peter stepping out of the boat, or Jesus stretching out His arms on a crossbeam. To be truly Beat was to be truly Christian with a wild and reckless joy, life more abundant. But somehow I didn't think it would play well down at the First Baptist Church. It seemed the security most church members wanted was something more temporal and conventional than the security of the believer.

I finished up the page and ran the gauntlet of The Rack for a bio break. I nodded in his direction as I passed without looking at him. He was laying in wait for my return.

"Hey, preacher boy," he growled. "Working on the Christmas edition of your yellow sheet?"

Despite the whipping he gave me before, I saw no point in running scared. "He's the preacher boy." I nodded at Weissman. "I'm the photographer."

"Oh yeah, the king of the snapshots. You know this whole Christmas thing is just a pagan holiday hijacked by the Catholic Church. No basis in history for it at all."

"What?" This one caught me completely by surprise.

"Jesus wasn't born in December. If He was born at all, which I seriously doubt, He was born sometime in the fall, probably October."

"How do you figure?"

"That's when shepherds camped out with their flocks. This whole December thing came about because the Roman Saturnalia festival happened then, and the Catholics couldn't keep their followers from celebrating the pagan holiday. So they just declared it God's birthday and gave the Christians permission to celebrate the same time as their neighbors. Same thing with Easter. You can't even come up with anything original. The whole religion is just a ripoff of other religions."

"Christianity is based on Judaism."

"Right, which rips off other religions. Monotheism? Borrowed from Zoroastrianism. Baby Moses set adrift and discovered by royalty? Borrowed from the Sumerians and the Hindus. Moses receiving the law from God? The Minoans, Egyptians, and

Spartans all beat him to the punch. Shoot, the Ugarit library excavated in 1928 showed most of the same myths, rituals, and gods of the 'chosen' people in Canaan, but it predated them by centuries."

"Uh . . . OK." That wasn't exactly the most snappy comeback, but I thought "Sez you!" might ring a little hollow, and it was all I had. I headed to the sanctuary behind the glass wall.

"Nice talking to you again," I said over my shoulder. "Merry Christmas."

On Saturday, Lori and I joined the trickle of people going to the lecture but detoured into the maze of hedges next to the chapel, picked a space deep in the middle, and spread the blanket. Over cold-cut sandwiches built from items smuggled from the cafeteria, we took turns forcing the other to listen to our favorite songs on the little recorder I borrowed from Fillmore, who used it to tape lectures. I rolled my eyes over Barry Manilow and the Carpenters; she gritted her teeth through Uriah Heep and Deep Purple. We agreed on Cat Stevens and Steely Dan.

We had another date the next week, missing the Christmas cantata so she could help me with my backhand for the tennis final. After she blasted enough serves past me to obliterate my masculinity, she came on my side of the net and gave me pointers on a two-handed grip. We discarded our coats as the exercise warmed us. I had no objections when she positioned my hands for me on the racket and then stood behind me and reached around to grab my wrists and guide the swing and follow-through.

By now the little voice had laryngitis and only spoke in scratchy whispers.

The night before the Christmas break we took a long walk down Grove Street, to the train overpass and back. We said good-bye on the porch of Merle Bruce at ten to avoid the rush.

We stood there awkwardly, saying things like "See you next year" and "Take care during the holidays" and "Be careful." There was a long silence. We just looked at each other. I knew the moment had come.

*No, it hasn't!* the voice rasped in my head. *She's just standing there because you're blocking the door.*

*Hey, Rhymin' Simon.*

*What?*

*Look into those eyes and tell me that.*

There was a long silence.

I said, "Good night," and leaned forward. She closed her eyes and leaned into me. I caught a hint of baby powder and shampoo. We kissed—a long, slow kiss. The taste of cinnamon gum teased my tongue as we pulled apart. I stepped back, smiled, and opened the door for her. She smiled and waved as she disappeared within.

I never heard the voice again.

# CHAPTER TEN

The month break allowed me to catch up on the home front. Bubba, Ralph, Darnell, Jimbo, and I had a reunion at the rest stop where we had celebrated graduation.

Ralph regaled us with stories of welding and derring-do at the refinery. Darnell was halfway through a trucking school, ready to graduate and start driving by the summer.

Jimbo got the occasional work hauling hay and so on, but otherwise lived unencumbered by the expectations of society, a Fred Beat if there ever was one. He even recited a few poems he had picked up from various bathroom walls over the years. Allen Ginsberg had nothing on Jimbo when it came to crudity.

It was a tough act for Bubba, the preacher boy, to follow. He didn't dwell too much on the content of his classes. Instead, he told the story of how Jolene became engaged. Ralph started laughing. We found out why soon enough.

On the previous Saturday morning, Turner McCullough knocked on the Culpepper door. Jolene invited him in. He crept in nervously and perched on the edge of the couch.

"Nice day," he blurted.

"Yup," Jolene answered. She couldn't make any sense of his behavior. She assumed he was there to see if Bubba was back in town, but he didn't seem to be in a hurry to find out.

"Got yer Christmas shoppin' done yet?"

"Yup," she said again.

"Hey," he said. "Would ya marry me?"

"What?"

"Do ya want ta get married?"

"Uh, not really." She looked at him curiously. "I mean, Turner, we aren't even datin'!"

"OK." Turner jumped up. "Well, I got ta go," he said loudly. He bolted for the door and was gone before Jolene could get up from her chair.

Fifteen minutes later Ralph knocked on the door. Jolene let him in. "Ralph, you'll never believe what just happened–"

Ralph interrupted her abruptly. "Nice day."

"Yeah, yeah, but Turner was just here and–"

"Got yer Christmas shoppin' done yet?"

"Yeah, yeah, but," she began, but she stopped and looked at him strangely. "That's exactly what Turner just said."

"Hey," he said. "Would ya marry me?"

"What?" Jolene stared. "But, Turner just–"

"Look, do ya want ta get married or not?" Ralph demanded.

"No! I don't. At least, not ta you," she retorted.

"Fine," Ralph answered and disappeared as quickly as Turner.

The rest of the day every boy she had humiliated over the years showed up at fifteen-minute intervals and proposed marriage with the exact same words. She declined at fifteen-minute intervals until late that afternoon. As the sun was setting, Buddy appeared at the door.

"You'll never believe the day I had," she said as she walked with him to the couch and they sat down.

"Nice day," he said abruptly.

"Not you too!" She jumped up.

"Got yer Christmas shoppin' done yet?"

She looked at him silently.

"Hey," he said. "Would ya marry me?"

Jolene shook her head. "Not a chance . . ."

Buddy looked up in alarm.

". . . that you could get out of it that easy. Yer stuck with me now."

One evening when the womenfolk were on a last-minute shopping spree, I ventured out of my room for a break. I was listening to Leonard Cohen and reading *Dharma Bums,* which I acquired by surrendering *On the Road* and a few Asimov books. It got me thinking about The Rack and the Christmas/Saturnalia thing. I found Dad in his study, working on the Christmas Eve sermon. When I came in, he pushed his commentary aside and looked at me over his glasses.

"The leviathan hath emerged from the depths. Speak and I shall attend thee."

I handed him a cup of hot chocolate, dropped into the armchair, and asked him my questions. He leaned back, rested the cup on his round belly, and verified everything The Rack said. He followed with a question of his own.

"Does it really matter what day we pick to celebrate the birth of Christ? Would you care if we celebrated your birthday in August instead of April?"

"March," I said.

"We can do it then, too, if you like."

"Thanks."

"Paul said, 'Do not let anyone judge you by what you eat or drink, or with regard to a religious festival, a New Moon celebration or a Sabbath day.' God isn't worried about technical details; He looks at our hearts. We could celebrate a holy day on the exactly proper day using the exactly proper rituals, but if we did it for show instead of sincerely worshipping God, it would be pointless."

"What about some other religion with a name that starts with a Z that I can't remember that came up with the idea of one god instead of many gods before Abraham did? What about the library of tablets that was dug up in the Twenties somewhere in what used to be Canaan? He said it had tablets written before the Israelites arrived that contained stuff in the Bible."

"This guy has done his homework. Too bad he's not only missing the forest for the trees, he seems to be lost in the woods. He is right about the details. It's hard to keep the truth a secret. It comes out in the strangest places. Even from the mouths of atheists."

"What? You're saying these other religions are also true?"

"Think of it this way. There are physical laws that describe how the natural world works. Like the speed of light. It's not just a good idea, it's the law!" He chuckled at his joke.

"Yeah, I heard that one already."

"Ah, I guess they're up on all the new stuff at the college."

"You were saying."

"The law of gravity is self-evident. It may have taken centuries for someone like Newton to get hit on the head with an apple and to deduce its inner workings and characterize its effects with mathematical formulas, but even cavemen with no scientific knowledge whatsoever knew they should avoid walking off a cliff."

"Of course."

"In the same way, there are spiritual laws that describe how the spiritual world works. People noticed these things, even before Moses started writing it all down. For example, Paul taught the law of reaping and sowing. 'A man reaps what he sows.' Hinduism teaches the principle of karma: a person's actions will determine his destiny in his next incarnation. While the details vary, the principle is similar. There are echoes of the truth in all religions. But Jesus is the truth, not just an echo of it.

"This is the time of year we acknowledge the coming of the truth, even if it is a few months too late. 'In him was life; and the light was the life of men. And the light shineth in darkness; and the darkness comprehended it not.' Sounds like this guy sees the light, but he doesn't comprehend it."

"See, you can just pull all this stuff out. I need you to come up there and straighten him out."

"Or maybe it's time for you to be ready always to give an answer to every man that asketh you a reason of the hope that is in you with meekness and fear."

"I have the meekness and fear part down. I just need to work on the answer part."

———

When I wasn't thinking on The Beats and The Rack, I contemplated my last few moments with Lori. A few days into the break I spread the eight-by-ten-inch prints on the desk in my bedroom and thought back on the kiss. Then I pulled out some stationery and tossed off a few pages, mainly keeping to events and a list of Christmas gifts given and received. I mentioned that I had given our last visit considerable thought and was awaiting our reunion with anticipation. A few days into the new year, I was stretched out in the den listening to the Brandenburg Concertos and finishing up *Dharma Bums* when Hannah sauntered in and dropped a pink envelope on my chest. It was addressed in a feminine hand and smelled of baby powder.

"Mail call, Romeo. Did you write this in Marshall and mail it to yourself, or is this an actual, bona fide love letter?"

I scanned the front. "You will notice it has a Louisiana postmark. How do you account for that detail?"

"You and Bubba drove over the state line to mail it and then came home. It's only thirty miles from Marshall."

"So you've established means and opportunity. Have you come up with a motive yet?"

"Insanity is its own motive."

"In that case, you should have a whole shoebox of letters from Louisiana."

"So, who is this Lori Street?"

"She is the lady who comes in and cleans the rooms once a week, makes breakfast, and takes dictation. This is her monthly report."

"And the scent?"

"She is hopelessly in love with me. I told her it's no good, my heart belongs to another, but she persists in this hopeless charade. It's kind of sad, really."

"It's more than kind of sad, if you ask me."

"Remind me to ask you one day. Until then, I ask that you depart. You are taking up space I require for other purposes."

She tossed her head and slammed the door behind her. I ripped the letter from the envelope. It was filled with details similar to the one I sent Lori. But the postscript stopped my pulse with a spasm of electricity. It read, "At our next parting, don't be so stingy."

---

The end of the break couldn't come fast enough for me. Five months earlier I thought nobody could be more ready to leave a town than I was. But I was mistaken. Then, I was consumed with but one desire, to get out of Fred as quickly as I could. But it was a negative desire, a desire to escape something. Fred was the vacuum that defied all known laws of physics and pushed me away rather than sucked me in.

But now I counted the days until I could see Lori again and be more generous. Bubba evidently felt restless as well. We agreed to drive up Saturday, a day earlier than most people returned. That's when we discovered the dorm didn't open until Sunday afternoon. Which explained why most people returned that day. We sneaked in the fire escape when nobody was looking and kept quiet.

We didn't have enough people to play dominoes. You need three to play moon, four to play 42. I rummaged through the Phils' room, found the Hava Tampa Jewels, and Bubba and I smoked cigars and listened to Ray Wiley Hubbard. After a long silence, Bubba spoke up.

"I've been doin' some thinkin'."

"Don't strain yourself."

"I'm swearin' off the pranks."

I arched a brow and peered through the smoke. "You appeared to enjoy them well enough."

"That's the problem. I ended up spendin' too much time thinkin' up pranks and not enough time on the real reason I'm here."

"Studying is for those who can't handle pranks."

"Mark, why exactly are you here?"

I pondered the question for a minute. "I live here."

"Why?"

"Mainly because they won't let me live in Merle Bruce." I attempted to blow smoke rings without success. "Is there a point to this?"

"I don't know. Just seems ta me that yer floatin' through this thing. What's yer major?"

"Beats me."

"What do you want ta do?"

"Right now, I want to enjoy this cigar and think about Lori coming back tomorrow."

"Seems like an expensive way to get cigars and meet women. You could do that a lot cheaper at Lamar back home."

"You would think that, wouldn't you? But as it turns out, because I'm a PK, I can go here cheaper than a state college."

We sat in silence for awhile. Shadows crept up the wall and the room slipped into gloom. I switched on the desk lamp next to my bed. Bubba's cigar glowed on the other side of the room.

"I'm just taking it one day at a time," I said. "Consider the lilies of the field, how they grow; they toil not, neither do they spin, is the way I see it. Take no thought for tomorrow, for tomorrow will take care of itself. Sufficient until the day is the evil thereof." I blew a smoke ring with greater success.

"The same guy said, 'Which of you, intending to build a tower, sitteth not down first, and counteth the cost, whether he have sufficient to finish it? Lest haply, after he hath laid the foundation, and is not able to finish it, all that behold him begin to mock him.'"

I should have known better than to get into a Bible-quoting match with Bubba of the ten-pound KJV family Bible and the photographic memory.

"Look," Bubba said, "I'm not tellin' ya what ta do. It's yer nickel. But it seems ta me you got a head start over most the rest of us. Both yer folks got degrees, right?" I nodded. "And with yer photographer job, you got a free ride here, right? And yer not the dullest knife in the drawer."

"Very kind of you to say, I'm sure."

"Ya only get one shot at college. Most folks don't even get that much. You really want ta risk it all drinkin' and smokin' dope?"

"Correction: drinking. I do not smoke dope."

"Drinkin' is enough to get you kicked out. But you hang with Phyllis, who does smoke dope. If he goes down, he's goin' ta take you with 'im. Don't blow it, is all I'm sayin'."

I inclined my head in his direction. "I'll take your comments under advisement and get back with you."

"You know why they don't send donkeys ta school, don't ya?"

"Yes, I believe I do," I answered.

"Touché," I added, after a few minutes.

# CHAPTER ELEVEN

The second semester proceeded much as the first, but this time we had the benefit of experience. We knew to research the right professor for a class and not to schedule any MWF classes before ten or after three.

My reunion with Lori was everything I imagined it might be. I still could not fathom why a girl such as she would consort with a guy such as me, but I chose not to question fate. I continued to solve calculus problems for no apparent reason, take photos, lay out the paper, endure the intermittent abuses of The Rack, play 42 each Monday, and pull the occasional prank.

Lori and I were spotted swapping saliva so often that our status became common knowledge. The eight-by-tens migrated from my notebook to my wall, and I supplemented my collection.

Too soon I was cramming for finals and trying to figure out how I would survive three months without my daily Lori quota. We had our tearful farewell, and before I could comprehend the change, I was back in Fred for the summer.

Friday night I called Jolene to hear the latest news.

"So, you haven't heard," she said.

"Evidently not."

"Remember Elrick Williams?"

Of course I remembered Elrick. He was the black student who came from Dallas my junior year and took the school by storm. Before Elrick, the school was effectively segregated although officially integrated. Whites did their thing, and blacks did theirs. An unspoken line ran through the classrooms, the cafeteria, and the bleachers. There wasn't any apparent tension or unrest. Each group just preferred it that way, dealing with the familiar and keeping the unfamiliar at a comfortable distance.

On his first day, Elrick sat down at lunch with a group of white guys. Granted, he was escorted by C. J., who was oblivious to the unspoken code. But a few weeks with Elrick convinced me that he would have done the same thing on his own.

Elrick and I were brothers in arms, even though he was as black as a Nubian and I was as pale as a Brit. Our shared fate as PKs forged a bond that my white compatriots and his black brothers would never comprehend. Bubba and I even attended a Sunday night service at his church, where Bubba was declared in possession of an inordinate degree of soul. I hadn't seen him in a year, but I would never forget Elrick Williams.

"Sure," I answered.

"Remember Becky Tuttle?"

I forgot to breathe. I had done my best to forget Becky Tuttle. And with Lori's help I almost succeeded. I had spent years building a shrine to Becky, a shrine of unrequited love. Knights bent on chivalry were puling punks in knickers compared to the torments of chaste longing I inflicted upon my unwilling flesh. Not that I desired to be chaste when it came to Becky. My myriad stratagems had singly come to naught up to the final barricade, which I assaulted with vigor until I heard the dread word *friend*. No suitor was proof against this hideous word.

Jolene knew better than to ask me if I remembered Becky. "Yes," I whispered hoarsely into the phone.

"Becky danced with Elrick at homecoming last year." She paused. "Hello?"

"Yes."

"Did you hear me?"

"I heard you. Is that the end of the story?"

"Not by a long shot. Before the dance was over, her daddy showed up and took her home. We think a teacher called 'im."

"Figures."

"I thought it was just one of them things, but turns out she loves 'im. Least that's what she says. I don't get it. I mean, Elrick is a nice guy and captain of the football team, but . . . Well, you know."

"Yeah, I know."

"So, now she's practically a prisoner in her own house. And at school they spy on her and report any contact, and her daddy will come there at the drop of a hat. We even had a few Klan meetin's this year."

"Klan meetings?"

"Yep, that's what I hear. Ain't actually seen one, of course."

The conversation turned to the wedding, which was only a month away, and other less sensational news. I hung up the phone and pondered these things in my heart. At first I felt slighted. How is it she would have taken to Elrick and passed me by? After all, I was at least white. Then I realized with some private embarrassment the racism my instinctive reaction revealed. On the other hand, it would explain why she had not found me desirable. It mitigated the lingering wound I nursed for half a decade. But only slightly.

Saturday morning Heidi called me to the phone. "Some girl," she said as she handed it to me.

"Hello?"

"Mark, is that you?"

"Yes."

"Hi, this is Becky."

My pulse doubled. "Hi. How's it going?"

"Not too good, really. I guess you heard about what happened?"

"I heard a little."

She filled me in on the gory details. Just listening to her talk so passionately opened up all the old wounds that she never knew were there. She told me how they had danced at homecoming and how all hell had broken loose and her dad came and hauled her away in disgrace. How she tried to run away. How her love survived on a starvation diet of clandestine notes passed through sympathetic friends.

When the senior prom arrived, she couldn't get a date on a bet. The only taker was a freshman, and when his mother found out, she locked him in his room. "Which brings me to why I called." There was silence as I sat, very moved but equally mystified. "Mark, would you go with me to the prom?"

I was sure all my vital signs stopped. My mouth opened, but no sound came out.

"Hello? Are you there?"

"Yes, yes," I blurted out. I took a deep breath. "Yes," I said with conviction.

"Yes you're there?"

"Yes, and yes to the other question too."

"Oh." There was a long silence. "You mean it?" she asked quietly.

"Yes, I mean it. I want to."

"Oh," she said in a softer voice. "Thanks." This time her voice was a little shaky.

Then I remembered Lori.

I said a word not normally heard in the Cloud household. Probably not ever said in the Cloud household. I looked around guiltily.

"What?"

"I'm sorry. There's something I forgot."

"You're busy that night. No, I understand, Mark. It's too much to ask. I just thought—"

"No!" I yelled before I regained control. "No," I said more calmly. "It's just that I'm dating this girl at college. We made a vow: no secrets from each other. I need to talk to her about it. Can I call you back?"

"Sure."

I hung up in a daze. After years of silent agony, I finally had a date with Becky, but first I had to ask permission from my girlfriend. God had a sick sense of humor. I dug out Lori's home number, but when I picked up the phone, I discovered that someone had acquired the phone in the meantime. We had a party line, and when the other parties got the urge, they would talk for hours.

I cursed my fate, grabbed some change, and headed to the pay phone at Fred Grocery. Lori and I had a long and rather tedious conversation that I tried to keep private, but Fred Grocery is no place to discuss secrets. I finally convinced Lori there was no danger in me taking pity on this poor girl and escorting her to the prom. Unfortunately, I wasn't able to convince myself of the same thing. The beast, once reawakened, was prowling with a renewed vigor after years of denial.

---

That night I walked the half-mile to the pool hall, strolled in, and stopped just inside the door, aware my appearance would cause a minor sensation. My straight blond hair now hung to my shoulders. I was wearing a dilapidated straw cowboy hat after the style of Dr. Hook and the Medicine Show, sides pressed up against the crown, front and back pulled down. I was also wearing a western shirt, skinny brown suspenders, faded jeans, and square-toed boots.

The buzz in the room lowered to near silence for a few seconds, the Tom T. Hall song on the jukebox suddenly audible, then shot up to an artificially high level. You get used to things like that when you have long hair in East Texas. But I didn't figure there would be any trouble in Fred; just about everybody knew me. I nodded to a few familiar faces as I walked through the cigarette haze past the pool tables.

I lurked near the foosball table, noting that the players were rank amateurs. During the past year I learned to play goalie and got steady work, leaving all the flash and glory to the guys with the quarters. I had perfected a bank shot from the backfield that beat major league batting averages. Noting the line of quarters on the table, I decided to wait awhile. I went outside to smoke one of the cigars I had requisitioned from Phyllis.

Tyler was a dry county, but most of the vehicles in the parking lot had a cooler in the back. From such a truck came a young cowboy, weaving his way through the lot with the deliberate stride of a drunk, despite obviously being under eighteen, the legal limit. He was wearing a blue F.F.A. jacket with Spurger stitched on the back and a black felt cowboy hat jammed down so far it covered his eyebrows.

He came to a stumbling halt at the entrance, glared at me with distaste, spat in the dirt, and staggered in, smelling of beer and hair grease. I looked across the road at the pine trees silhouetted against the Milky Way and reflected on life and green things in general and Becky things in particular. The cigar and the scenery did nothing to relieve the growing disquiet in my soul. I thought of calling the date off, but knew I couldn't do that to her, regardless of what I was doing to myself.

A few minutes later the drunken cowboy staggered back out, leaned against the wall, and glared. I nodded to acknowledge his presence and resumed my reflection. I didn't know him, but I inferred from his behavior that he took exception to my preference in hair length.

Joe Bob broke the silence with a comparison of my cigar to a certain portion of the anatomy of a male donkey. I smiled enigmatically and blew smoke in his direction. He repeated the analogy. I debated whether to speak. One can go a long way with silence if carried with the proper attitude.

But I found Joe Bob's crude familiarity offensive. I expected good country boys to respect their elders. I cut him a measure of slackage for two reasons. People frequently thought I was at least two years younger than I was. Also, he was from Spurger.

In the end I weighed these factors in the balance and found them wanting. Joe Bob needed a lesson in manners. In Texas, if someone needs straightening out, we just take him out back. Unfortunately, I felt unqualified to give him the lesson in the only manner likely to register, a good thrashing. I resorted to my weapon of choice—words.

I cleared my throat, took in the entirety of his short, stocky frame in a withering glance, and replied that he had a surprising familiarity with the private parts of a donkey. For good measure, I also raised certain vague speculations as to how he acquired such an intimate knowledge. Can't afford to be too subtle in an East Texas pool hall if you want your point to register.

A girl appeared at the door and watched Joe Bob nervously. I knew her from high school, Kathy somebody. She could see Joe Bob wanted to beat me like a rented mule. The look she gave me was a mixture of apology and pleading. I nodded to her.

There were rules to this kind of thing. Joe Bob couldn't just walk up and start pounding me. He had to annoy me to the point that I would throw the first punch or goad me into an insult offensive enough that he could throw the first punch. I knew the rules as well as Joe Bob did. I had spent years developing the skill of extricating myself from potentially violent confrontations. Joe Bob didn't pose a threat. I wouldn't be throwing any punches, and I could see he was too drunk to recognize anything short of a vulgar insult to his mother.

But the best way to win a fight is to avoid it altogether. I tossed the cigar in the dirt, returned to the foosball table, and found a partner. I had almost forgotten about Joe Bob when he appeared at my left shoulder.

"Say, when's the last time ya got yer hair cut?" he demanded and leaned on me just as the opposition made a shot. It rolled in for a point. Amazed that I missed such a slow ball, everyone looked up and saw the growth on my shoulder. With a few well-chosen curses, my partner shoved Joe Bob and told him he was going to pay for the games if he made us lose.

Joe Bob muttered under his breath, puzzled at the lack of support from his friends. He moved to the end of the table, bristling for the sake of his self-respect.

"Hey! I asked ya a question." I raised an eyebrow at him and returned my attention to the game. "When's the last time ya got a haircut?"

I answered casually as I continued to play. "Do you remember your last haircut?" I glanced up at Joe Bob. "Do you even remember your last name?"

My partner tried to turn his laugh into a cough and almost missed a shot. I noticed the other team was grinning even though they lost a point.

"Hey! If ya look like a hippie, how come ya dress like a cowboy?"

"It's required for officers in the Willie Nelson Fan Club."

Kathy appeared and attempted to save Joe Bob from further humiliation.

"Come on, Jimmy, let's go play a game of pool."

Ah, so his name was Jimmy. I liked Joe Bob better; it fit him so well. But pool held no allure for Joe Bob this night, regardless of how the game may have entranced him in days past. He may not have been bright, but he was persistent. He knew what he wanted, a chance to flatten the face of a hippie, and he wasn't quitting until he got it.

"Hey! Long hair, jeans, boots. You ain't no cowboy. Yer a cowgirl!" He sneered, certain he had hit his mark this time.

I shook my head. "Nobody else in here is confused about my gender." I paused to block a shot and pass it up to my partner. "Are you getting enough oxygen to that vestigial brain of yours? Perhaps your hat is screwed on too tightly."

Joe Bob blinked at this flurry of words and frowned. Kathy resorted to direct pleading.

"Jimmy, leave him alone. His daddy's the preacher."

"Hey! So you're the preacher's daughter. How about a little date, honey?"

I was disappointed. I considered this comment beneath even Joe Bob's level. I almost didn't reply, it was such an easy shot, but I felt compelled since there were witnesses.

"You pick the pool hall on a Saturday night as the time and place for coming out of the closet? And with such a pretty girl-friend. You surprise me, Joe Bob."

"Who's Joe Bob?" he asked.

"Jimmy, he's from 'round here," Kathy yelled at him. "He's taking Becky Tuttle ta the prom."

My head jerked up as the room fell silent. How did she know that? Then I remembered. She was in Fred Grocery while I was on the phone to Lori. The news had just been released for mass distribution.

Everyone stared at me. The foosball game came to a halt. Joe Bob seized the opportunity Kathy laid in his lap.

"So, yer takin' that coon-lover ta the prom! Then ya must be a coon-lover too." He took a step toward me, and even Kathy saw the futility of trying to stop him.

I stepped back from the table and turned to face him. "I don't follow your logic, or lack of it, Joe Bob. I'm taking Becky to the prom, not Elrick."

"You coon-lovers like ta stick together, don't ya?"

The blood rushed to my head. "Hey, I'm just taking one of the prettiest girls in the school to the prom. I don't think that qualifies me as a coon-lover."

I spat the last two words out with scorn. In my rage I lost control and offered Joe Bob the opportunity he had been fishing for all night.

"Since Kathy is dating you, that makes her an idiot-lover. You're probably taking her to the prom, so you must be an idiot-lover too! I hear you idiot-lovers like to stick together."

Joe Bob roared a volley of curses and rushed me. I was almost as surprised as he was when he came crashing down in front of me. Ralph Mull leaned over and pulled him up from the floor by his shirt collar.

"Jimmy, you're not bein' very friendly ta my buddy."

Joe Bob turned to take on Ralph, but even in his inebriated state he could see Ralph was at least a foot taller and outweighed him by a considerable margin. Instead, he turned to me and snarled, "Coon-lovin' hippie."

Ralph shook him a little. "Jimmy, didn't your mama never teach ya no manners? I think ya should apologize ta Mr. Cloud."

Joe Bob shook loose Ralph's grip and shuffled off, muttering. My heart was pounding almost as hard as when Becky asked me to the prom.

Ralph watched him go and turned back to me. "Hey, Mark. Back from college? Let's go outside and get a beer."

"Hey," my partner interjected. "We're in a game here."

"Find another goalie," Ralph said, and ushered me out into the parking lot.

He twisted his way through the cars and I followed, looking for his old '61 Falcon. Instead he came to a halt at the back of a new Ford pickup. He flipped open a cooler and held out a beer. I shook my head. I knew better than to ask if he had any wine coolers. He slammed the lid shut, sat on the tailgate, opened the beer, and took a long drink. I took a seat next to him and fired up a cigar. We sat in silence for awhile.

"So, you're taking Becky ta the prom."

"Yeah."

"I guess you know what happened."

"Yeah." We sat in silence for several minutes.

"Well, it's your nickel," he finally said.

"OK, Ralph," I said with a bit of irritation. "Name me one girl that's prettier than Becky. Just one."

"Jolene Culpepper," he said without a second of hesitation.

"Fine. Jolene Culpepper. Name another one," I said with a bit more irritation. I waited for a minute or two, but he didn't say anything. "So, give me one good reason not to take Becky to the prom."

"Elrick Williams," he said, again without hesitation.

"Fine. Elrick Williams. Name another one." He snorted. "I rest my case," I said with a flourish of the cigar. "Oh, and by the way, thanks."

"Shut up and git in the truck. I'll give ya a ride home."

**CHAPTER TWELVE** I kept my mind off the prom by finding a summer job. The lumberyard where I worked the previous summer hired me, and before I knew it I was getting up at 4:00 A.M. and pulling plywood off a belt by five. Summer jobs really have one purpose, to convince you that college isn't so bad after all. This job was no exception. However, physical labor leaves the mind free to wander, and mine relentlessly returned to the subject of Becky Tuttle.

What kind of fool was I, agreeing to take Becky to the prom? It made about as much sense as a reformed alcoholic joining a fraternity.

Then there was the matter of Lori. While it was incomprehensible how she could be crazy about me, it was also indisputable. I had ample firsthand evidence. So a girl who has ignored me all through high school calls me up and announces that she's in love with somebody else as a preamble to asking me to the prom. What kind of idiot jumps at the chance to go on this date when he has the affections of someone like Lori? The Mark Cloud kind, evidently.

----

Fredonians didn't rent tuxedos for something as mundane as a prom. A wedding, maybe, but definitely not a prom. I didn't own a suit, but that wasn't a problem. The other guys would be wearing leisure suits and cowboy boots. On Saturday I threw together a garish combination of slacks and sports coat and jumped in the car.

To my surprise, when I arrived to pick Becky up, her parents treated me like royalty. I was unaccustomed to such a reception in East Texas because of my shoulder-length hair, but all they saw was my lily-white complexion. A hippie was a welcome change to them.

Becky was wearing a long formal. Like a movie preview, it showed just enough to make you want to see the rest without giving away the ending. As soon as I saw her I knew it was a mistake. How could I treat this vision of beauty like a friendly date? And if I didn't, how could I escape being torn to bits by both Elrick and Lori? They would sell tickets and take turns.

We drove to the dance in awkward silence punctuated by fits of strained dialogue. I had no idea what she was thinking, but I was contemplating the cruel jokes played by fate. Here I was, alone with the girl of my dreams and owing it all to the fact that she was desperately in love with someone else.

At the prom I confessed to Becky that I didn't know how to dance. It's an occupational hazard of being a Baptist preacher's kid. She looked distractedly around the room and said she didn't feel like dancing anyway.

I made a trip to the refreshment table, noting that there were sufficient chaperones to assure that Becky and Elrick had no contact. I returned to find her staring across the room. I followed her gaze and saw Elrick. The expression on his face triggered a revelation. He knew nothing of the arrangement. I realized I should have at least made a phone call to him, if not a visit. Now it was too late. And the ferocity in his eyes told me that in this case, late was not better than never.

It wasn't difficult to guess the thoughts torturing his mind. He came to Warren High School from the big city. For all I knew, such things as a black guy and a white girl dancing were common in a place like Dallas. He revolutionized the football team, becoming the first black team captain in the history of the school. He ran for and won student council representative for his class. He was in the Beta club, the Debate Society. He initiated the acceptance of funk as a serious contender to country on the cafeteria jukebox. He had, from all appearances, scaled the color barrier and single-handedly integrated the school. Not that the school wasn't integrated before, but whites and blacks clustered in cliques before his arrival. He changed that. At least he must have thought he changed that.

Then he stepped across the line. He dared to believe that he really had changed something, that the surface changes reflected a tectonic cultural shift. It's not surprising that Becky would be drawn to such self-confidence and vision. There were more differences between Elrick and me than our skin color.

But now Elrick was trapped in the Jim-Crow corner the blacks staked out for themselves in the wake of the backlash, while I escorted the girl he loved because my skin happened to be the right color. How could he know that my own personal torment was to sit next to her throughout the night, tortured with that same knowledge? Yearning to be desired for who I was but admitted to her presence through a perverse kind of affirmative action? I was not selected for my merits, but only to meet the racial quota of one white male for every white female.

And Becky was forced to sit and stare longingly across the room at the unattainable object of her affections. We sat together, each burning with desire for something we couldn't have.

Late in the evening the band played one of my favorite tunes, "Autumn" by Edgar Winter, who was, in a case of ironic over-kill, an albino. Overcoming my two-left-feet self-consciousness, I asked Becky to dance. She consented and we walked out onto the dance floor. I shuffled awkwardly around, attempting to mimic the moves of the other dancers and grateful for the semidarkness to hide my inexperience. I lacked the detachment I achieved the night I danced with Jolene. Too many things conspired against me to return to that nirvana.

I tried to absorb every nuance of the experience, knowing it was as close as I would ever come to my dream. I felt the softness of her right hand nestled in my left and the pressure of her left hand on my shoulder. My fingertips rested lightly on her back, desiring but not daring to stroke the smooth skin. My chin brushed against her hair, the scent of lavender rising from her slender neck. The Marquis could hardly have devised a more exquisite torture.

The music ended but Becky just stood there. I muttered, "We can go sit down if you like."

She whispered, "You're standin' on my dress."

I stepped back and glanced at Elrick. The dark looks he flashed my direction were disconcerting. They suggested the rage of a caged animal, a pent-up fury threatening at any moment to explode.

Several glasses of punch later I made a trip to the bathroom and ran into Elrick in the hall. He moved to brush past me, but I stepped in front of him. He stopped abruptly to keep from running me down and glared into my eyes, breathing heavily through his nose.

"Make a hole, Cloud, or I'll make a hole in you."

"Elrick, who do you think I am?"

"One of them."

"Them?" I moved to the wall on my right, as if to let him pass.

"Don't start with me, Cloud. I'm givin' you fair warnin'."

I released the stinger. "And who is Becky? She's white too. Is she one of them?" I bit off the word *them* the same way I bit off *coon-lover* the week before.

Elrick swung heavy with his right and I ducked to his left. His knuckles crashed against the wall an inch from my left ear. Before he could roar with pain, I put my left foot against his chest and pushed with all my weight, which was not much. It was sufficient to stagger him back several steps. He recovered sooner than I expected and rushed me. I backed to the bathroom door. He faked with his right, which was bleeding, and caught me on the cheek with his left. It drove me through the door onto the floor of the bathroom.

He came charging in after me, but I rolled to the nearest stall, slammed the door, leaned on it and locked it just before he hit it. It held.

"Elrick," I hollered from the stall, bracing my feet against the toilet. "Have you gone crazy? It's me, Mark."

"I'll make a mark on ya." He slammed against the door again. The metal around the screws on the latch warped out but held.

"Why do you think I'm here?" I called over the partition.

A short silence followed, then his leg whipped under the partition and caught one of my feet, almost knocking me off balance. I jumped to the toilet and looked over the partition. He was crouched for another attempt.

"She called me and asked me to the prom," I called down to him.

He sprang at me. "Liar."

I jerked backward and lost my footing. My left foot dropped into the toilet. My right leg hit the handle. Water swirled around my left foot. I braced myself against the walls and lifted my dripping shoe.

"Didn't she tell you?"

"How would she tell me?" His voice was a sudden wail.

I awaited the next assault, but it never came. I peeked over the partition. Elrick was on his knees. His shirt was missing a few buttons and hung open, dotted with blood from his fist.

"If you'll quit trying to pound on me, maybe we can figure something out."

He looked up at me, uncomprehending in his pain. But he didn't move. I decided to chance it. I climbed down from the toilet and unlocked the stall.

I peeked around the door. Elrick stood up. I stepped out. The bathroom door opened and a short kid came in, probably a junior.

"The bathroom's out of order, use the other one," I said. He looked from me, disheveled and winded, to Elrick, shirt torn open, blood dripping from his fist.

"What other one?"

"I don't know. Use the parking lot. Just get out of here." He left. I looked at Elrick. "Go wash your hand."

He looked at his hand and moved to a sink. I stepped up next to him.

"I heard about this mess when I got back in town. Becky called me and said the only way she could get to the prom was if I would take her. All her other options bailed on her, and her parents wouldn't let her go unless she had a date."

The blood from Elrick's knuckles swirled down the drain.

"I'm just here for the summer and I'm out of here. I have a girlfriend at college. I just did this as a favor to Becky, so she wouldn't miss her senior prom." I figured this was close enough to the truth. My history of burning with desire for Becky was immaterial. Nothing was going to come of it, so there was no need to complicate the picture. The inside of my head was complicated enough.

Elrick glanced up in the mirror. I caught his glance and raised my eyebrows, waiting for a response. He looked back down.

"How did this happen, Elrick?"

"I don't know. It happened slow and all of a sudden. One day I looked up and knew I loved her for a long time. From there on out, it burned me 'til I couldn't stand it and had to say somethin'."

"I know just how you feel. Drove me crazy too." He jerked around. "With Lori, I mean. At college." He searched my face, then ripped off a paper towel. "So, what did your folks say?"

He dried his hands for awhile and tried to straighten up his shirt. "They think I gone crazy. And that I'm bringin' down trouble on their heads with no cause." He tossed the paper towel at the trashcan. "I guess they're right, but I can't help it."

"Let me give you a little advice. Play it cool for now. In a week you'll both graduate and then the school won't be able to interfere. You have enough trouble with her parents and yours. Don't stir up more with the school."

He grunted.

"And it'll never work here. You'll have to leave home if you want to pursue this thing. You might even have to leave your family behind. I'd say you have to count the cost."

Elrick stood in silence for awhile. I looked around and caught my reflection in the mirror.

"Man, what did you do to me?" I stepped closer. My cheek was split and a trickle of blood ran down my face. The huge red bruise would be purple by morning. "Great."

I saw the barest hint of a smile from Elrick in the mirror. "You were provokin' me."

We returned to the ballroom through separate doors. Becky gave me a strange look when she saw my cheek.

"Floor was wet in the bathroom. I slipped and hit the sink."

She looked across the room. Elrick walked in, looked at us. Even from that distance I could see his face harden back to the mask he had been wearing all night. He looked away. She looked back at me but didn't say anything.

On the drive back I allowed myself a final bout of aching desire for the girl leaning against the other door. I wondered what she would do if I told her how I had endured years of silent longing for her. Would she abandon the unattainable Elrick and settle for me? Or would she recoil in disgust? After all this time I still had no idea. I didn't ask.

I walked her to the porch. I could hear *Saturday Night Live* playing behind the front door. We looked at each other in silence. I wondered if I should kiss her. After five years, I felt I deserved something for my devotion.

"So, what will you do?" I asked instead.

"I don't know."

"Well . . ." There really wasn't anything to say. I could see it was hopeless. "I hope it works out for you."

A tear brimmed and trickled down her face, leaving a trail of mascara. I guess she knew it wouldn't.

"I'm sorry. I shouldn't have said anything."

"No, that's OK. It's not your fault." She smeared the mascara on her cheek with the back of her hand. "He hit you, didn't he?"

"No, I threw the first punch. Got lucky and cracked his knuckles with my cheek. It just took all the fight out of him."

She let out an amalgam of chuckle and sob.

"Thanks for going with me, Mark."

"Thanks for asking." We looked at each other for a second. "Good night."

"Good night," she said and slowly walked up on the porch.

I turned and walked to the car. I backed out of the driveway, shifted into first, and took one last look. Becky was standing on the porch. I nodded and drove away.

---

When I got home Mom was sitting at the table with a cup of hot tea and Sandburg's *Lincoln*. The light in the study indicated that Dad was working on a sermon.

"Mark, what happened to your face?" She jumped up and filled a dishtowel with ice.

"You should see the other guy."

"Who was the other guy?" She held the ice to my cheek, her hand against the back of my head. I winced and took the ice from her. We sat down at the table.

"Elrick."

"Reverend Williams's boy? Why would he hit you?"

"I took his girl to the prom."

She gasped. "You went to the prom with a Negro girl? I thought you were going with Becky."

"I did." I sat in silence, watching her face as it flitted through several expressions.

"I think Hannah said something about that. Didn't something happen last fall?"

"They danced at homecoming."

"Yes." We sat for awhile. She sipped her tea. I repositioned the towel to prevent the melting ice from dripping on my pants. "That's too bad."

"What's too bad?"

"Those two. They should have stayed with their own kind."

"Mom! Their own kind?"

She looked at me with an indulgent smile, as if explaining something to a slow child. "Of course. Love is hard enough without complicating it with something like race. Look at how many people don't make it as it is, without having to worry about everybody in the county trying to break them up.

"On the other hand, we don't necessarily pick who we fall in love with. Sometimes love picks for us. I never figured I'd marry a preacher, but here I am, in Fred." She shook her head with a small smile.

During all those years of ulcerating in this wilderness, it never occurred to me that anyone, especially Mom, was dissatisfied with the arrangement.

"You didn't want to move here?"

"Oh my, don't be silly. Who wouldn't want to move to East Texas with its giant flying cockroaches and little scorpions and rattlesnakes and copperheads and armadillos? And then think of all those dreary plays and symphonies and galleries that those poor people in the city endure. It must be dreadful for them."

This was mind-boggling. "Where did you want to go?"

"I would like to try San Francisco. Just think of all that fog."

"Then why did we come here?"

"Life is like love. You don't pick it; it picks you. I fell in love with a preacher boy, and the rest fell like dominoes. You can decide which domino to thump, but the rest go without your help."

"So you're saying be careful who you fall in love with?"

"Yes, if you can." She got up to pour more hot water into the teacup. "If you can."

All kinds of questions were awakened by this unexpected view into the past. I hesitantly voiced one. "Do you think you made a mistake?"

Mom smiled and came back to the table. "Oh no, dear. I'm not sure I had much choice. Once I saw your father, the domino thumped itself. But I was lucky. If you and the girls do half as well, I'll be happy."

I fixed a Dr Pepper and wondered about Lori. Should I thump her domino?

# CHAPTER THIRTEEN
Between slaving away at the lumber mill and being pummeled by youthful Othellos, my time was pretty full. But across the highway, others had busy lives of their own. The Culpepper-Jowett wedding was fast approaching, and Jolene was orchestrating the arrangements with the frenzy of a whirling dervish. But as often happened in Jolene's presence, things didn't exactly turn out as planned. The details of most of the unexpected developments were known only to a select few; in some cases, only to Jolene and Buddy. I eventually came to know even the most intimate details and pieced together the full story from multiple sources over the stretch of a decade.

The week of the wedding was a typical searing Texas June that sapped their energy. Jolene and Buddy finished up the last details on Thursday night. They sat on the porch swing awhile, watching the kamikaze June bugs buzzing around, thudding into the light and skidding along the floor. After awhile, Buddy stretched his legs and got up.

"Hey, I don't guess I'll see ya tomorrow. A lot of folks are comin' into town and I promised Toni we'd go swimmin' at Toodlum Creek."

"Tony?" Jolene asked. "Do I know Tony?"

"Nope. But we used ta go swimmin' a lot when we were kids, and I promised one last swim for old-time's sake."

"Well, I guess that's better than a stag party," Jolene conceded.

Buddy raised an eyebrow. "Who says I'm not havin' a stag party?"

Jolene shot him a look that would have sobered Dean Martin. Buddy responded with his lopsided grin, kissed Jolene on the forehead, and left.

By sunrise on Friday it was already hot. Jolene took the wedding dress to the one-hour cleaners in Silsbee in Bubba's Corvair. It had no air-conditioning. She basted in this mobile convection oven for an hour. By the time she returned, she was ready to toss all the venison out of the deep-freeze and climb in. Bubba met her at the car door, grabbed the car keys, and left.

Jolene decided to join Buddy and Tony at the creek, but all the cars were gone. She pulled a bicycle out of the shed.

By the time she found Buddy's truck, she was as limp as a banana peel and considerably sweatier. She tossed her bike in the back of the truck and took the trail to the swimming hole. What she saw when she parted the bushes made her hotter.

Buddy was there all right. And he was handing the swinging rope to a blonde in a yellow bikini with ample features even a boat tarp couldn't conceal. And Buddy wasn't bashful while helping her get on the rope.

Jolene started to barge through the brush when Buddy gave the girl a push from the bank and she went swinging across the water with a disgusting squeal. She stayed on for the return swing and tried to get off, but Buddy laughed and gave her another push. She dropped to the water, feet first. The shock caused a minor but significant wardrobe malfunction.

Jolene opened her mouth but nothing came out. Instead, it slowly shut and bent itself into a smile. It was not the kind of smile a fiancé would like to see on his bride-to-be the day before the wedding. It had a suggestion of the burning pirate ship about it.

She retraced her steps down the path, slipped into Buddy's truck, pulled a set of keys from behind the air-conditioner, and smiled smugly. She let the truck roll back and popped the clutch.

A fifteen-minute ride put her at home, where Bubba was washing his Corvair.

"Hey, Bubba. Buddy asked me to drop his truck off at his aunt's house. Could you follow me and bring me back?"

He eyed the brilliant blue finish appreciatively. "I always wanted ta drive this thang. You drive the car. The keys are in it."

Jolene shrugged and traded places. She raced out of the driveway in the Corvair while Bubba took his time adjusting the seat and the mirrors. A lot of time had passed, and she was worried that Buddy might have found a way back home already. She glanced in the rearview mirror. "Dang it, Bubba, get a move on," she muttered. She checked her watch and punched the gas.

She stopped on the side of the road by the aunt's house and waited for Bubba. Five minutes passed. No Bubba. Ten minutes passed. No Bubba. She muttered all the way back to her house but saw no sign of Bubba. She returned to the aunt's house and came back again without seeing a trace of her brother.

"Great!" She stomped into the house and slammed the door. "Just great!"

Her tantrum was interrupted by the phone. She snatched it off the wall. "What?" she barked into the receiver.

"Jolene, what the heck is goin' on?"

"Bubba!" She glared at the phone. "Where in the world are you? You were supposed to follow me!"

"I'm in jail."

"What?"

"I been arrested for stealin' a pickup truck. You wouldn't know anything about that, would ya?"

"Uhhh. Listen, Bubba. I can explain the whole thing. You see, I saw Buddy out at Toodlum Creek with some girl, and I was so mad I decided ta teach him a lesson."

"Very funny. The officers down here are really gonna buy that one."

"Sure they will. Put 'em on the phone and I'll explain it."

In a second she heard a gravelly voice. "Deputy Lynch."

"Hello, Mr. Lynch. This is Jolene Culpepper. I'm Bubba's sister. You see, this whole thing is just a little joke I was playin' on my fiancé."

"We don't look on grand theft, auto, as a laughin' matter, Miss Culpepper."

"But I didn't steal the truck. As a matter of fact, I was in the process of takin' it ta Buddy's house when all this happened."

"Ma'am, you ain't bein' charged with stealin' the truck. Mr. Bodean Culpepper is."

"But he didn't take it. I did."

There was a moment of silence. "Ma'am, are you confessin' to conspiracy ta steal a vehicle?"

"No! No! We didn't steal it! It's just a joke. It's my fiancé's truck. If you'd just let me explain."

"This truck belongs ta your fiancé?"

"Yes," she said, emphatically. "He was out at the creek when I came along and–"

Lynch interrupted. "Is this truck insured for theft?"

"How should I know?"

"If you was in a conspiracy ta defraud the insurance company, you'd know."

"Really, Mr. Lynch!"

"Ma'am, I believe you'd better come down here and straighten this thing out. We'll be keepin' Mr. Culpepper here nice and cozy 'til you show up. Oh, and you might want ta bring a bondsman along."

Jolene didn't panic. A lifetime of practical jokes had trained her to think fast. She called Mary, and a few minutes later they were on their way to Silsbee. At the police station, Jolene announced herself to the dispatcher, who called Lynch. Jolene tried to explain.

"So," she concluded, "if we can just get ahold of Buddy, he would clear this all up."

"When you say Buddy, do you mean Melvin Cuthbert Jowett?" Lynch asked.

"Yes. I'm sure he'd laugh about it."

"I don't think so."

"Why not?"

Lynch pointed through the glass. An officer was escorting someone in handcuffs out the back door.

"Buddy!" Jolene jumped up and ran out the door before Lynch could stop her. "Buddy, what happened?"

The officer stepped between them. "Sorry, ma'am. No contact allowed with a prisoner."

"Prisoner? Buddy, what did you do?"

"What did I do? What did you do?"

"Me? You're the one out skinny-dippin' with some hussy the day before our weddin'."

Buddy strained at the cuffs. "We weren't skinny-dippin'. And she's my cousin, Toni Jowett. We were born on the same day, and we grew up together."

"Like brother and sister, I suppose?"

"Yeah. Exactly. And she's gettin' married next week to some guy who isn't stealin' his fiancé's truck and gettin' him throwed in jail!"

"But, Buddy, why are you in jail? You didn't steal any truck."

Lynch stepped between them. "Mr. Jowett has a matter of a few outstandin' tickets ta take care of."

"Where are you takin' him?"

"The Justice of the Peace."

"Oh." Jolene considered for a second. "Before you haul him off, can we get Bubba out? I mean, we need Buddy ta clear it up."

Lynch stepped forward. "Mr. Jowett, do you intend ta press charges against Bodean Culpepper for grand theft, auto?"

"No."

"OK." Lynch turned to the other officer. "I'll take charge of Mr. Jowett. Mr. Culpepper is free ta go." He escorted Buddy out the back door.

When Bubba joined them, his mood wasn't much better than Buddy's. Jolene latched onto his arm.

"They've taken Buddy ta the Justice of the Peace because of outstandin' tickets."

"Yeah, he told me."

"Don't you see what this means?" Bubba shook his head. "You're here. Mary's here. I'm here. Buddy's here. And we got a Justice of the Peace handy."

"So?"

"Yeah, so?" Mary echoed.

"So, we have the bride, the groom, the maid-of-honor, and the best man. My wedding dress is in the trunk, and we have a Justice of the Peace."

"You don't mean . . . ," Mary whispered in disbelief.

"That's exactly what I mean."

———

Jolene walked into the J.P.'s office in her wedding dress and announced, "Judge, I want ta marry this man."

Lynch looked at her without comment, although he blinked rapidly. The judge had a spasm that sent his pen flying across the room. Buddy shook his head.

The judge retrieved his pen. "Missy, you'll need a marriage license."

"Got it," she answered, waving the copy she had retrieved from the county clerk.

"You'll need two witnesses."

"Got 'em," she answered as Bubba and Mary walked in.

"You got ta wait 'til I'm through with 'im," Lynch said.

The judge hastily concluded his business. "OK, Missy." He motioned to Jolene. "You're up next."

The bride came rustling up to the desk and grabbed Buddy's arm. Buddy maintained an ambiguous expression. Jolene looked back at Bubba and Mary.

"Come on, y'all," she said with impatience. She looked at the cuffs and then at Lynch. "Could you take these things off?"

Lynch removed the cuffs. The judge retrieved a book from a shelf and dusted it off.

"Hmmmm. Do y'all want all the trimmin's, or the *Reader's Digest* version?"

"The short version," Jolene said.

"Thought as much." He put on a set of reading glasses and flipped through the book. "Hmmmm. Here we go. Do you, uh . . . ," he consulted the arrest warrant on his desk, "Do you, Melvin Cuthbert Jowett, take this—"

"Melvin Cuthbert!" Bubba howled and staggered around the room.

"Put a cork in it, sonny," the judge said. He looked back down at the book.

"Do you, Melvin Cuthbert Jowett," he glared at Bubba over the top of his reading glasses. Bubba turned red and made a choking sound. "Take this woman ta be your lawful wedded wife?"

"Not a chance . . . ," Buddy said.

The judge's head jerked up. Bubba and Mary looked at Buddy with their mouths hanging open. Lynch lost his composure to the point that one corner of his mouth twitched.

". . . that you could get rid of me that easy," Buddy concluded. "Looks like yer stuck with me."

"Oh. Do you . . ." The judge looked around on the desk, then leaned over and jerked the marriage license from Jolene's hand.

He flipped it open and consulted it. "Hmmmm. Do you, Jolene Janice Culpepper, take this man ta be your lawful wedded husband?"

"I do."

"Good. Then by the power divested in me by the state of Texas, I announce you man and wife. That'll be thirty-five dollars and don't forget ta sign the register by the door." He slammed the book shut and shoved it back on the shelf.

Buddy and Jolene looked at each other, almost surprised that they were actually married. He kissed her. She grabbed a vase of plastic flowers from a filing cabinet, turned like a bride with a bouquet, and threw them. Lynch was forced to catch them to keep the vase from breaking on the floor.

Buddy paid the judge. Jolene swore them all to silence.

The next day their wedding drew the biggest crowd ever in Fred. It was sure to be the funniest wedding in the history of matrimony. But even more, everyone feared the pranks that might befall those who failed to attend. I sat in the auditorium along with everyone else, wondering at the delay. Thirty minutes after the ceremony was supposed to start, Dad came out and announced that neither the bride nor groom were there.

When we emerged from the church, we discovered that every car was decorated with shoe polish and tin cans. There has never been so much cussing at a wedding before or since. Not even at a Perkins wedding.

---

The couple drove to a cabin in Louisiana for the honeymoon. Jolene had slipped a bag filled with ammunition for practical jokes under the front seat. Buddy had buried his under the luggage in the truck bed. When they parked in front of the cabin, Jolene grabbed her bag and rushed inside while Buddy smuggled his bag under the hanging clothes.

Buddy made a pit stop before dinner. He discovered too late the Saran Wrap stretched tightly across the commode. Undaunted, he disposed of the wrap and greased the seat down with Vaseline. He stepped out to see Jolene smiling sweetly at him.

"Are you ready ta get something to eat?"

"Sure."

They found a cafe nearby. Both took precautions. They checked the lids and tasted the contents before they used the salt or sugar. They kept their drinks well away from their plates and the edge of the table. In this manner, they completed the meal without incident. Satisfied that he had circumvented all traps, Buddy dropped his napkin on his plate and got up to pay the bill. When he walked away, the tablecloth followed him. As everything crashed to the floor he looked down to see the tablecloth pinned to his shirttail.

"Oh, my!" Jolene said in calm surprise.

"Oops," Buddy said dryly, removing the safety pin.

Back at the cabin, Buddy took a shower. He mentally reviewed the contents of his bag of tricks for a response to the cafe catastrophe. His meditations were distracted by a clinking noise. A shadow against the shower curtain caught his eye. It slid back to reveal Jolene holding an olive-green ice bucket full of ice water.

"No!" he gasped as he scrambled clumsily for the curtain. He seemed to see everything in slow motion, the swinging bucket, the shimmering metallic arc of water undulating toward him, the trail of smoky vapor left by individual water drops.

Then the water hit. Jolene disappeared through the mist with a giggle and a slam of the door. Buddy closed the curtain and grabbed the soap with a shivering hand. He scrubbed vigorously with no results. He inspected the soap. It was coated with a layer of clear fingernail polish.

Buddy twisted off the water and stepped onto the mat. He rubbed the condensation from the mirror and stared at his reflection. Something must be done. Yes, but what? He sat on the toilet to think and remembered too late about the Vaseline.

Something snapped inside. He sprang from the toilet with a roar, jerked the door open, and stormed into the bedroom. Before he took three steps he halted abruptly and stood dripping.

The room looked like a chapel, illuminated by candles scattered over every available surface. Incense burned on a nightstand.

Jolene sat in an armchair, wrapped in a full-length silk nightgown of midnight blue. The candlelight transformed it into a collage of soft highlights and suggestive shadows that beckoned to him. Her dark hair was an abyss of shadows, streaming over her shoulders like an ebony waterfall. Her black eyes glistened with expectation and promise from behind a set of Groucho glasses.

Bushy eyebrows, bushy mustache, and gargantuan nose. Buddy approached her quietly. She offered him an identical set of Groucho glasses, and he led her to the bed. But not before he checked the pillows for shaving cream.

# CHAPTER FOURTEEN

I had the day off for July Fourth. On Friday Bubba and I took a three-hour road trip to Stanley. Since he was driving, I was forced to listen to his Hank Williams collection. Just before noon I called Lori's number from the pay phone at the Dairy Queen in Center. She answered.

"Hey, Lori. It's Mark."

"Mark?"

"Cloud. Mark Cloud."

"I know that. I was just surprised to hear from you."

"I have another surprise for you. I'm at the Center DQ with Bubba. If you give me directions to your house we'll come by and visit." There was silence on the line. "Hello? Lori?"

"I'm here."

"Did you hear me?"

"Yeah."

"So, I have a pen."

"Now isn't a good time. We're going to my aunt's cabin on Caddo Lake for the weekend. We're getting ready to leave."

"We could come help you pack, and you could ride with us up to the lake. We could even hang at the lake a little before we have to drive back down to Fred. Where's your aunt's cabin?"

"Uncertain."

"Surely your dad knows where it is. He can give us directions."

"It's in Uncertain."

"What?"

"Uncertain, Texas."

"Oh, so you know how to get there."

"Mark, I don't think you should come here."

"Why not?"

"You don't know?"

"Should I?"

"Are you kidding?"

"No."

I heard a heavy sigh over the phone. "Just think about our last conversation."

It was a month back, when I talked to her about taking Becky to the prom.

"You mean the prom?"

"Of course."

"But you said it was OK."

"Don't be an idiot, Mark. You really think I'm OK with you dating your old girlfriend?"

"But you said it was OK!"

"I was being sarcastic. I mean, how could you have the nerve to call me up and ask me a stupid question like that?"

"But, but, but . . ."

"I have to go now."

"Wait! Wait, she's not my girlfriend. I mean, she's not my old girlfriend."

"Right."

"I never dated her in high school. Last month was the only time we have ever been out together and I just did it as a favor. I told you the story."

"Yeah. I told my brothers that story. They thought it was real funny."

"Lori, seriously. I never dated Becky. In fact, she told me I was a good friend, like a brother."

"Did you kiss her?"

"No!"

"Did you hug her?"

"No."

"Did you put your arm around her?"

"No."

"Did you dance with her?"

I hesitated. Just as I had told Becky, Lori and I had a vow: no secrets. It didn't seem like a good time to tell the truth, but I had given my word. "One dance."

"Slow or fast?"

"Slow."

"Right."

The phone went dead. I hung it up slowly and went back inside where Bubba was eating a DQ Dude. I sat down across from him.

"Well?"

"She's out of town."

"Bummer."

"Yeah."

It was a long summer. I called Lori, but she was never home. At least that's what I was told. I wrote her, but the letters came back unopened. A few hundred times I debated calling Becky, but I knew in that way lay madness.

I spent my time sweating in the lumber mill and luxuriating in the muddy waters of Toodlum. One late afternoon I drove out the river road, my destination the hill where I used to sit in the green Bonneville watching the sun and Vernon sink into oblivion while we discussed moss-covered three-handled family credenzas and green things in general. I figured we could smoke a cigar and he could give me questionable advice on my love life. I rounded the corner and let the Falcon drift to a stop next to the field. It was empty. I looked across the road at the old frame house. The porch swing hung motionless.

I shifted into first and drove the mile to Vernon's trailer. A waist-high moat of weeds surrounded it. The driveway was empty. The cinderblock steps were scattered in front of the door like a white-trash Stonehenge. I was about to ease the car into the overgrown driveway and try the door when I noticed a new driveway twenty yards down with a mailbox and red reflectors on either side of a culvert. I pulled forward. The old Crowley place came into view.

Vernon's Pontiac was there alongside Parker's F150. Beyond them lay the house I could have leveled with a good sneeze last year. It always seemed to be slouching in the background, a poor relation, self-conscious in the shadow of the opulence of the trailer. Now it stood at attention, fresh wood here and there along the exterior, mainly around the eaves and along the pier-and-beam foundation. The skeleton of a new porch was framed in, orange in the afternoon sun, towering over the piled bones of the old porch that used to tilt opposite to the general leaning of the house.

I parked the Falcon behind the Pontiac and walked the planks that were the only path over the studs to the house. The door was open. I peered in. Vernon and Parker were off to the right in the kitchen, sitting at a deal table next to a window that faced the sunset.

"Mark boy. Git yerself in this house."

I stepped over the threshold. Vernon pushed a chair back from the table with his foot. A cigarette was wedged between the middle stubs on his left hand. The fingers on his right hand were wrapped around the handle of a chipped mug.

"Pour yerself some coffee. Parker made it."

I nodded at Parker. He nodded back. His face didn't move, but I could see a smile lurking in his good eye. "Used an old recipe. I call it second-chance coffee."

I looked around the place. It needed a lot of work. Obviously they chose to fix the outside while the weather was good, saving the inside for the winter. I filled a mug and dropped into the chair. The coffee was strong and bitter. I pulled a five-pack of Hava Tampa Jewels from my shirt pocket and tore the cellophane from the top.

"Give one of these a try."

I pushed a cigar across the table to Vernon. He looked at it like a calf looking at a new gate.

"I ain't had a cigar since the war." He peeled it open and pulled it out of the cardboard shell. "But they didn't have these fancy wooden tips." He mashed the cigarette out in the saucer full of ashes and picked up the Bic lighter.

I held one out to Parker. He looked at it. "Never did take much ta smokin'."

I shrugged and fired it up instead. The bite of the stale tobacco rolled back on my tongue. I blew out the smoke and cut the edge by washing the bitter coffee over it. I suddenly felt that everything was as it should be.

I was still wearing my steel-toed boots and faded work clothes grimy from the sawmill, the sweat of my labors dried on pale, thin arms. I rubbed rough hands over the rougher table. The top edges of the grooves were worn smooth from decades of Crowleys eating breakfast before setting out on a circuitous route to a hard day's work at the still. I looked from the spare living room furnished with handmade furniture to the potbellied stove in the corner. I scanned the kitchen, taking in unfinished cabinets and countertops. A bare bulb hung above the table; a string hung from the bulb.

I had crossed a portal into the true Texas, had achieved a cosmic state of bubba enlightenment. Here I sat, scorned in love by a woman I didn't understand and who didn't understand me, sipping coffee strong enough to choke a heifer and smoking a cheap cigar between two old outlaws, one with half a hand, the other with a patch over his left eye. All we lacked was Guy Clark playing us a song about a train on Willie's beat-up nylon-string guitar with the gash in the front.

We didn't talk much, just watched the pink-orange passion play of the sun fade into the final curtain of nightfall. I asked a few questions about the renovations. They were spawned by a chance meeting of Parker and Vernon at Fred Grocery. From what I could see, the two were settled into the comfortable rut of old friends, much like my sessions with Vernon in the Pontiac my last year of high school. Only they fit together more naturally, like a pair of old loafers scuffed and worn down on the heels. I felt a warm sense of satisfaction that I could nestle between them like I belonged. It eased the frustration of Lori's rejection.

I took to hanging at Vernon's place a couple evenings a week. Sometimes on weekends I hooked up with C. J. and we cruised through Warren and Silsbee and Beaumont, trying to stay out of trouble. We were usually successful. Most of my money went into a savings account. I spent some on film and trekked back roads, looking for shots. My portfolio grew.

Finally, September arrived and my exile came to an end.

---

I breezed through registration, talked Dr. Fulton into hiring me again as *Compass* photographer, and checked to see if Lori would come down when I paged her. She wouldn't.

During the first Annual Monday Night 42 game, we discovered that some lunatic had made The Captain a wing rep. I guess they figured that as a senior, he must have some sense of responsibility.

During the summer Phyllis experienced a greater measure of success with Sam than I had with Lori. He probably didn't start the summer off by dating an old flame either. The first Monday back he was out with Sam. The rest of us were dateless and bored. The Captain stopped by, and we began the game early.

Around 10:30 P.M., while his partner, Fillmore, went nello for the third time, The Captain wandered listlessly around the room, picking up things and looking at them. He plopped down on Bubba's bed in exasperation.

"Gentlemen, it is entirely too calm out there this evening. I fear this new crop of freshmen lack the verve of their forbearers. They need a good shaking up."

He stood up, reached into a back pocket, and pulled out a pistol. He checked the chambers, spun the cylinder, and closed it.

"Whoa," Fillmore said. "No need to get crazy. I won't go nello again, I promise."

"What is up with that?" I asked, pushing back from the table.

"This, sir, is the tool with which I shall foment the chaos latent in this somnambulistic generation. Desperate measures, true, but these are desperate times, and the hour produces the man."

He stood up with resolution and stepped dramatically to the door. He opened it slowly, looked out, thrust the pistol into the hall, and squeezed the trigger. The noise was deafening. We all jumped to our feet, knocking over chairs. The smell of gunpowder drifted into the room, The Captain closed the door gently, scurried back to the dresser, and buried the pistol in my sock drawer.

"Hey!"

"Fear not, my good fellow. I will retrieve it later. However, it would be inconvenient to have it on my person while interrogating freshmen to discover who has created this disturbance."

He strode out and banged on the door across the hall. I looked out in the hallway. It was filling up with guys looking around and asking each other did they hear that? Morris the Crew Cut Prophet came up the stairs three at a time. He stopped at the top and surveyed the scene, his disapproving glare coming to rest on me. The Captain nearly bowled over the poor freshman who answered the door and began interrogating everyone in the room.

Phyllis walked up the stairs, pushed past Morris, and edged into the room. "What's going on?"

I shook my head. "Nothing. Just The Captain. Come on in, we're set up."

---

A month later I was working on *The Compass* with Weissman. I took a bathroom break, and as usual The Rack stopped me on my way back. I was in no mood for harassment. Lori still refused to talk to me. I had hay fever and was hopped up on antihistamines. At this point I really didn't care about much of anything except keeping the headlines straight and putting the issue to bed so I could do likewise.

I listened numbly to his ranting for awhile, shrugging my shoulders when he asked a question. He launched into the issue of evolution, ridiculing a six-day creation and six-thousand-year-old earth. He mentioned carbon dating. I held up my hand like a traffic cop.

"I really don't care about any of this. I will now go back to my little corner and work on my yellow sheet. But I do seem to remember hearing about a live clam that carbon-dating said was thousands of years old."

"I see you read Jack Chick tracts."

"Maybe that was where I heard it."

"Predictable. You rely on a comic strip to learn science. Your kind should not be allowed to reproduce."

I thought of Lori. "I wouldn't worry about that if I were you. There doesn't seem to be any danger of it occurring."

"Clams build their shells from the matter suspended in the water around them. Those growing in an environment rich with limestone will have a disproportionately low amount of carbon.

Consequently they will appear to have lost an amount of carbon that would normally take thousands of years to lose, but only because they started out with less."

"I'll keep that in mind."

"Do you know the speed of light?"

"No, but if you hum a few bars I'm sure . . ." He didn't even smile. "Sure, 186,000 miles per second. Give or take."

"How do you explain that we can see light from stars five billion light years away?"

"Huh?"

"There are stars that are so far away, it would take the light from them five billion years to get here. If the universe was created six thousand years ago, as you people claim, the first beam of light from those stars should still be 4,999,999,994 light years away. But it's not. We can see the light from those stars."

"Right now I can't see the light at the end of the tunnel, much less light a gazillion miles away. I just want to see the inside of my eyelids. It's been nice chatting with you. I have to go now."

I toddled back to Weissman and finished the paper.

---

In my drugged delirium I hatched a plan to get through to Lori. It required an accomplice, but once I explained the plan, all prospective accomplices declined to assist.

My salvation came from the most unexpected source. Weissman agreed to assist in my desperate scheme. Sam agreed to bring Lori to the Quad at the appointed time. Weissman and I met on the Quad early in the afternoon on an October Saturday. The rest of the gang, while declining to participate, chose to observe.

Bubba pulled his Corvair up near the fountain, put the top down, and plugged the Edgar Winter tape in the stereo. Fillmore and The Captain sat on a bench. Sam and Phyllis joined us.

"Weissman, this is Sam and Phyllis."

Weissman held his hand out to Phyllis. "Good to meet you, Sam."

"I'm Sam." She waved.

"You're Phyllis?" he said, looking at Phyllis.

"No, I'm Phil Lancaster and this is Samantha Phillips. I believe you already met Mark, the pinhead."

I butted in. "I'll explain later. Right now Sam has work to do."

I nodded at her, and she disappeared into the dorm. Phyllis took a ringside seat. I nodded to Bubba, and he hit play. The strains of "Autumn" washed across the Quad. He turned it up and took a seat next to Phyllis. I turned to Weissman.

"Shall we?"

"Don't mind if I do."

I held out my hands, and we began dancing around the fountain to the music, stumbling and making exaggerated swoops and turns. Soon a crowd gathered. A confused crowd, but large enough to encircle the fountain. As the last verse began, Sam pushed her way through the crowd with Lori in tow. I spun Weissman around so I could see her reaction, and we continued to dance.

At first she was puzzled, then she saw who it was. She did not seem to be amused.

"Weissman," I yelled over the music. "I think somebody wants to cut in."

"Oh, no, my dear," he screeched in a piercing falsetto, "even though we have only shared this one dance, you have stolen my heart."

"Sorry," I said as the music died away. I stepped back. "I gave you one dance, but I gave someone else my heart."

I turned to Lori.

"I'm sorry," I said. "I was an idiot, just like you said." The next song started up, a rocker called "We All Had a Real Good Time." I held out my hand. "May I have this dance?"

She was silent. I couldn't read her at all. Sam leaned to her.

"Go on, Lori. He's really sorry. I mean, he apologized in front of all these people. He must mean it."

I thought I saw a glimmer of a smile in Lori's eyes. Sam pulled Phyllis from the bench and started to dance. Weissman grabbed a girl from the crowd and started dancing. She blushed but joined him. Others started dancing. Soon nobody was looking at us. We stood in a crowd of Baptists dancing on a Saturday afternoon.

"Lori, will you forgive me?"

She smiled. "OK. But you're lucky to have me. You better remember that."

"I will," I said and pulled her into the dancing crowd as "Frankenstein" came on.

We all had a real good time until Morris the Crew Cut Prophet showed up, turned off the stereo, and demanded to know what was going on.

A month later Phyllis was in the doghouse. I never got the whole story, but I think it had something to do with Sam's new hairdo. She had it cut very short, almost shorter than his. He said something about her looking like a choirboy, and it disintegrated from there. When she started making comments about him having a preference for choirboys, it became obvious there was a rift in the lute.

Not everyone greeted this news with the shaking of the head and the clicking of the tongue. The Captain was heard to mention that he had always felt that Sam had paired beneath her station and that perhaps it was for the better that she recognized this before it was too late.

I'm not sure if this gave her the idea, but I do know that on Saturday she was seen eating lunch with The Captain and by that evening had a date. The news reached Phyllis the next day. Three floors down the guys in the lobby had to turn up the TV to hear the game. In Cragmont's the posters vibrated on the walls, and Bubba's shaving mug fell off the shelf and shattered.

Phyllis called The Captain a ham and a hack. He cataloged every slight and insult he had suffered, starting with the dinner at Neeley's a year before. He cast aspersions on the decrepit Valiant The Captain drove, on his taste in clothes, on his haircut. He even criticized his skill at 42.

Then he was suddenly silent. In the vacuum of sound that followed, I tiptoed to the bathroom and peeked into his room. Phyllis was sitting on his bed, smiling. I closed the door and locked it.

Monday afternoon I was working on calculus in my room. Through the open door I saw Phyllis pass by with a bayonet at his side and a purposeful stride. A few moments later I heard a familiar sound.

At dinner that evening The Captain plopped down at the table next to Lori and me.

"I am at a loss for words," he said with great emotion.

Somehow I doubted it.

"You will never in your most fevered imagination guess what that foul pervert has done."

"He sawed a six-inch gash in your door with a bayonet," I said.

"However did you discern that?"

"Have you looked under the sign on my door that says 'Abandon hope all ye who enter here'?"

"Sir, you astound me."

"He happened to see me last Thanksgiving when I dropped a water balloon on him from the window."

"I assure you this deed shall not go unanswered. The cad shall pay, and dearly."

I strongly advised him to let it go. I told him it was Phyllis who died him blue the year before. I reminded him of the pencil shavings in the cigarette. I told him several other stories of his retaliations. But I could see I was having no affect.

Hours later I had forgotten the conversation and was in the middle of our Annual Monday Night 42 game when the door to the room burst open and The Captain stormed in. With three steps he approached Phyllis, who looked up from his dominoes to see a pistol pointed at his chest. His eyes grew as large as a Petri dish, and the cigar dropped from his mouth.

Before he could react, a roar filled the room and the stench of gunpowder overwhelmed the stale cigar smoke. Phyllis grabbed his chest, closed his eyes, and fell from his chair, landing on the floor on his side. He rolled to his back and lay there. The Captain turned on his heel and strode out as he came in, stuffing the gun in his jacket pocket before he got out the door.

The whole thing took no more than five seconds. Through the ringing in my ears I heard doors opening up and down the hall, people running up the stairs. A few guys followed the smell of powder to our open door and looked in.

Phyllis lay on the floor, eyes closed, hands clasped to his chest. He opened one eye and looked around. He opened the other, then looked down at his hands. No blood. He looked at his chest. Wadding from the blank cartridge was plastered against his shirt. He began laughing.

Soon after, Phyllis and Sam were reconciled. Before the Thanksgiving break, Phyllis and The Captain were close friends.

**CHAPTER FIFTEEN** The following February an ice storm hit campus. Declining to ride on the back of a motorcycle on the icy streets, I called Phyllis from the *News-Messenger* for a ride back to the dorm. I was holding my hands over the heater vents when I noticed we were driving the wrong direction.

"Hey, I'm supposed to meet Lori at nine to study Spanish."

"Keep your shirt on. Just got to run a quick errand."

He stopped behind a dark ramshackle house a block or two from Wiley College, hopped out, and ran to the back door. A sliver of light fell on Phyllis as it opened. A black guy looked around and gestured him in. Half a minute later he emerged, ran to the trunk, and then jumped back in the car.

"What was all that?"

"Replenishing basic supplies."

I grunted and pushed my hands deeper into my pockets. As we approached campus, Phyllis turned off Grove and took a spin around the Quad at a speed unsuited to the conditions. I had flashbacks of Darnell Ray and the Hound of Hell.

"Hey, take it easy."

"What, scared of a little ice?"

"No, I'm scared of a little stupidity. If I wanted to die on the road, I would have taken the motorcycle."

"Take a chill pill." We slid down past the chapel and came to a full stop at Grove. "Check this out," he said.

He gunned the engine and spun the wheel to the left. The Chrysler did a 180 and went sliding down Grove sideways. I watched the cars parallel parked in front of Feagin Hall pass by in front of us. Phyllis spun the wheel to the right and gunned it again. We did another 180 and watched the cars across the street zip by.

"What are you doing?" I screamed. I was leaving permanent indentions in the armrest.

"Driving." Phyllis spun the wheel back to the left, gunned the engine momentarily, and then stepped on the brakes. We came sliding to a halt in the middle of the street directly in front of the dorm.

"You idiot! Have you lost your mind?" I reached for the door handle. "See that car coming? What if it was closer? We would have hit it." I shoved the door open. "What if it was a cop?"

As the words left my mouth, red lights ignited on top of the approaching car. Phyllis muttered a curse at me as if I had conjured up the cop car. It stopped in the street next to us. The driver's window came down. Phyllis rolled his window down.

"Pull your car over into that lot," the cop said, pointing his flashlight to the parking lot across the street from the dorm.

The cop pulled up behind us and got out. He shined the flashlight into our faces. He flashed the light in the backseat, which was empty. "Get out of the car." Phyllis got out. "You too." I got out.

"License." Phyllis gave him his license. "You too." I gave him my license. He compared them to our faces. "Registration."

Phyllis crawled across the seat and pulled the registration from the glove box. The passenger side of the cop car opened and another cop got out. I shoved my hands into my pockets, stamped on the ground, and looked at the first cop. He was wearing a down-filled jacket, earmuffs, and gloves. His nametag glinted in the mercury-vapor light over the parking lot. It said Smithers.

Phyllis handed the registration to Smithers. He looked it over. "Have you been drinking?"

"No," Phyllis said.

I said, "No, sir."

"What would you call that little maneuver you just pulled?"

"I was reaching for the brake but my shoe was wet and it slipped off and hit the gas. I had difficulty regaining control on the ice."

The other cop walked past us to the door of the Chrysler. I checked his nametag. It said Hansen. He began rooting around in the car.

"What is he doing?" Phyllis demanded.

Hansen walked to the back of the car and opened the trunk. "Just taking a look around," he said. "You don't mind, do you?"

"Yes, I do. You don't have any right to search my car."

Hansen walked up from the back of the car. Phyllis squinted into the beam of the flashlight. "Son, I think the best thing you can do right now is shut your punk mouth before I shut it for you."

I saw Smithers wince, but he didn't say anything.

Hansen walked back to the trunk and flashed the light around. Smithers moved so he could see what Hansen was doing. We moved with him. My stomach felt as if I had lived on nothing but stale coffee for several days. I shivered and looked at Phyllis. His eyes were on Hansen, who dug around in the right wheel well, tossing an oilcan out on the ground. He moved to the left wheel well, moved a jug of antifreeze out of the way, and lifted a rag. Then he smiled. It was not a smile that spread joy to those around him.

He pulled out a baggie that looked like a roll of quarters. A green roll of quarters. I heard a high-pitched whine in my head. I began shaking, but not because it was cold. He dangled the bag in Phil's face.

"Is this yours, Mr. Lancaster?"

"What is that?" I whispered to Phil. He didn't answer either of us.

Hansen slammed the trunk closed, looked at Smithers, and nodded to Phil. He turned to me. "Hands on top of the trunk, feet spread apart."

"Wait," I said loudly. "What's going on? What is that?" I began to feel nauseous.

Hansen spun me around facing the car. "Son, we'll ask the questions around here. Hands on the trunk and spread 'em."

Next to me, Phil was being patted down. Smithers pushed his feet farther apart with his foot and searched for weapons. Then he pulled out a set of handcuffs and began saying, "You have the right to remain silent . . ."

"We're being arrested? What for?"

Hansen grabbed the back of my shirt and threw me against the trunk.

"Shut up and put your hands on the trunk."

I leaned against the car, the cold seeping up from the metal into my bones. He kicked my feet apart and began searching for weapons.

"Don't you have to tell me what I'm being arrested for?"

"Don't act stupid, kid. You already know. If you want to see it written down, you'll get your chance when you're booked."

I looked up through the hair hanging in my face. The red-and-white lights of the cop car flashed on the dorm. Faces peered from half the windows. Somebody stood on the front porch.

Hansen grabbed an arm, slapped a cuff on it, did the same to the other, and started reciting his lines. It wasn't real. It couldn't be happening. I looked at Phil. He didn't look back. Even after they shoved us in the backseat, he wouldn't look at me.

"Phil," I whispered to him. "Tell them." He ignored me. "I didn't know it was there. It's not mine."

He said nothing.

"Phil," I whispered more fiercely.

He glared at me. "Shut up. If you know what's good for you, you won't say another word until there's a lawyer in the room."

I glared back at him and looked away. All the what-ifs echoed through my head. Why hadn't I taken the motorcycle instead?

Why didn't I get out of the car when he first stopped it instead of sitting there hollering at him? The speculation followed. Would they believe me? Would Phil tell them I had nothing to do with it?

Unfortunately I was the one who looked like the doper. I had blond hair to my shoulders. I had on bell-bottom jeans and a thick denim work shirt with an ecology flag stitched to one sleeve, an American flag held on with a pin on the other. Phil had short dark hair and was wearing a flannel shirt, jeans, boots, and a pea coat.

We were escorted through a thick sliding door into a small room. The door rolled shut behind us with a solid clunk, then a door on the opposite wall screeched open. Hansen nodded at the guy behind the counter.

"Hey Bert, got a couple of punks for you." He handed Bert our licenses and took our cuffs off. "Empty your pockets here." He pointed to the counter. "Your shoes up here. And your belt too."

"What's the charge?" Bert asked, rolling a form into a typewriter and picking up Phil's license.

"Felony possession of a controlled substance, marijuana, greater than one ounce and less than four ounces."

"Felony?" I blurted out. "I didn't have anything. It's not mine."

"Tell it to the judge," Hansen said. He grabbed a clipboard, sat down at a table, and started filling out a form.

Smithers came in with two cups of coffee, shoved one to Hansen and sipped the other. "Slow night, Bert."

"Yep. These fellers is our first customers all night."

"Too cold."

"Got that right. Ice storms are tough on the troopers, but I sure like 'em. Gives me a break."

Bert started asking Phil a bunch of questions about things like tattoos and blood type. At first he refused to answer until the cops pointed out that it had nothing to do with his crime–it was just information for the form. Then they rolled his prints and took his picture while I answered the questions.

They were sitting around, smoking, drinking coffee, and talking about the weather. To watch them you would think we were applying for a driver's license or registering for a class. But I was watching the end of my world. I didn't usually think about the future, what it might be like. I tried now. My brain jerked in spasms like the dry heaves. Nothing came up.

Even though my mind was racing like an engine in neutral, I felt as if I was moving underwater. All the surfaces looked hard and shiny, like a fellowship hall in a backwoods church, all folding tables and chipped tile and benches and fluorescent lighting. The stale smell of decades of cigarettes seeped from the dingy walls and mixed with the scent of scorched coffee and fresh tobacco smoke.

We were escorted to a large cell. It was empty, but the fragrance of its previous occupants lingered. I speculated what it would have been like if it were a full moon on a warm night and shuddered. The door slammed closed, and I flinched like when The Captain pulled the trigger.

When we were finally alone, I cornered Phil. "What is going on? Why didn't you tell them that wasn't mine?"

"Get a clue, Twinkie brain. If I tell them it's not yours, it's the same as telling them it is mine."

"But it is yours," I hissed.

He grabbed the front of my shirt. "Don't make me say it again. If you want to get out of this, you will not say anything else until there is a lawyer present." He pushed me away.

"Have you done this before?"

"No, but I have friends who have. And my dad's a lawyer, remember? They didn't have probable cause to search the car and I didn't give them permission. They think reckless driving gives them probable cause. But my story about losing control on the ice will hold water as long as nobody contradicts it. The thing will be thrown out as unreasonable search and seizure."

I looked at him, trying to decide if I should trust my future to his speculations. I didn't think so. I went to the bench on the other side of the cell and lay down, listening to the slam of the door echoing into the emptiness of my future.

The next day a guard showed up and escorted me to a room with a table and three chairs. The cop deposited me in a chair. An old man in a suit sat opposite me at the table. He put on reading glasses and consulted some forms.

"Mark Thomas Cloud?" I nodded. "I'm Judge Herman. You are being charged with felony possession of marijuana, more than one ounce and less than four ounces. Your hearing will be set for," he looked through a calendar, "Tuesday, February 24. If you don't have a lawyer, one will be appointed for you."

"But I don't know anything about any grass. I was just catching a ride from work."

"That is immaterial."

"What? Some guy who gives me a ride secretly has dope stashed in his trunk and I can go to jail for it?"

"Yes."

"So you're saying I should search the car of anyone who gives me a ride in case they have dope?"

"I'm saying you are charged with possession. If you want advice, I would say choose your friends more carefully."

"I've known him for over a year. I had no idea he smoked dope. How is that my fault?"

"You can plead your case at the trial. Do you have a lawyer?"

I decided to play Phil's idea in a desperate bid to get out. "No, but I guess I need one. I need to ask him about probable cause and unreasonable search and seizure."

The judge looked at me over his glasses. "What?"

"See, we were at a stop sign and Phil's foot slipped off the brake and hit the gas and the car skidded all over the road, but he got it back under control. That's when the cops pulled us over. While one cop was checking our licenses the other, I think his name was Hansen, took the keys out of the ignition and searched the trunk. We didn't do anything illegal to give him a reason to do that."

"Did this Hansen ask the driver for permission to search the car?"

"No. In fact, when Phil asked him what he was doing, Hansen told him to shut up." I looked at the judge. He was not happy. "But I guess I should just wait and tell it to the lawyer."

The judge said a word not allowed in the courtroom, closed the folder, and scooped it into a briefcase. "Johnson, you can take Mr. Cloud back to his cell."

After the guard left, Phil stepped in close to me. "What did you tell them?" he whispered.

"I told the judge Hansen searched the car without probable cause or permission."

"What did he say?"

"I won't repeat what he said, but he closed my file and had Johnson bring me back here."

Phil smiled and sat down on the bench. "We're out of here."

---

The next day a note was delivered to my calculus class indicating I should proceed to the office of the Dean of Students with all due haste. It didn't sound good, and it wasn't good. Phil was just leaving as I got there. I asked him what was going on. He shook his head. I walked through the door he left open and was directed to a second office, where the dean sat behind a monstrous desk. He pointed to a chair.

"Mr. Cloud, I have spoken to the authorities. I regret to

inform you that we have terminated your status as student. You may go to the registrar's office to get the refund available to you at this point in the semester."

"But the charges were dropped."

"A legal ruling of not guilty is not the same as being innocent. There were drugs in that car."

"But they weren't mine. It wasn't even my car."

"Perhaps, but there have been other incidents. All taken together, they indicate that you present more of a liability than an asset to the college."

"What incidents?"

He picked up a file folder. "There were reports of a gun being fired in your dorm room this semester. Last semester it was reported that you organized a dance on the Quad, even though dances are specifically prohibited in the student handbook. Last year there was strong suspicion that you were party to a series of pranks that involved defacing the campus and theft of private property, although conclusive proof was not forthcoming."

He set the folder back down. "Individually these incidents are insufficient to warrant disciplinary action. However, taken together with a criminal arrest and evidence of possession of drugs on campus, they are more than adequate to justify this action. Indeed, I would be irresponsible if I did not remove you from this institution."

"That's it? Judge, jury, and executioner all in one? No appeal?"

"Mr. Cloud, attending college here is a privilege, not a right. Your behavior indicates you have failed to earn this privilege. It is indeed unfortunate because you showed such promise. We all regret that you did not live up to that promise."

I got my meager refund from the registrar's office and went to the cafeteria. Lori was sitting at our table.

"Where were you last night? I waited for you until curfew."

I looked at her, drinking in her face, memorizing it.

"What?" Her eyes narrowed. "What is it? What happened?"

I took her hand and held it on top of the table. "Lori, Wednesday night I was riding back from the *News-Messenger* with Phil Lancaster. We were stopped by the cops. They found a bag of marijuana in his trunk. I spent the night in jail."

"No!" She jerked her hand back and searched my face. "Mark, is this supposed to be some kind of joke?"

"It's as serious as a heart attack. The charges were dropped on a technicality, but the school has kicked us out anyway. I have to be off campus by the end of the day."

Tears came to her eyes. "Mark, stop it. This isn't funny."

"I'm not laughing."

Lori pushed back from the table and ran out of the building. I found her in front of the admin building between the stairs where we had our first date. She was crying. I put my hand on her shoulder, and she turned around and buried her face against my neck.

"Tell me it isn't true."

"I've been telling myself that, but it doesn't help. I know it is true."

"That Phil. I hate him."

"I'm not too crazy about him, myself."

"Mark . . ."

She was crying. We didn't say anything for a long time. It might have been twenty minutes, but when she pulled away it felt like it had been only a minute. Already my arms began to ache for her the way they did the first time I saw her. I brushed away a strand of hair that was stuck to the tears smeared on her cheek, held her chin in my hand, and kissed her slowly.

"I'll probably get a job and apply at SFA. It's less than two hours from here and from Stanley. We can spend weekends together. It won't be so bad."

"That doesn't sound so bad."

We kissed a few more times, and I walked her back to the dorm. I spent the afternoon packing my stuff, remembering Bubba's comments. *You get one shot at college, don't blow it.* Thanks, Bubba. I'll get right on it.

I put off the phone call as long as I could, but I had to do it before I left. Bubba would be out of class any minute, and we'd pack up his car and go to Fred. Him for the weekend, me for much longer. As much as I hated to tell Dad I had been kicked out of college over the phone, it was preferable to telling him in person. On the phone I wouldn't see his face, the disappointment. I felt bad enough. Right now I didn't need that.

I took a handful of quarters to the phone booth at the head of the stairs. Dad answered.

"Hey, Dad, it's Mark."

"Mark. I was just picking up the phone to call you when it rang."

Oh, no! Did he already know? How did he find out? I hadn't even told Heidi yet. "Really? That's weird."

"Yes. Mark, I'm afraid I have some very bad news. You remember how your mother has been so tired lately."

I recalled Christmas wore her out last year, which was unusual because she would usually leave the Ghost of Christmas Present begging for a break. "Yes, sir."

"It's been getting worse. Last week she woke up in pain. We took her to the hospital in Silsbee and they transferred us to Beaumont. There's no easy way to say this, son." The next breath he took was loud and ragged. There was a long pause. I waited. "Your mother was transferred to MD Anderson. She has cancer. Pancreatic cancer. It doesn't look good."

"What?" I stopped breathing. "Mom? Mom has cancer?"

"Yes."

"But . . ." There was no but. There was nothing.

## CHAPTER SIXTEEN

I dropped my laundry by the washer and walked into the den. Dad was sitting in the overstuffed chair staring at the TV. It was off. He looked like an overstuffed marionette after the strings were cut. He saw me and smiled a weary smile. Heidi came in behind me. After I hung up, I called her and told her she could ride with Bubba and me. She cried most of the drive home. After an hour she settled down and I told her about the arrest. She agreed to say nothing until I discussed it with Dad. I would choose my time.

Heidi dropped her overnight bag and rushed to Dad. He stood and wrapped her in his arms. She cried again. He didn't say anything, just held her.

I found Hannah in her room. She was sitting on the bed, staring at the security light in the backyard. I went to the window. A layer of frost coated the brown grass around the light. A wheelbarrow lay on its side at the edge of the shadows.

I turned around. She didn't look at me.

"We're here. Heidi and me."

She looked at me and tears brimmed. "Yeah."

She looked back out the window. I went to my room. I knew I should be crying like everyone else, but I wasn't. I wondered why. After all, she was my mother too.

Not for the first time I wondered what was wrong with me. I recalled Peggy and Kristen's funeral. The whole church was in tears, and I didn't even get misty. I tried to feel something, but you can't really make yourself feel something. Either you feel it or you don't. Deciding doesn't make it happen.

I thought of other times I should have cried but didn't. The guy in my class who committed suicide. The girl who was killed by a drunk driver. They were sad things and I felt bad for the families, but that was about it.

But this wasn't just anybody, this was Mom. What kind of a monster was I? I couldn't even cry when my own mother was dying of cancer. At least I figured she was dying. Dad was the king of understatement. When he said it didn't look good, it meant it really didn't look good.

Maybe I was like a guy born without a leg or some vital organ. But the thing I was missing was less tangible. It wasn't like I couldn't feel emotion at all. Perhaps it was just certain emotions. Maybe it was like being colorblind, where red and green look the same. I was emotion-blind. Overwhelming grief and mild sadness felt the same to me.

Or maybe I was just an unfeeling jerk. That was always a possibility.

Saturday morning on the three-hour drive to Houston, Dad gave us all the details. The cancer was detected late and had spread. They didn't know how far. The next set of tests would determine if radiation or chemotherapy would be of any use. I agreed with Dad. It didn't sound good.

Like most people, I didn't like hospitals. Just the smell of them made me nervous. Things were too intense. Too many people facing impossible decisions, hearing the worst news possible. Not many smiling faces. Even the people who didn't have bad news weren't smiling.

I didn't like being in situations where I should be feeling something that I didn't feel. I didn't need any reminders of my weirdness. But maybe the weirdness wasn't like colorblindness. Maybe it was like having a high pain threshold. Maybe I couldn't register emotional pain until it was really high. That was an unsettling thought.

What would happen when something painful enough finally broke through? Would it be a blinding pain that fried all my circuits? Would I have the emotional equivalent of smoke rising from the cinder that used to be my psyche? Would seeing Mom in the hospital be the trigger?

I walked into Mom's room like it was a minefield. Her eyes were closed. She was hooked up to several machines. Normally slender, now she was so frail she didn't even make a dent in the mattress. I checked my meters. No overload.

Dad put a hand on her shoulder. "Happy Valentine's Day. We're here."

She opened her eyes. "We?" She saw us and smiled. "Hi. Sorry to ruin your weekend with a drive to Houston." Her voice was soft, mainly breath.

"Don't be silly," Heidi said, being very brave and collected. "We came as soon as we heard." She put a rose in Mom's hand.

"Bubba drove us down. He was coming home for the weekend anyway," I added.

"Tell me all the news then."

Heidi looked at me. I looked away. This wasn't the time for true confessions.

"I can listen if I close my eyes. Don't feel much like talking. Still sore and tired."

"They did surgery to get material for the next set of tests," Dad said. "Nobody ever feels good after surgery."

Heidi tried to put Mom in a coma by talking about what was happening in her classes and which of her friends was dating whom and who wasn't talking to each other and a million and one other things of complete inconsequence in my estimation. I couldn't imagine Mom caring a whit for any of those things. But Mom smiled and nodded at all the right times, so maybe she did want to hear.

Hannah talked about the senior portraits and final projects and planning for beach trips in May and all the things high school seniors do. Thankfully, before my slot on the program, Dad cut in and said Mom could use some rest. We had lunch in the cafeteria and dropped in for good-byes before heading back to Fred.

The car was quiet. I stared out the window at the marsh grass and oilrigs and thought about Mom. I wasn't devoid of emotion after all. I finally felt something—anger. In the hospital, while Heidi and Hannah prattled on, I stood in the corner and watched Mom. Her china features now looked like Melmac, used and worn down to a dull shine. She was obviously drugged and struggling to stay awake. Hooked up to those machines, she looked like a torture victim recovering from the last session, trying to talk to the good cop before the bad cop came back.

She didn't deserve this. She wasn't even fifty. Never made it to San Francisco. Just followed her preacher boy around the country and ended up stalled in a backwater town, cooking dinners and killing cockroaches and raising ungrateful kids. Or at least one ungrateful kid. One who couldn't even feel sad when she was dying. Who would do this to a woman like her?

Sunday, Dad gave the congregation the news from the pulpit, and there was an extended time of prayer. We brought home covered dishes for lunch and supper—fried chicken and potato salad.

That afternoon I found Dad in his study, the inner sanctum where all serious conversations inevitably took place. He was sitting in grandmother's chair, his feet on the ottoman, one hand over his eyes, glasses dangling from the other. I sat in the swivel chair at his desk. He dropped his hand from his eyes.

"You never asked why I called Friday."

He looked confused for a second. "Oh. That's right. You called me."

"Once I heard about Mom, I didn't want to bother you with my news." I paused and took a deep breath. "I'm not going back to school with Heidi this afternoon."

"You're not what?"

"Last Wednesday I got a ride from the newspaper office with a friend of mine. The cops stopped us. They found marijuana in his trunk. I spent the night in jail."

"In jail?"

"They had to let us go because the cops illegally searched the car. But when the school found out, they kicked us out."

"It wasn't yours, was it?"

"Of course not. But they won't take my word for that."

He sat up in the chair. "They most certainly will! We'll drive up tomorrow and straighten this thing out."

"Well . . ."

"Yes?"

"There's more to it."

I told him the rest. Sort of. I didn't tell him about the wine or the cigars or about knowing Phil had the drugs in the car. I didn't tell him I had shed my family and faith like an outgrown jacket, that I had taken my own road.

I told him about the pranks from the year before. He was not amused. I told him about The Captain and the pistol. He was not amused. I told him about Lori and the dance on the Quad. He smiled and put on his glasses.

"Mark, most of this is circumstantial evidence. You were never directly charged with doing any of these things. If they're going to kick you out, they should do it properly."

"We could go up there and make them file formal charges and go through all the process. Do you think that would change anything?"

"Maybe if you got your hair cut and got some decent clothes."

"Dad, I spent the night in jail. All we will accomplish is to make it a public event with all the charges on the record."

He considered my comments. I sighed inwardly at my own naiveté. Had I really thought I could escape the specter forever looking over my shoulder, circumscribing my choices? PK expectations would probably follow me to my grave.

"How is Deacon Fry doing these days?" I asked. "Meek as a lamb?"

Dad regarded me as if recalibrating his measurements. "I see your point."

"I figure I'll get a job, save some money, and apply at Stephen F. Austin for the fall."

"Why not Lamar? It's closer to Fred."

"SFA is closer to Stanley."

"Who's Stanley?"

"Louisiana. That's where Lori lives."

"You're serious about this girl?"

"I think I am."

───────

There was a spot open at the plywood mill where I worked the last two summers. The foreman didn't exactly like me, but he knew I would give him a full day's work. I got the early shift, which meant the Falcon was freed up by the time Hannah got home. Heidi went back to school. Dad took the Galaxy to Houston, living out of a suitcase and sleeping in the chair next to Mom at nights. Hannah buried herself in her senior year. I ate the covered dish suppers dropped off by the prayer chain, read Kerouac, and went to bed in an empty house.

On Tuesday, Lori called. She'd heard about Mom from Heidi. I told her what little I knew, about the job, about how I missed her. She cried, making me feel twice as miserable. I began to feel like the arrest was my fault. When I hung up, the house felt emptier.

After three nights of isolation, I was ready for a break. I stood outside the garage and watched Hannah drive to the Beta Club awards banquet in Kountze. Two hours 'til sunset. I dug behind some boxes and pulled out the old Spyder bike. It was dusty and rusty. A few minutes with an oilcan and a rag freed up the chain. I raised the seat, adjusted the handlebars, aired up the tires, and set out for the river road.

I got there an hour before sunset. The porch was finished. The house was painted white with dark blue trim. Parker's truck was out front. I walked in without knocking, poured myself a mug, and sat in the chair Vernon pushed out for me. I looked around. The kitchen was the same, but the living room had sheetrock, paint, lights, and some decent furniture. I grunted and sipped my coffee.

We sat in silence, waiting for the sun to sink behind the world. I fired up a Hava Tampa Jewel. Vernon cocked an eye at me, and I passed a cigar to him. We watched the grass grow for awhile.

Vernon cleared his throat. "It's a shame about yer ma. Sorry ta hear about it."

Parker cleared his throat and nodded. "She's a fine woman. Pastor Matt is a lucky man. I mean . . ." He searched for the right words in confusion, panic on his face. Then he just looked at me, and I could see everything he wanted to say in his one good eye. He nodded and looked at the sunset, taking a sip of coffee.

I didn't welcome the topic. I had avoided thinking about Mom, instead trying to concentrate on my mindless job and reading Kerouac to keep the anger at bay. I felt it rising up like nausea. I pushed it back down. "Thanks."

We let the silence settle in a bit. The awkwardness passed, but the resentment kept pushing back, wanting to bloom into rage.

"Vernon," I said suddenly in the quiet of the gloaming, "whatever happened to that flask of yours?"

He studied my face. "What about yer pa?"

"I don't think he wants any."

Parker made a noise down in his throat that would have been a laugh if he had let it out. Vernon glanced at him and back at me. I waited. He wasn't changed much since the day I met him. There was a little more gray in his jet-black hair, a few more wrinkles on his broad face. But his eyes were different. The rheumy pink was gone. They were clear and sharp, digging past my question into my brain.

"I don't recall where I left it." He released me from his gaze and turned the end of his cigar against the saucer, the ash dropping away to reveal a red, glowing point.

"The bottle should be around here somewhere, right?" I looked around the kitchen. "You always had a spare, didn't you?"

Vernon took a slow drag off the cigar and blew out the smoke. "You can look. I don't reckon you'll find anything. I got ta workin' on this place with Parker, here, and it just slipped my mind. I ain't seen it in over a year."

I looked at Parker. He looked back without comment.

"Ain't missed it much, ta tell the truth," Vernon said.

"What about your business?"

"I'm retired."

I looked at him. "There ain't no fairness in the world, Vernon."

"I hear ya."

"Just when I could use a drink, you go and swear off drinking." I sipped my coffee for awhile and thought on the unfairness of life. "Consider this," I said. "I have never smoked dope. And yet I am thrown out of college because somebody else smokes dope."

"How does that work?"

"For five years the girl of my dreams ignores me. Then out of the blue she invites me to the prom. But only because she loves somebody else."

"Come again?"

"That's what I said. On the other hand, they didn't charge me for the gash in the door, so maybe it balances out. On the other hand, they might stick Bubba with it at the end of the year. Which is unfair to him, since he didn't throw the water balloon."

Vernon looked at me, puzzled, but evidently gave up on getting an explanation.

I thought about the bubba nirvana I had attained on my last visit. If Willie were here, we would get drunk and come to a full understanding of the unfairness in the world. Profound pronouncements would be made that would morph into a song about loss and sunsets and sadness. We would sink from the fading glory of the day into the oblivion of night and whiskey. Somebody had it wrong, but I couldn't figure out who.

# CHAPTER SEVENTEEN

Friday afternoon Dad brought Mom home. She was still weak and dependent on pain medication. Dad set her up in the bedroom and spent most nights on the chaise lounge across the room so as not to disturb her. She had a bell she could ring if she needed anything, but she rarely rang it.

Sunday I stayed home with Mom, drinking coffee in the kitchen, reading Asimov on evolution, and listening for the bell that didn't ring. I wondered about the things The Rack said. I had not made an extensive study of origins, but I had reservations about Bishop Ussher's six-thousand-year-old earth from my trip to the Grand Canyon. And I was learning that, Morris's proclamations notwithstanding, the theory of evolution was based on more than the wishful thinking of humanistic, atheistic, devil-worshipping scientists. It was based on actual scientific investigations that warranted more response than the "I'm not going to let Darwin make a monkey out of me" comments I heard from the loyal opposition.

I began to wonder if my faith was merely a result of not knowing any better. Not that The Rack's bitterness was an attractive alternative, but he did seem to be more informed than the Bible-thumpers at the college. In fact, all of the people I knew who were believers were not very well educated, Dad being the notable exception. I didn't think I could be satisfied with the notion that it was good enough for Daddy so it must be good enough for me. I wanted to know. But, I suspected that once I set foot on a journey of enlightenment, there would be no turning back. It was almost a certainty that it would take me where no one in my family would follow.

At noon a crowd arrived, people from church to pray for Mom. They filed through, nodding to me or smiling softly as they passed the kitchen. Scooter walked through, Brenda taking the kids to the den to keep them quiet. Some of the deacons came but not Deacon Fry. I pulled some chairs aside to let Mac through in his wheelchair. Even Parker was there. Dad brought up the rear, indicating I should join them. I reluctantly followed Hannah down the hallway and lurked near the door.

The church members crowded around the bed, standing at the head and foot, kneeling by the side, many placing their hands on Mom or the sheets. They prayed for a long time, praying for healing from God, praying against harm from Satan, praying hedges of protection and coverings. I thought of barn doors and horses.

I didn't feel the urge to pray and wouldn't have known what to pray if I had. If God was that concerned, He could have stopped it before it started. Or did they think this happened when He wasn't looking. That a polite little, "Oh, by the way, You might have missed this one," was all that was required. He let Mom get cancer in the first place, didn't He?

A Bible scene seeped into my mind. The disciples seeing a blind man, asking Jesus who sinned for this to befall him. Jesus saying nobody sinned, but that he was born blind so that the work of God could be seen in his life. Of course the man is healed, and he is happy, but I wondered about the first twenty or thirty years of his life. Seemed like a big price to pay for the pleasure of being healed in the end.

I did have a short prayer. "Why not use somebody else's mom for show and tell?"

Then I had a sickening thought. I slipped from the crowd and headed out to the Fortress of Solitude, the tree house that was the scene of so many previous wrestling matches. I stood in the middle of the wobbly floor, facing the acres of pine wilderness.

"You did this because of me, didn't You?" I hollered, my words floating in pale patches of fog before me. "I'm the one who messed up." I pointed a finger into the woods. "Leave her out of it; she's got nothing to do with it."

The wilderness was silent. My words fell flat on the pine needles that carpeted the half-roof of the Fortress, the plank flooring, the bed of the forest all around me. It didn't feel as if they even reached the low awning of late-winter clouds.

"You want to punish somebody? Punish me. I'm right here." I stretched my arms out and turned around. "Go ahead. Zap me." I faced the woods and stretched my arms 'til they hurt. "Zap me. I'm not going anywhere."

I waited in the silent forest, my breath hissing in and out between my teeth. In my anger I had stormed out of the house without a jacket. I shivered in the flannel shirt; my arms quivered as I held them out. I turned away and jammed my fists down into my jeans pockets.

"OK. You've made Your point. It's blackmail, not punishment. You want me back. Fine. But she lives. I'll quit drinking. I'll quit smoking. But she gets healed." I pushed my gaze above the tree line. "You hear me?" I yelled to the sullen gray ceiling. "Do what You want to with me, but leave her alone."

I suddenly felt like an idiot. What did I think I was doing screaming at the sky? I jerked the ammo case from the secret compartment, pulled the pack of cigars out, and ripped it open. I broke them all with a single motion and crumbled them, tobacco trickling between my fingers to the ground twenty feet below.

"There," I whispered under my breath. I threw the fragments from me. "There," I said loudly. "This is my covenant. You take me, give me cancer if you want. But you leave the innocent alone."

I took to coming home, taking a shower, and sitting in her room. She was always propped up on the pillows, asleep. I didn't say anything, just sat and looked at her. I realized I had never really seen her before. She was there in my memory, a part of the background like the furniture, a requisite component of the infrastructure of my life. Like a car or refrigerator. She did what she was supposed to do, and life went on.

Only once before had I bothered to see her. The night she nursed the injuries Elrick inflicted on me in his misery. For a brief moment the fog of self-absorption parted, and I saw Mom as a person with dreams and desires. But before she even left the table, the fog enveloped me as I wondered what to do about Lori. I had lived for twenty years with this woman and had treated her no better than a hired housekeeper. I really was an unfeeling jerk.

But surely I could change that now. I whispered, "She has cancer," and waited for a feeling to come. It didn't. I thought, *She's dying,* but I didn't cry. Didn't even get misty.

I was a leper watching the doctor poke me with a needle and ask, "Do you feel that?" Was part of my heart dead? Would it spread? What would go next? What if I got married and then one day I found out I couldn't love my wife anymore? What if I had kids and discovered that part of my heart was already dead and amputated and I didn't care anything about them?

I wondered if I should warn Lori in the daily letters I sent, like you would warn somebody you might marry if there was insanity in the family. It wouldn't be fair to her to get married expecting a normal husband and end up with an unemotional mannequin.

Dad usually came in while I was there and woke her up with something to eat, a cup of soup or something so small it looked lonely on the saucer. Sometimes she woke up before he came in. She would see me sitting there and tell me about a dream she had or ask me about work, which was always the same so there was little to tell.

Heidi came home for spring break and spent most of her day with Mom. I didn't tell her she usurped my afternoon slot. She had only a week to catch up. I had all the time in the world. Or as much time as Mom had left.

The news came that Friday on my birthday. Hannah got home as I was getting out of the shower. Dad gathered the three of us in the den and told us the results of the tests. The cancer had spread throughout her body.

"What about radiation?" I asked. He shook his head. "Chemotherapy?"

"Both are basically poison. The idea is to poison the body, hoping the cancer cells die before the patient does. Because it has spread so far and because your mother is very weak, there's almost no chance that she would survive the treatment long enough to kill the cancer."

Hannah was crying. I stared at him.

"You mean they're not going to do anything?" Heidi demanded.

"Sometimes they can't do anything," Dad said quietly. "This is one of those times."

"You mean they're going to let her die?" Heidi asked, crying.

Hannah jumped up from the couch. "Figure it out, Heidi! She's dying. She's going to die." She wiped her nose with the back of her hand. "They're not letting her die; they can't stop it."

Dad's eyes followed Hannah as she ran from the room.

"Does she know?" I asked. "Mom, I mean. Did you tell her?"

Dad nodded slowly, and I saw his lip tremble for a second. He looked away and blinked a few times. But his voice was steady when he answered.

"Strangely enough, she's taking this better than the rest of us. I don't think she needed a doctor to tell her. She already knew."

"But how can she die? She can't die. She can't die," Heidi said.

She leaned over and crashed into me. I put my arm around her, and she leaned her head against my chest, shaking and muttering between ragged breaths. Dad nodded to me and went back to Hannah's room. I pulled up the tail of the flannel shirt I wore open over a T-shirt and held it out to Heidi. She laughed the smallest of laughs and wiped her face with it, but she didn't move. We sat there for a long time.

I sat dry-eyed and recited my covenant like a rosary.

I watched the sunset with Vernon on Saturday, but in keeping with my vow, I omitted the cigar. Hannah, Dad, and I went to church Sunday. Heidi spent most of the time with Mom until she had to leave for college. I didn't mention Mom in my letters to Lori, but she found out from Heidi Sunday night and called me. It was good to hear her voice, but I felt hollow when I hung up the phone.

Monday afternoon I took a shower and went to Mom's room as usual. She opened her eyes as I sat down on the chaise lounge. I asked her if she needed anything. No. How was she feeling? OK. We sat in silence for awhile.

"I've cut back on my medication," she said.

"Your pain medication?"

She nodded. "I don't want to spend the little time I have left sleeping. I'll trade a little pain for some time with my family."

"In that case, I brought a book." I held up a copy of *Roughing It*. "Want me to read to you?"

"That would be nice."

I started about two-thirds of the way through, when Mark Twain arrives in San Francisco. Mom's eyes twinkled when I read about the weather and the earthquakes. We enjoyed it so much that we spent the rest of the week reading about his trip to the Sandwich Islands as a correspondent for the San Francisco *Enterprise*. It took place after Europeans settled there but before the U.S. overthrew the Hawaiian government. We found the stories of the missionaries to be of particular interest. Twain pointed out their successes and their follies with the same satirical style.

The next week I started at the beginning. When things got a little tedious, like the long section on the Mormons, we blithely skipped to the next chapter. When we caught up with San Francisco, I asked her if she would like to hear another book. She pointed to the three-volume biography of Lincoln by Carl Sandburg.

"I was reading those before and haven't had the energy to read more than a few pages since I came back."

I took the third volume, the second half of the war years, and opened it at the bookmark.

Each afternoon when I came in, she would have the Lincoln book out if she wanted me to read or leave it on the shelf if she wanted to talk.

One day as I finished a chapter of Lincoln, she said, "I think I named you wrong. You're not a Mark Twain; you're an Abe Lincoln."

"How is that?"

"Twain was flamboyant and ostentatious. And he became very bitter. That's not like you at all."

"So, what am I like?"

"You're more of a misfit, like Lincoln. You've always been reserved. When you were a year old, all our friends called you The Judge because you just looked at them and didn't smile. You've never been like the others in your class, starting from the beginning. You're not an outcast, but you don't completely fit in. But that's because you've been given more than others. You just don't know it yet."

"What?"

"Like Abe, you're the one who stands above the others. Not in height, of course, but in more important ways." She smiled at me. "You're going to do some great things."

"Me? I have no idea what I want to do with my life. I almost got Dad fired a couple of years ago. I can't even go to college without getting kicked out."

"I know you can't see it, even though it's right in front of you. You've already played a part in the lives of so many, but you don't even know it. As far back as elementary school." I frowned at her. "Remember Pauline?"

"Oh."

"You saved her life."

"Not for long. She died a week later."

"How many fifth graders would have done that? Her son would have grown up without a father if you had not done what you did.

"And what about Mr. Crowley? You saved his life too."

"Anybody would have done that."

"Darnell didn't. Until you talked him into it. Then there's Deacon Fry."

"How did I help him?"

"You brought him the grace of God. He was humbled, and God gives grace to the humble."

"Does he act like it?"

"Not particularly, but I'm sure his soul is being refined." She smiled.

We spent many other afternoons reading and talking, but one topic remained untouched. Sometimes she would close her eyes, and I would wonder if it was because of fatigue or pain. Other times I knew it was pain by the way her jaw clenched and she breathed loudly through her nostrils. It began to happen more frequently. One afternoon I put down the book and held the pain medication to her. She opened her eyes and shook her head.

"I know you're in pain. Why won't you take them?"

"These minutes are too precious," she said between labored breaths. "I won't have them stolen from me by narcotics."

"It's not the drugs that are stealing your minutes."

I was breathing loudly through my nose too. She looked at me sternly in silence as she clenched her jaw and breathed in through her teeth and out through her nose. Then her breathing settled, her gaze softened, and she took the bottle from me.

"Mark, sit down here." She patted the bed. I sat and stared at the wall. "What do you think is stealing my minutes?"

"Who, you mean."

"Who, then."

"Who had the power to keep you from getting cancer, but didn't?"

"I see. You're blaming the wrong person. Satan is the destroyer of life, not God."

"But I always hear that Satan can't do anything without God's permission."

"Mark, there's no use in arguing with God over this and blaming Him. Things happen in this world, good things, bad things. But God uses them all for good, if we let Him."

I stared at the wall in silence, my jaw muscles clenching and relaxing as Mom's had done earlier.

"Mark, of one thing I am certain. God's love and mercy are infinitely deeper than I will ever know or understand. He's given me almost fifty years of a life better than I deserved. I'm not going to throw a tantrum because it wasn't twenty years longer."

She set the pills on the nightstand and smoothed the sheet over her legs. "Many people live twice as long as I have with half the blessings. I'm not going to walk greedy and grasping into the presence of one who has been so generous to me, pouting because the end is sooner than I expected."

It sounded good, but I couldn't dispel the cloud of resentment swirling in my head. How could she be content when she was the one who was dying? Didn't she see the injustice? I wanted to shout out, to force her to realize how unfair it was, how angry she should be. But I couldn't bring myself to say the words.

I knew it wouldn't change her mind. It would only sadden her and make her concerned about me, as if I were the one needing consideration. I went back to the chaise lounge and picked up the book.

# CHAPTER EIGHTEEN

Ten weeks after I made my covenant, one week before Mother's Day, she died. All the aunts and uncles and cousins converged on the house, taking over our beds and sleeping on sofas. There were a few tears, but mainly they sat around the den and talked about Mom, telling stories about their childhood. I sat in a corner and listened. Heidi joined in, asking questions. Hannah didn't come out of her room. Lori called and asked if she should come down. I told her the house was packed and there was no place for her to stay.

The funeral was on Tuesday. The church was full. They had to bring in folding chairs. Bubba showed up with Lori, driving from Marshall that morning. I saw them pull up while I was standing outside the church. She ran to me and I hugged her. When she pulled away she was crying. I kissed her.

I didn't hear a thing said at the funeral. In my mind I was in the Fortress, shaking my finger at the sky. "I kept my side of the deal; I kept my promise," I whispered through clenched teeth. But I sensed that I was bargaining with empty air that day. I was just a foolish boy trying to control the relentless machinery of a blind universe with words and venom. The grinding juggernaut inched on, missing me but taking out Mom.

By Wednesday the house was empty. Dad spent more time in the study. He usually fell asleep in grandmother's chair, waking up about the time I left for the lumberyard. I'd leave him sitting at the table in rumpled clothes, drinking coffee. When I got home he'd be off visiting the hospitals or mowing the field behind the church or something.

The next week Heidi left to take her finals. Hannah, on the home stretch for graduation, spent very little time at the house. I had plenty of time to think.

One day I came home from work and was startled to see Dad in the den. He was writing slowly in a small black three-ring notebook. When he saw me, he left the book in the chair and stood up.

"A Dr Pepper sounds good about now. Want one?"

"Sure." I dropped into a chair at the table and kicked off my steel-toed boots.

Dad sat opposite me and shoved a glass across. "I hope the next item on your agenda is a shower. You'd stun a goat at fifty paces."

"I work at a plywood mill, not a perfume factory."

"True. Here's mud in your eye." He held his glass up and took a drink.

"What's the occasion?"

"Occasion?"

"I'm not used to actually seeing a person in here while it's still light, much less having a conversation."

"Ah." He took another drink, leaned back in his chair, and looked at me. "How are you holding up?"

I shrugged. "How are you holding up?"

He took off his glasses. "I've been better." He looked over my head out the window. "Yes, I've certainly been better."

"Dad, can you explain it to me?"

He pulled back out of his trance. "Explain what?"

"How can God let something like this happen?" He looked hard at me. "I mean, do you know a nicer person than Mom? Do you know anybody who deserved this less?"

"No." His voice was quiet.

I blew out a lungful of air and waved a hand at him. "Look, I know it sounds shallow. I've heard people who are fine with God until somebody kicks their sandcastle down, and then they are all outraged at God and sounding stupid. At least they always sounded stupid to me. But that was before I got my sandcastle kicked in." I calmed down a little. "It looks different from this side."

"Yes, it does."

"What are you saying? You're the preacher. You're supposed to have the answers."

"Oh, I know the answers. I've recited them plenty of times to people on the other side. People on the side we're on now."

"Well?"

"You want to hear the answers? 'All things work together for good to them that love God and are called according to his purpose.' 'For me to live is Christ, to die is gain.' 'Precious in the sight of the Lord is the death of his saints.' 'To be absent from the body is to be present with God.'"

He stopped and looked at me. "There. Did that help?"

"Not one bit."

"Exactly."

"You're saying you don't believe it?"

"Oh, I believe it. I have to believe it. I don't feel it, but I believe it. That's about all I have left."

"What do you mean, it's all you have left?"

Moisture glistened in his eyes from the light of the kitchen window. "Mark, have you ever been in a fight?"

"No, not really."

"You've never had the wind knocked out of you? I mean completely knocked out. Never found yourself clawing the air, desperate for another breath?"

I shook my head.

"You feel like you'll never get air in your lungs again. You don't see how you're going to get the next breath, but you believe it'll come, that God isn't going to leave you gasping forever.

"Well, I've had the breath knocked out of me. Clean out. I don't really trust myself to talk to anyone. That's part of the reason I've made myself scarce around here."

"But you're still preaching."

"I'm preaching sermons from a seminary notebook I dug out of the closet." He shook his head. "The sad thing is, I don't think anybody's noticed."

"But you still believe?"

"Yes, I still believe."

"Even when you don't feel like it's real?"

"Especially when it doesn't feel real. I can't follow my feelings, or I'm lost. Now more than ever, I believe. I must believe. When this thing started, I grabbed the hem of His garment and held on until I tore the corner off. So now I'm just holding onto the scrap I have left, believing one day I'll be able to join the little piece I'm holding back to the rest of the garment."

"But you're a preacher. You devoted your life to God. Why should you be kicked in the stomach? It's not right. Mom didn't have to die. She wasn't supposed to die. Not like that. It's wrong. It's just wrong."

"I know."

"You know? It's wrong. God let it happen."

"Ever hear of Job?"

"Yeah, and it makes no sense. God wipes out a whole family, ten kids, all the servants, thousands of cattle, just to win a bet? It's wrong. Then, after He's killed all these people, He gives Job ten more kids and somehow that makes it OK?"

"The Book of Job is there to ask all those questions so we can see the answers. Job questioned why these things should happen to him, but he never quit believing in God. And when he got the audience he demanded, he realized his perspective was limited compared to God's. He repented of questioning God's motives or His right to do with His creation as He wished."

"Maybe Job was a chump."

"Maybe, unlike you or me, Job knew what it means to be in the presence of a holy God."

"Holy or not, I'm not sure I like Him. He jerks people around, blackmails them, tortures the people who love Him most, kills their families."

"Mark, you have good reasons to be angry, but you have to make decisions based on what you know, not what you feel. Feelings are nothing more than chemistry. I could change a few of the chemicals in your body, and you'd be the happiest man on earth. But feelings don't change facts. You remember Art Linkletter's daughter?"

I remembered. The story was that she was on LSD and jumped out of a sixth-floor window.

"Due to a little chemistry, she felt like she could fly, but that didn't change the law of gravity. My feelings, or lack of them, don't change the facts or the law of God's grace.

"The facts are God let Mom die. Those are the facts I see."

"None of us are going to get out of this thing alive. Man's perspective is that this life is all there is. Well, this life is precious, but God's perspective is that there are things more important than this life."

I stood up. "God let Mom die, and you're sitting there taking His side. Well, I can't do that. I'm sorry, but it's wrong and I'm not going to pretend like it's not."

I opened the garage door and ran into Hannah. I pushed past her and slammed the door behind me.

---

I took the bike. By the time I reached the county line, the adrenaline was burned off. A fresh layer of sweat brought out the delicate bouquet of the plywood mill. I coasted down the hill to the creek that marked the separation between Tyler and Jefferson counties, stood and pedaled up the other hill, and swerved off the road to the right into the gravel parking lot of the store we called Last Chance Liquor. I tossed the bike down and slammed the door

open. A little bell jangled violently, announcing my arrival and attitude to the guy behind the counter. He met my glare and his eyes
narrowed. He didn't like customers with stringy, shoulder-length
blond hair who looked like they'd been dragged to jail behind a
truck and smelled like they'd escaped through a sewage ditch. Fine.
I didn't like redneck bubbas. We could compare notes later.

I stalked the aisles looking for something familiar. I grabbed
a flask of Jim Beam and took it to the counter. The man looked at
the whiskey then at me.

"We don't sell liquor to sixteen-year-olds."

I looked around for a sixteen-year-old. "I didn't say you did."

"Then take this on back over ta where ya got it and git out of
here."

The adrenaline was gone, but the rage was still there. I
slammed my license on the counter. He picked it up and checked
it out closely, turning it over and peering at the back and the
edges.

"Well, it don't look fake."

"That's because it isn't fake." I plucked it from his hand and
shoved a ten in its place. "I assume you take cash."

While he sullenly dug through the register for change, I
twisted the cap off the flask. He turned toward me as I was raising
it to my mouth.

"What do ya think yer doin'?" he roared.

"It's paid for."

"Is this some kind of TABC setup? I ain't gonna git my
license pulled 'cause of you. Get out of here."

He dropped the change on the counter. I screwed the cap on,
shoved the change in my pocket, and stomped out into the parking lot. Cars whooshed by on Highway 92, heading home from
work. I ignored them. Standing over the bike, I twisted the cap
back off, raised the flask in my fist toward the sky, and shook it.
Then I took a big swig, swallowing with gritted teeth.

"There," I said and broke into a coughing fit. It was like drinking gasoline. Burning gasoline.

I wiped my mouth with the back of my hand and, to prove it wasn't a whim, took another swallow, a big one. I let the fire roll back in my throat and slide down into my gut. It sat in my belly with a dull glow. My ears were glowing like a branding iron. A vicious euphoria crept into my head. I suddenly saw the genius of my plan.

"Yeah," I hollered, thrusting the flask at the passing traffic. "See?"

I took a third swig. This time it was less like drinking lava and more like taking medicine. I thought of Kerouac, of Dean Moriarity, who I remembered was supposed to be somebody named Neal Cassady. I whooped and slapped my leg.

"Yes, yes, yes," I said, trying out his manner of speaking in the book. It had always seemed strange before; now the essential rightness of it was opened to me like the mystery of a koan. I heard the tinkling of bells and turned, expecting to see a Buddhist monk with finger cymbals. The enraged guy from behind the counter startled me.

"Are you crazy? Get out of here before I call the cops."

"Yas, yas, yas," I said, attempting to twist the cap back on. It wouldn't go on. I looked down and realized I didn't have the cap. I spun around on the heel of one steel-toed boot and spied it in the gravel under a bike tire. I bent over, elaborately inserted two fingers between the spokes, snared the cap, and extracted it. Then I cleverly screwed it back on the flask, pushed it into my back pocket on the second attempt, and jerked the bike from the ground. I threw my leg over the seat, saluted the scowling clerk, and pedaled back down the hill to the county line.

I focused all my attention on the bike, and it responded to my touch like a well-trained horse to its master. Never before had I ridden the bike with such skill and daring. Four miles later I came across the river road. I veered into the sand and stood up on the pedals. The whiskey was fading, and so was I. I pulled into the ditch, took two more hits of medicine, and resumed my pilgrimage.

A fuzzy calm descended over me, and I whirled serenely past Parker's house, past all manner of barking dogs and lumbering log trucks, past the hill and the empty porch swing, to the Crowley manse.

I tossed the bike into the yard, clumped across the porch and into the kitchen. Vernon was there. So was Parker. They looked at me with mild curiosity as I deliberately poured coffee and collapsed into my appointed chair. I pulled the flask from my pocket, screwed the cap off, and held it toward Vernon.

He shook his head. "I'll give it a miss."

I turned to Parker.

"I'm good."

"Suit yourself then." I poured a generous amount of whiskey into my coffee and sampled the mixture. It was strong, raw, and bitter. It suited my mood. I sipped my cowboy cocktail while the others examined me. The silence mellowed like the contented lull after Thanksgiving dinner. I considered the sunset and the thoughts that drove me from the house.

"Vernon."

He grunted.

"What was that girl's name you met in Italy? At the farmhouse."

He waited awhile before answering. "Sarah."

"Yeah, Sarah. When she died, were you angry?"

"I don't know if that's the right word." He started up a cigarette, waiting a few draws to continue. "More like you would feel if ya came home from a party and saw yer house burnt down. Sure, yer angry, but that's only part of it."

"So, who were you angry at? The German that shot her?"

"No. That was self-defense. He didn't aim ta shoot anybody when he come ta the house, but she pulled out the Luger I left behind. Looked like she got all three of 'em afore he took her down."

"Then who were you mad at?"

"Weren't nobody ta be mad at, in particular. I could a got mad at myself fer leavin' but ain't no percentage in goin' down that road." He took a sip of coffee. "Can't spend yer life second guessin' yerself. Ain't no way ta live."

"Did you ever wonder why God didn't stop it? Why He let it happen?"

Parker nodded to himself and sipped his coffee. Vernon let out a cloud of smoke in a protracted sigh.

"Mark, I seen a mess a killin' and worse in Italy. There was a lot of things that shouldn't a happened, but they did. That's how life is. That's all. It's just how things is."

"But it shouldn't be that way."

"Might could be. But I ain't settin' myself up ta be the one that says what should be."

"It's not right."

"There's a lot a things that ain't right in this world. But I think yer puttin' the blame in the wrong place."

"Why? God is in control, right? He could stop it if He wanted to. But He doesn't. Maybe because He can't. Maybe because He isn't really there."

Parker cleared his throat. "Brother Williams says God lets things come into our lives to chip off all that don't look like Jesus."

Vernon considered this. "The way I hear tell, God set us down here, and He lets us make our own choices. He don't go jumpin' in and undoin' ever little mistake we make."

"So what mistake did my mom make?"

"Ah, I figured that was it. She didn't make no mistake, far as I can see, but this world is busted, and it ain't gonna get fixed this week, nor the next. Your pa says it won't be fixed, it'll just be scrapped and we'll get a new one. Might be right."

"So, you just let it go at that?"

"Not much more I can do."

"That's not good enough for me."

Vernon sat silent for awhile. "Is that what the whiskey is all about?"

"It's about a vow I made. That somebody else broke." I poured more in the coffee to make my point.

The sun slipped below the tree line. The room slipped into gloom.

"Mark boy, that could be a slight detour yer takin' or it could be a long road. More like a tunnel that's hard to git out of once yer in it."

Parker leaned forward in his chair, elbows on the table. "Mark, there's some of us have ta learn the hard way." He nodded at Vernon and looked back to me. "There's others that's had the benefit of a good home and good teachin'."

The anger boiled over. I pushed the chair out and jumped to my feet. "I'm done with that. You people think just because my dad's the preacher, I'm not really human. That I'm some kind of holy robot that doesn't have the same feelings of normal people."

I glared into Parker's good eye. He looked back. I could see he didn't really think that, but I was too angry to back down. I looked at Vernon. His face was impassive, waiting. I grabbed the chair, dragged it up violently, and dropped into it.

I jerked a finger at Parker. "Of all people, I figured you guys would understand it. I would expect a sermon from Deacon Fry, but not here."

Parker looked at Vernon. Vernon looked back and shrugged almost imperceptibly. Parker took a deep breath and turned back to me.

"Mark, I . . ." His voice trailed off. He took another breath and tried again. "You seen how it is. You seen where that got the both of us." He nodded at the flask. "I ain't sayin' you ought ta be some kind of saint. I'm sayin' yer a lot smarter'n the two of us put together. You already know that ain't gonna get ya anywhere you want ta go."

I slapped my hand down on the table. The mugs rattled. "I had a deal. I kept my side."

"What kind of deal?" Parker asked. "With who?"

"It's complicated. But if He had kept His side, I wouldn't have this." I picked up the bottle and took a swig from it. It ran down my throat like water. I didn't even feel it anymore. "So that's how it is. From now on I make my own decisions, and He can just like it."

Vernon looked at me for a full minute. I glared back for a few seconds, then looked away and sipped my coffee. Finally he spoke.

"OK. Let me know how that works out fer ya."

---

When the alarm went off at 4:00 A.M. I reached for it and knocked it off the nightstand. My face was buried in the pillow. I couldn't see the clock, but it quit making noise so it faded from my consciousness. In the place of my brain, a giant fist was clenched inside my skull, which felt as brittle as an eggshell. Every time my pulse beat, the fist tried to open. This occupied my attention for awhile, until I tried to swallow. Then I realized that someone had swabbed all the moisture out of my mouth with cotton balls and then left them in there.

I tried to roll over. On the third attempt I dragged my legs to the edge of the bed. They dangled until my boots hit the floor. I leaned over, elbows on knees, feeling a sucking vacuum of fatigue in all my limbs where my energy used to be. I squinted at the bed. It was wrinkled but still made. I was wearing my work clothes. I smelled as dead as I felt.

A plan. This much I remembered. I repeated it between the clenchings of my brain. *A plan. I have a plan.* The plan didn't involve feeling like death on a Popsicle stick, but I would work around it somehow. I slithered to the bathroom and took a shower hot enough to clean a hog carcass. I dragged fresh clothes across my bones and left the house at the same time as always and drove to work.

I parked in the back of the lot, climbed in the backseat, and slept until the sun came up. Then I hung out at a diner eating runny eggs and limp toast until the savings and loan opened. I emptied out my account, almost four hundred dollars. I bought a pack of cigars, then went to the army surplus store and bought a backpack and a sleeping bag. As I expected, the house was empty when I got back. I filled the pack with clothes I thought could take some mileage. I also packed my camera.

I left a note on the table. It said, "I'm taking some time off to think. I'll let you know where I am when I get there."

Then I took the bike to Darnell's place. He was out of school and driving his own rig. His mom fixed us lunch, and we rumbled off to Beaumont. He dropped me off at a grocery store while he picked up the trailer because he wasn't supposed to have riders. Following Kerouac's lead, I bought a loaf of bread, mustard, and a package of ham. I took them out under a tree and made sandwiches, piling them to one side and putting the stack of them back in the bread bag. They didn't all fit, so I ate one while I waited.

An hour later we were on I-10 to Ft. Worth via Houston. Darnell asked me where I was headed. I told him I didn't know, but Ft. Worth was as good a starting point as any. We talked about what he'd been doing since graduation, about Jolene's wedding, about Becky and the prom, about being busted for drugs. We didn't talk about Mom.

The seven-hour drive afforded ample time for reflection. Each day since the funeral the injustice impressed itself on me with greater intensity, but nobody else seemed to care. Hannah just disappeared. Dad took the company line. Not surprising, really, but it galled me to see the one who should be most offended meekly acquiesce instead. Even Vernon and Parker seemed to be a party to this conspiracy of apathy. The way I saw it, inaction was consent, and I didn't consent.

As I sat in Vernon's kitchen, I had realized that I had to do something. God, if He was there at all, was doing His thing and didn't seem to want or need my input. Fine. I would do my own thing. My plan didn't extend further than getting out of town. I tossed about for a destination. All roads seemed equally likely. Maybe I should go to San Francisco for Mom.

As the miles rolled by, I wrote a long, semilegible letter to Lori telling her about my decision. I warned her that I would not have an address for awhile but that I would continue to write.

In Ft. Worth, Darnell dropped the trailer and we hit a truck stop for pie and coffee. We would sleep in his rig, him in the bed in back, me in the front seat. The next morning he would head back to Fred, and I would set out west. While we waited for our pie, Darnell looked out the window. He let out an exclamation, intercepted a guy coming in the door, and dragged him to our table.

"Mark, this here's Darren. We was in the same class at the school." We shook hands. "Mark here is hittin' the road. He's gonna see the country on his thumb."

Darren nodded, flagged down the waitress, ordered a steak, and turned back to me. "I can take you as far as Texarkana. I'll be pulling out at dawn. You can sleep in back if you want."

"Actually, I'm heading west. Maybe go to San Francisco."

"Suit yourself. Don't know anybody headed west right now. I might be going to El Paso next week."

"Mark," Darnell said, "is there some reason you picked San Francisco?" I shook my head. "Well, seems ta me ya got a ready ride right here. Why not go to New York instead?"

I thought it over as I ate my pie. East. What did I want to see in the east? M! I hadn't been back to Middletown since we left eight years ago. I would look up M and see what he was doing.

# CHAPTER NINETEEN At 10:00 A.M. Darren

let me off on State Line Avenue. I walked across to Arkansas, got a Dr Pepper in a 7-11, and looked through a highway map to verify my route—Little Rock to Nashville to Cincinnati. Then I walked back to I-30. A hundred yards past the entrance ramp I set down the pack with the sleeping bag lashed to it. I opened the Dr Pepper, took a drink, turned around, and held up the sign I had made from the side of a cardboard box in Darren's truck—Little Rock—in patchy block letters.

I stood for thirty minutes, my back to the sun, watching cars go by. An Arkansas state trooper appeared, slowed down, and suddenly swung over and screeched to a nose-dive stop right in front of me. I jumped back, stumbled over my pack, and fell into the grass.

The trooper walked up as I scrambled to my feet. "Son, what do you think you're doing?"

"Uh, just headed to Little Rock, sir."

"It's illegal to hitchhike in Arkansas."

"It is?"

"You want to go to Little Rock, you take the bus like decent folk. We don't take to bums traipsing along our highways."

"Yes, sir."

"If you get off the road right now, I won't take you in."

"Yes, sir."

He left, and I walked back to State Line. I found a diner and ordered eggs and toast from a cowgirl with bleached hair. Her mustard yellow uniform had an olive green collar and cuffs, and *Wanda* stitched above the pocket. Things were a lot easier in Kerouac's time. They had places where people needing rides could hook up with people wanting help with gas money. And hitching was more common too. But at least I was doing better than Weissman. Nobody had beaned me with a brick, and the trooper didn't pistol-whip me or anything.

Wanda brought me my breakfast, looked at my pack, and asked me where I was headed. I told her I was planning to hitchhike to Little Rock before I found out it was illegal.

"Whoever told you that?" she asked in an accent thicker than the syrup stuck to the Formica table.

"The state trooper who almost took me to jail."

"Right. You wanna know why he didn't take you to jail? 'Cause he knew he couldn't. There ain't no law against hitchhiking. And I can tell you why he ran you off too." She reached over and flicked my hair over my shoulder with her pencil. It had been two years since my last haircut. It hung well below my shoulders. "You wanna hitchhike around here, you're taking your life in your hands with that hair."

"You're not serious."

"Didn't you see Easy Rider?"

"No."

"You are gree-een. You better do something about that hair."

---

I walked down State Line 'til I saw an Albertson's. I found the cowboy hats, picked out a nice white straw one, pushed my hair up under it, and crammed it on tight. I looked in the mirror. "Hey, Bubba." I winked at the mirror. "Hey, Joe Bob. Who's yer daddy?" I nodded. "Yep, it's a doofer."

At the checkout the girl looked at me expectantly. I smiled at her.

"Well?" she said.

"Oh, the hat. I'll take the hat."

"Can you take it off? I need to see the price tag."

I handed her the hat. My hair fell out and she jumped back, knocking the hat to the floor. I picked it up.

"I'm sorry," she said, "just startled me, is all."

That was as good a test as any. I headed back to the highway and walked a few miles on the access road in case the trooper came back. Then I set up shop again, sipping the warm Dr Pepper and holding the sign. After an hour, a brown Dodge Dart slowed to a stop next to me. A thin guy with black hair plastered on his head and a metal stud in his ear leaned across the seat and rolled down the window.

"I'm headed to Memphis. I can drop you off in Little Rock."

"Memphis is even better." I shoved the pack through the open back window and dropped into the passenger seat. The hat hit the doorway and fell to the ground, my hair tumbling around my shoulders.

"My, aren't we full of surprises." He smiled at me and held out a hand. "I'm Bruce. What's your name, cowboy?"

I fumbled with the hat and held out my hand. "Mark."

"Well, Mark, hang on for the ride of your life."

He stomped on the gas pedal. The tires spun in the gravel next to the shoulder and the door swung shut as I pulled my foot into the car. I checked the speedometer, surprised that a Dart had such power.

Bruce noticed my shock. "I have a friend who knows a few things about cars. He's tinkered with it."

Bruce asked me questions about where I was going and where I had been. I kept my answers light, giving only sketchy details. Bruce was more forthcoming. He was from Kansas City but was spending the summer with a friend in Memphis who was starting a punk rock band. He had stopped in Dallas to get a guitar amp.

"I had to come by here. I grew up in Hope." He took the exit and drove through town. "Hated every minute of it. Got out as quick as I could."

"So why come back?"

"To sneer at the locals, of course. How about a hamburger?"

He pulled into the parking lot of a rickety hamburger joint. I followed him in. He ordered us both a deluxe and collapsed into a booth.

"She doesn't recognize me. Her brother used to beat on me after school. He never figured out who put the sugar in his gas tank."

We ate lunch while he told me stories of his past in the town he hated. Back in the car he turned down a back road.

"Here, I'll show you something. You'll like this."

He took a few turns in a wooded area, crossed over a creek, and darted over an overgrown cattle guard. Behind a thick stand of trees he pulled to a stop behind a rock house and turned off the car. I looked around. I couldn't see more than twenty yards in any direction.

"Cool, isn't it? It's called Rockwood. Land for miles around belongs to a rich guy who lives in New York. A director or producer or something. I used to hang out here with a few guys back in the day. Nobody ever comes out here."

We stared at the house for awhile. The humid air pressed the silence down on us. I could feel the sweat trickle down the hollow of my back. The minutes stacked up, and Bruce just sat there, staring at the house. I looked at it for awhile, but soon bored. It was a nice rock house, but in the end it was just a house.

More minutes passed. I began to wonder why we were just sitting there. I took a sideways glance at Bruce. Sweat was trickling down the side of his neck onto the white T-shirt. He stared forward like he was waiting for something. A sign.

Then, in a sickening flash I knew why we were sitting there, what he was waiting for. For a few seconds I doubted it, argued with myself, and then a certainty settled on me like dread. My pulse quickened. I rubbed my hands on my jeans. I realized I was breathing shallow and took a deep breath and let it out.

Bruce turned to me as my hand slipped to the door handle, his elbow on the seat back, his hand settling on my shoulder.

"Mark," he began, but I was already tumbling out of the car. "Hey, where you going?"

"Sorry, gotta go." I slammed the door and reached through the back window, pulling out the pack.

He crawled halfway to the passenger window. "But what about Memphis?"

"I just realized I left my wallet back in Texarkana."

I leaned into the back window to retrieve my hat, and he grabbed my wrist. "I'll give you a ride back. It's only thirty miles."

I jerked my hand out the window, jammed the hat on, and grabbed a strap on the pack.

"Don't trouble yourself," I hollered over my shoulder as I bolted around the house.

I thought I heard the car door open, but the underbrush was so dense that within a few seconds I was hidden from view, crashing through the trees. After a hundred yards I stopped to rest and get my bearings. I listened but detected no sound of pursuit.

It took me more than an hour to get back to I-30. With my hair safely under my hat, I put my thumb out, watching closely for any sign of a brown Dodge Dart. I got lucky after ten minutes. I ran up and climbed in the semi. I kept the hat on.

He was headed to Hot Springs. He was a talker and didn't pause for replies, hollering over the CB radio or sometimes grabbing the mike and yelling into it and slamming it back into the cradle without a break in his rhythm. At first I said, "Ah," and "Yeah," and "I see" until I realized that he talked right over them, so I quit.

Mile after mile he talked without a discernible pause for breath. I thought he must have mastered the circular breathing technique required to play the didgeridoo. He talked about the Cowboys, the Astros, the hippies, disco, Nixon, Ford, Carter, Lucille Ball, Ernest Tubb, Ralph the Diving Pig, hot tubs, wallpaper, brake jobs, boudin, and cockroaches. I nodded off a few times, but the flow never stopped. When he dropped me off in Hot Springs, he was still talking to me as he drove away. I wandered the area, taking pictures. Then I bought a Dr Pepper and a bag of chips, found a quiet street, and walked down it for awhile. After a few blocks I came across a sign that said Whittington Park, grabbed a bench, ate two sandwiches, and wrote Lori.

By five I was east of town on Highway 70 holding my sign. I watched cars pass for three hours until the light began to fade. I needed a place to stay the night. I headed back to the park. It was dark when I got there. I unrolled the sleeping bag behind a bench and lay there willing myself to go to sleep.

It was my first night on the road. I'd spent the afternoon avoiding thinking by watching the sun, recalculating my anticipated arrival time in Little Rock, and peering at each vehicle as it approached, wondering if this would be the one. Now I was lying on the ground trying to go to sleep without thinking about what I was doing because I didn't really know what I was doing. God or no God, blackmail or not, what did I hope to accomplish by hitting the road?

I wondered who found the note first. Probably Hannah coming home from school. If she came home at a normal hour. Graduation was only a few weeks away. She probably was out at some student government party or rehearsal or something. So Dad might have beat her home and read it first. Would he think I left because of our argument? Probably. Was that the reason I left? I didn't know.

I left because I couldn't stand staying. The reason wasn't very clear to me. I just knew that one minute Fred was endurable; the next, it wasn't. The instant the thought of leaving crossed my mind, the discontent that had grown to a chaotic din in my pea brain faded to a comforting white noise, masking the questions and accusations that clamored for answers. The future, instead of a bleak wasteland stretching to the horizon, became an intriguing fog, indistinct but seething with possibility.

I had no idea what lay ahead, and that suited me down to the ground. I would greet it with the open hand. America was out there waiting. I pictured it in my mind, dotted lines marking the states like cuts on a side of beef.

In the meantime, working out the logistics left little downtime for the clamor to break through. As long as I kept moving, I could outpace it.

# CHAPTER TWENTY

I awakened in a spasm of flailing limbs to find a dog licking my face. It jumped back. The tatters of a morning fog drifted through the park. I grasped at the edges of the dream fading from my mind, closing my eyes tight to remember it.

I recalled a woman with translucent skin passing through a fog. She seemed to emanate light. She was clothed only by her hair, which was whiter than her skin and flowed over her shoulders in all directions, down past her waist and faded into the swirling mists. I felt a desire for her, but not a sexual desire. It was the sense of expectation that filled the days before Christmas when I was very young. Not excitement but more a longing for things that were too good to be true.

The pale woman leaned over me. I could feel her breath on my face. She dipped her finger in water and held it over my head. A single drop hit my brow and trickled down. Then she stepped back and held up her right hand, palm forward, like the taking of a vow, and her left hand out, palm up, as if accepting something. A phrase echoed back to me. *All is empty but the open hand.*

Then the dog and the flailing. As I brushed the dew off the sleeping bag and rolled it up, I rolled the dream around in my head, but gained no clarity. It was vivid, but mystifying. The sense of longing persisted. Or perhaps I was just hungry. I shoved my hair in my hat and set out for a date with a cup of coffee and Highway 70. The dog followed me for a bit, found a trashcan, and bid me farewell.

I was a mile out of town and almost awake when a white pickup stopped. Three young guys in work clothes and hardhats were crammed into the cab.

The beefy one by the window hollered, "Hop in back."

"Thanks."

I tossed my pack into the bed and jumped in after it. I leaned against the back window on the driver's side and watched the pine trees file past me on either side. We were a few miles out when a gust of wind tossed my cowboy hat into the ditch. My blond hair blew around my head, blinding me. I was attempting to wrangle it back into a ponytail when I felt the truck brake and swerve to the narrow shoulder, slamming me against the side of the truck bed. Both doors opened.

"Well, boys," the driver drawled, "looks like we got us a undercover hippie." He was lean, cigarettes rolled up in a sleeve of his T-shirt.

"He's a freak in goat-roper clothes," said the guy riding shotgun.

The third guy climbed out. He was taller than the others. "Come on, guys. Just let him out and let's get to the site."

That startled me. Instead of what? I scrambled to my feet, grabbed my pack, and walked to the tailgate.

"Hey, I have to go find my hat. You go on and I'll get another ride."

The first two guys followed me and rounded the back of the truck as I put my foot on the tailgate and jumped to the ground. Shotgun lurched for me. I had the pack on my right shoulder. I grabbed the strap in both hands and swung it around. It slammed him against the tailgate. His hardhat bounced into the bed of the truck. I ran past him, tossed my pack over a barbed wire fence, and followed it in one smooth motion, hands on a fencepost as I vaulted over. I scooped the pack up without slowing down, crashing through the underbrush and looking to see if I was being followed.

The driver must have won all-district in track. He vaulted the fence in a running leap with a good foot to spare. His hardhat tumbled to the pine straw without a sound. I fled, head down, the pack in front of me to push back the limbs. I made twenty yards before he slammed against my back. I went down on top of the pack. He rolled over my back and came up in front of me.

I crawled to my hands and knees. Through the screen of my hair I saw a cowboy boot swinging sideways at my head. I pulled the pack up as I rolled the other way. The boot ricocheted off the pack; the heel grazed my ear. I completed the roll on my knees a few feet away. He was off balance from the roundhouse. I rushed him and shoved him with the pack. He staggered back, hit a pine tree and went down, tearing flakes from the bark.

I turned and ran straight into Shotgun. He grabbed the pack, pushed me backward, and jerked the pack, ripping it from my hands. My foot caught a root and I fell. Shotgun tossed the pack aside. His shirt was ripped, and a long scratch on his arm was ridged with blood. Probably from the fence. He smiled. It wasn't a reassuring smile.

The driver crawled to his feet. They converged on me. I stood up slowly.

"Look, guys, I say we just let bygones be bygones. You don't want to be late for work."

Shotgun snorted. "Don't matter. His dad's the foreman."

He toed a pinecone, one that wasn't open, green, dense and spiky as a pineapple. He got his work boot under it and kicked it at my head. As I ducked it, the driver rushed me. Before I could react I was pinned to the ground. He grabbed the pinecone in his right hand and slammed it against my head. I felt the thorns tear the flesh on my ear and rip along my cheek, pulling my hair across my face. I rolled my head away before it got to my eye and swung a fist at his head. He rolled off of me, and I rolled the other way to get to my feet.

That's when Shotgun kicked me in the stomach.

The woods went dark around the edges, telescoping to a pin-point that receded from me. I curled inward, arms crossed over my gut, fingers clutching at my ribs. My mouth opened, but nothing went in or out. I was caught at the terminus of a long exhale, one that might last a year. I was aware of the pain in my stomach as a detail, noted along with the thin edge of individual pine needles pressed against my right cheek, the tickling crawl of blood seeping down my left cheek, the musky smell of rotting timber, the sound of wind rushing through my head, and a pressure against my ears like I was at the bottom of Toodlum Creek. I gaped like a fish, but it was as if a sock had been stuffed down my throat. I quivered with the spasms in my gut and turned in a small arc as my legs ratcheted back and forth, but the long exhale would not end.

Then, just as I thought I had passed out, the fist clenching my stomach released its grip and I sucked the cool humid air in ragged gulps. The forest pinwheeled back into view. My senses seeped back into my brain, and I caught up with events, fast-forwarding through the driver kicking me in the back to the present. Shotgun was dragging me to my feet. The driver flipped open a pocketknife. I struggled, but Shotgun pulled my arms back and locked the elbows behind me.

"That's enough, Shane." We all looked to the voice. It was the third guy. "You've had yer fun, but now yer taking it too far."

"Mind yer own business, Jack," Shane said and nodded to Shotgun.

Shotgun shoved my face against a large pine tree, his arm against my back pressing my chest against the bark. He buried his fist in my hair and jerked my head back.

"Shane, I'm warnin' ya. I'm not goin' to prison because of you."

"Put a sock in it, Jack. We ain't gonna hurt him." He stepped around the tree. I could see him with one eye as Shotgun held my head back with my hair. He looked me in the eye and smiled. "Much."

I was breathing loudly through my nose.

"Ya see, Jack, he wants ta be a cowboy. He's got the hat, the shirt, the jeans, the boots. He just needs the haircut."

He reached up with the knife and hacked upward at my hair. I could feel it come away in clumps, the pain in the back of my head moving up my scalp as all the pressure was focused on the hairs still holding my head back. He sawed until the last strand was severed and my head fell forward.

Shotgun spun me around and slammed the fist full of hair into my jaw. I stumbled against the tree and slid to the ground. He opened his fist over me. Hair trickled over my legs. Shane looked at his blade, tried shaving his arm.

"I need ta sharpen this thing," he said and snapped it shut. "Well, boys, let's git ta work. We're wastin' daylight."

He picked up the crumpled pack of cigarettes that had fallen, rolled it up in his sleeve, and walked away without a backward look. Shotgun smirked at me and followed him. Jack stood with his hands on his hips, looking at me. He shook his head and turned to go.

"Hey," I gasped. He stopped without turning. "Thanks."

He paused, then left.

---

I didn't move for a long time. I leaned against the tree and listened to the morning traffic whish by on 70 like figure skaters. The long shadows of morning stretched out in front of me as stray beams of light filtered through the trees.

Shotgun hadn't bothered to gather the stray hairs on the sides into his grip. Hair stuck to the left side of my face, smeared into the blood. I explored my cheek with my fingertips. There were half a dozen scratches of varying length and depth running from my ear to my eyebrow. My fingers slipped down to my jaw. Even that light pressure hurt. I could almost feel the skin turning blue.

I rolled onto my knees and used the tree to help me stand. The pain in my stomach made it hard to straighten up completely. The pain in my back didn't care what position I took. It hurt equally in all orientations. I hobbled to my backpack and dragged it to a stump fifteen yards deeper into the woods. I pulled a Swiss army knife from a side pocket and sawed off my side locks.

After a few minutes I decided the pain had abated as much as it was going to. I gingerly shouldered the pack and headed back to the road. The outbound crossing of the fence was much slower than the inbound. I figured I was three or four miles out of town, which meant I was at least twenty-five miles from I-30. I headed back to town. In ten minutes I came upon my hat in the ditch. It wasn't even dirty. I put it on.

An hour later I was back in town. I found a gas station and got the key to the bathroom. I peeled off my shirt and inspected the damage. A large red spot was turning blue on my stomach. The skin was broken on the two smaller bruises near the middle of my back inflicted by Shane's cowboy boots. I washed the blood from my face and turned my left cheek to the light. The scratches were ragged and red, starting on the outer edge of the ear, skipping the half-inch by the sideburns, and continuing to the cheekbone and the edge of the eye. The washing opened them up, but blood was no longer running out. The bruise on the jaw wasn't as visible as the ones on my back, but it was sore to the touch. I figured it would take a few weeks to return to normal.

I turned the key back in and consulted a highway map from the rack in the station. I decided the better plan was to avoid the redneck express and get to the interstate as quickly as possible. I could get there in twenty miles on Highway 270 as opposed to the thirty miles by taking Highway 70. It would put me twenty miles further from Little Rock, but that wouldn't be a problem once I got a ride.

I got directions to the nearest barber. It was still an hour until opening when I got there. I found a place to get some breakfast and went back. I was his first customer. He gave me a queer look when I took off the hat and he saw the scratches down the side of my face. He was even more puzzled by the state of my hair. He asked if my last barber used pruning shears. I told him I had tried to give myself a haircut with a lawn mower, and he shut up. But he did offer to put some antiseptic on the scratches, so I tipped him a dollar.

I borrowed some string from the barber, tied the Little Rock sign to the pack, and set out for Highway 270. Halfway to I-30 a blue LeMans convertible blaring the Beach Boys pulled over as I was finishing a sandwich. The guy waved me to throw the gear in the backseat. I did and gingerly let myself down into the seat. I looked him over as he checked his mirror and pulled out. Young guy, crew cut, white shirt, blue pants and tie, RayBans.

"Whoah! What's with the face?" He hollered over the stereo.

"Fight with my girlfriend."

"Really? How many fingers she got?"

"I didn't want to turn the other cheek, so she scratched this one twice."

His name was Mel, and he was a salesman for manufactured homes, which took me a few miles to translate into trailer house. He covered dealers in Arkansas, Tennessee, and Kentucky. In the next hour he gave me a thorough education on the construction of premium mobile homes. He gave me his card and told me to call him first if I ever decided to buy a house. I assured him I would.

Mel was going to Nashville the next day. He dropped me off at the Motel 6 where he put up his brother-in-law when he was in town, promising to pick me up the next morning at five. There were still more than six hours of daylight left. I consulted the yellow pages in my room and located a movie theater not far from a used bookstore. A conversation with the desk clerk got me a bus schedule and directions.

I watched *The Seven-Percent Solution* at the matinee and went to the used bookstore. There I picked up a few tattered Doc Savage novels, a cheesy-looking sci-fi titled *Apostle from Space,* and a decent copy of *Our Man in Havana* all for under $2. Back in the room I ate my last two sandwiches and watched *Barney Miller* and *The Streets of San Francisco.* I wrote Lori, but I didn't tell her about Bruce or Shane. Then I read a Doc Savage.

# CHAPTER TWENTY-ONE
I was awakened by a pounding on the door. I rolled over and checked the clock on the nightstand: 5:03.

"Yeah, yeah, I'm coming," I hollered. I stumbled to the door, fumbled with the chain, and opened it. Mel pushed his way in.

"Let's get rollin'."

He stood by while I pulled on a shirt and pants, crammed the books into the pack, and carried my boots to the car. By the time I had my shirt buttoned and my boots on, we were on I-40 with Sha Na Na on the stereo and the sun cresting the pine trees to blind us.

Mel pointed to a thermos and two mugs in the floor by the transmission. "So, what's in Ohio?"

"Old buddy of mine." I handed him a cup and poured one for me.

"Can't be too old of a buddy. You're barely old enough to buy beer."

"Last saw him eight years ago. That old enough?"

"It'll have to do." He took a sip of coffee. "You got the look of a guy runnin' from somethin'." I looked out the window. "That's what I thought. Let me tell you as one to another: you ain't gonna get anywhere until you quit runnin' from and start runnin' to."

I waited for the explanation I knew would come. He seemed set to tell me something, and nothing on my part would stop him.

"You got somethin' in your past you want to get away from. You keep that up, you'll be runnin' all your life. Now, you set yourself

**183**

a goal, somethin' you want to do, and go toward that, you'll find success."

"Like you."

"Exactly. I wasted a couple of years bein' mad at the world. Then one day I woke up and realized life was passin' by, and I wasn't doin' nothin' but frownin' at it. I set my mind to go somewhere, and now here I am, with a territory of three states, nice car, nice house, girlfriend in every town I got a dealership."

I acknowledged that he seemed to have arrived. By judiciously asking questions at appropriate times, I kept him yammering about himself all the way to Nashville, declining his offer to help me fulfill my dreams by setting me up with a job and a cheap room. In Nashville he offered to buy me lunch at a gentleman's club, but I told him I was allergic to cigarette smoke. He bought me lunch at the Catfish Kitchen instead and headed off to his manufactured home dealer.

I decided to spend the weekend in Nashville. No telling when I might be back. A phone book and a quick call to the YMCA confirmed that rooms could be had cheap. I had set out with almost four hundred dollars and still had more than three hundred dollars. I thought I could afford a few nights at the Y.

I walked through downtown, past the Ryman Auditorium, and slipped into a hotel lobby for brochures. I spent the afternoon at the Parthenon taking pictures, mesmerized by the lines and perspectives. Then I picked up some groceries and made another batch of sandwiches in my room at the Y. Sitting on the single bed eating a sandwich, I realized I had accumulated three rolls of film that needed to be developed and printed.

On Saturday I dropped the film off at a 24-hour processing drop at Wal-Mart and spent the day wandering the riverfront with my sandwiches and camera. Sunday I picked up the prints. There was lots of junk, but I had about ten pictures worth keeping. I stored the negatives and the good prints in a tennis ball can I found at the Y and tossed everything else. No room to keep the mistakes.

———————

Monday morning I dropped a letter to Lori in the mailbox, took the bus to the north side of town, and walked up I-65 with a sign that said "Cincinnati" tied to the pack. Around noon I ate a sandwich and added a second sign that said "Will Pay For Gas." I got a ride to Louisville from a horse trainer headed to Lexington with two horses.

There was still plenty of daylight, so I set out for I-71. I didn't have any luck. As the light faded, I kept walking north until I came across a stand of trees in a depression near a creek. I crawled into the underbrush and spread the sleeping bag in the thick of it, feet toward the creek.

After three nights in a bed, I didn't find it easy to sleep on the ground. The occasional semi droning by reminded me that others were speeding to Cincinnati without me. My thoughts turned to M. It had been eight years. Would he be glad to see me? Would he even remember me?

It was a sobering thought, the possibility that I was no more than a passing acquaintance for M. He was the closest I had come to having a brother. Was I presuming too much?

After what felt like hours, I fell asleep and woke what felt like minutes later as the sky grayed in the east. Echoes of the dream in Hot Springs floated through my head, but I couldn't tell if I dreamed it again or was just remembering it from the last time I woke up on the ground. *All is empty but the open hand.* Made no sense to me.

I did what I could to make myself presentable and took my position back on the highway. Within the hour I was picked up by an elderly man in a car he probably bought before Pearl Harbor was bombed.

"Son, do you know Jesus?" he asked before we were out of second gear.

"Yes, sir."

"Amen and amen. When did you come to know him?"

"Uh . . . 1972."

"And have you received the Holy Spirit with the evidence?"

"Uh . . . yeah, sure."

"Then we will pray for my brother. We have a couple of hours, and it might take that long. He's in the hospital in Dayton dying without a saving knowledge of Jesus."

"Uh . . . OK."

The old man began muttering so low it was difficult to hear him, but he got gradually louder. However, even when he reached the level of shouting, I still couldn't understand a word he said. I sat in silence and stared at the road. After awhile he stopped.

"Son, aren't you going to pray?"

"I am praying. I was just praying silently."

"Son, the Word says where two or more agree on anything in His name, it will be done. Now how can I agree with you if I can't hear you?"

"I was agreeing with you."

His foot lifted off the gas and he peered at me. "Son, are you sure you know Jesus?"

"Oh, yes, sir. No question."

"And you received the baptism of the Holy Ghost."

"Yes, sir."

"With the evidence?"

"Which evidence would that be?"

"The evidence of tongues."

"Oh, the evidence of tongues. Right. Sure, just like you said."

We were still decelerating. Cars were honking and whipping around us.

"Then start praying for my brother." He kept the car going at about 30 mph, straddling the line to the shoulder.

"Yes, sir." I cleared my throat and closed my eyes. "God, I'm coming to you on behalf of . . ." I opened my eyes and looked at the man. "What did you say your name was?"

"I didn't."

"OK." I closed my eyes again. "God, there's a man in the hospital in Dayton we'd like You to keep alive long enough for"—I peeked at the old man, but he just stared back at me—"for this man here to get there and lead him to You." I opened my eyes and nodded. "Amen."

The old man inspected me with obvious distaste. "You're not a Christian."

"Yes, sir, I am. July 1972 in Barstow, California, around midnight. I even burned a copy of *The Mysterious Stranger*."

"You didn't pray in tongues."

"Sir, I'm sorry, but I can't pray in tongues. I just need a ride. Look, I'll even pay." I pulled some bills from my wallet.

"That won't buy your way to heaven."

"Will it get me as far as Middletown?"

He didn't take my money. He just stepped on the gas and preached a sermon starting with Acts 2:38 and ending with Highway 122. Somewhere in the midst of the two-hour ordeal, I interrupted him.

"Sir, how do you know there really is a God? What if belief in God is just a cultural manifestation of the fear primitive tribes had of the unknown? What if religion is nothing more than centuries of elaborate embellishments on their attempts to control their environment, a kind of pre-historical attempt at science?"

He stared at me for so long I was afraid he was going to run off the road. "Son, where did you pick up that hogwash? One of those atheistic universities?"

"No, sir. I've just been reading some books."

"You've been reading the wrong books, boy. What kind of tomfool talk is that? You're not a Christian."

"Sure I am," I said. But I was afraid he might be right. I wasn't sure I believed it anymore. Not sure I wanted to believe it anymore.

"If you was a Christian, you wouldn't ask questions like that. A Christian knows there is a God. He doesn't have to wonder. Shucks, everybody knows there is a God. The universe proves there is a God. 'The heavens declare the glory of God.'" He pointed out the window.

"Think of Romans, boy. 'For the invisible things of him from the creation of the world are clearly seen, being understood by the things that are made, even his eternal power and Godhead; so that they are without excuse.' You hear that? Without excuse. Everybody knows there's a God, but some are too proud or spiteful to admit it, like the next verse says. 'Because that, when they knew God, they glorified him not as God, neither were thankful; but became vain in their imaginations, and their foolish heart was darkened. Professing themselves to be wise, they became fools.' Now there's a verse written exactly about those books you've been reading. Fools calling themselves wise."

"But what about times when it seems like God is on vacation? Like in the Nazi concentration camps. How do you know there's a God when things like that happen?"

"You know down in your knower."

"Your knower?"

"The place where you just know things. Does your mama love you?" I didn't say anything. "Of course she does. How do you know it? You just know it. She doesn't have to prove it to you."

"So you have never doubted that God exists?"

"Never. 'He who doubts is like a wave of the sea, blown and tossed by the wind. That man should not think he will receive anything from the Lord; he is a double-minded man, unstable in all he does.' I have never doubted the Lord for a minute."

And so it went until he took the exit for Highway 122. He told me to repent, let me out, and got back on I-75. I walked west, past Blue Ball and the elementary school where I wrote my first love note with check boxes.

I found a gas station with a city map. Five miles later I was walking up Young Street, trying to place my old house. When I found it, I was shocked at how much it had shrunk. How did all the rooms I remembered running through fit into that small building?

I walked up to the school, down Girard, and turned down Curtis, stopping in front of M's house. It had shrunk too. I looked at it for awhile, suddenly nervous now that I was faced with it. Then I walked up the sidewalk, set my pack to the side of the door, and knocked. No answer.

I walked downtown, bought a Coke and chips, and found the gap between the auto shop and the liquor store. I squeezed through to the back. This place had not changed much since I found Pauline living here in the refrigerator box. More junk than before. I sat on the edge of an abandoned transmission housing and ate my lunch. I thought back on the story she had told me in a gin-thirsty rasp, the saga of an unexpected love disintegrating into a nightmare, of an abusive husband and a kidnapped kid. I wondered how they were getting along. Enoch should be finishing high school about now. I wondered if Vic ever told him about his real mother, how she saved his life. I doubted it.

I walked down to the middle of the block and the old movie theater. It looked seedier than I remembered, if that were possible. I took in the matinee of *Rocky* and headed back to Curtis Street.

———

This time Mrs. Marshall answered the door. I recognized her right away. She was still a tall woman, perhaps not as tall as I remembered, but taller than I was. Her hair was mostly gray, a nice contrast to her coal-black skin. She wore reading glasses.

"Hi, Mrs. Marshall, I'm Mark Cloud." There was no sign of recognition. "Ten years ago I lived in the house behind yours on Young Street. I used to play with M when we were in elementary school."

"Oh." She looked startled for a second, but then broke out in a gigantic smile. "Well ain't you jest all growed up. Come on in here."

She stepped back from the door. I grabbed my pack and stepped in. The room looked very different from the last time I was there. The heavy, broken-down furniture was gone, replaced with white wicker and floral prints. The streaked wallpaper was replaced with wainscoting and sheetrock. Carpet covered the worn boards the twins played on years ago. My surprise must have registered on my face.

"Yes, it does look different from the last time you were here, don't it? Sit down, sit down. Oh, honey, what happened to your face?"

"Oh," my left hand brushed across the narrow scabs. "Nothing much. Just got scratched by some thorns hiking through the woods in Arkansas."

"Well, you just sit right there and I'll get us some tea, and you tell me what you been up to all this time. Where did you move to?"

"Texas." I took a seat on the couch.

"That's right," she called from the kitchen. "I recall now that you was from Texas. Didn't you have a sister?"

"Yes, ma'am. Two."

"That's right. Your sisters and your folks, how is they doin'?"

"Fine."

"Well, that's good to hear." She came in, set a tea glass on the glass top of the wicker coffee table, and sat in a wicker armchair.

"Now what is you doin' up here in Ohio? Goin' to school down at Oxford?"

"No, ma'am, actually I came to see M. Is he still in town?"

Mrs. Marshall seemed to run out of steam and coast to a stop. She set her glass on an end table. "Marcus moved off to Chicago two years ago. I haven't heard from him since then."

"What's in Chicago?"

"A lot happened to Marcus since you left. He run into some trouble, and they helped him out of it. I don't take with their religion, them denyin' Jesus, but I can't deny the good they done my boy. I was afraid he was goin' to end up in prison like his papa."

"Prison?"

"Mark, there's a lot of misery that don't bear diggin' up in this old house. I done what I can to build an oasis in the desert, but some things can't be fixed. Harriet and the twins moved to Detroit and is startin' over. My church helped me fix up the house, and I'm takin' in boarders to make ends meet. When he gets out he can take a room here if he likes, but he won't get near those girls again, I'll make sure of that."

"Why exactly is M in Chicago?"

"He gone joined the Nation of Islam and moved to Chicago, where Elijah Muhammed has his big temple. But he died last year. I hear his son runs it now."

"M is a Black Muslim?"

She nodded. "He was trainin' to be in the Fruit of Islam when he left. Quit playin' music and everything."

"What did he play?"

"Drums. He played in the school jazz band; even started his own band."

I had never been to Chicago. It was as good a place as any. "Do you know how I can get in touch with him?"

"The day he left was the last time I heard from him. I don't even know for sure if he made it to Chicago."

I thanked Mrs. Marshall and prepared to go, but after a bit of interrogation, she discovered I was thumbing it. She insisted I stay the night and take the bus. It was less than four hundred miles to Chicago. I had already traveled more than three times as far in a week and now that I had short hair and was out of the South, I figured I could make good time. But as I lay on the crisp sheets and stared at the light from the street shining through the gauze curtains on the newly painted ceiling, I had to admit that I didn't look forward to standing on the road for hours with a Chicago sign on my pack or sleeping on the ground between rides. The next morning when I discovered the fare was less than thirty dollars, my mind was set.

# CHAPTER TWENTY-TWO

Wednesday morning Mrs. Marshall refilled my sandwich bag before she went to work. I walked down the alley M and I had taken so many times on our way to the library while talking of spies and bike wrecks and witches and secret loves. I browsed through the library's shelves once again and then waited on the steps for the church friend Mrs. Marshall had talked into giving me a ride. He showed up in an office supply delivery truck, and I helped on several stops before we got on the highway to the Greyhound bus station.

In Dayton I bought my ticket, ate sandwiches, and finished the second Doc Savage. Then I watched the traffic through the terminal until it was time for the afternoon Chicago bus to board. My previous experience was limited to school buses, so I wasn't prepared for the cloth seats that reclined. The bus was only half full.

I took a window seat on the left and watched the scenery until we got out of town and it became monotonous. I spent some time shaping my hat to match the old Dr. Hook hat I left behind. I pulled *Our Man in Havana* from my pack but set it unopened on the tray table. I thought back to the phone calls I had made the night before in the kitchen while Mrs. Marshall watched *Good Times* in the living room.

Hannah answered the first call. I couldn't tell if she was relieved or annoyed. She demanded to know where I was. I told her I wouldn't be there long in case Dad got some crazy idea to come after me. When she asked where I was going, I told her I hadn't decided yet. Then she asked me if I was crazy and what I thought I was doing.

"Not sure, really."

"You think Dad doesn't have enough on his mind that you have to disappear? That's just like you, only thinking about yourself."

"Hey, I'm not the only one who disappeared. At least I was honest about it and actually left. How many times have you been in the same room with him in the past week? How many conversations have you had with him this week? My guess is none."

There was a long silence. I felt bad, but I just leaned against the kitchen counter and stared at the phone number in the center of the dial.

"That's not fair," she finally said.

"No, it's not. It's not fair for you to hide in your schedule and your room and pretend like you're the only one who lost somebody."

"That's funny. A lecture from the runaway about hiding from reality." Her voice was shaky and becoming shrill. "I'll have something to write about in my diary tonight."

"Look, Hannah—"

"Was there a reason you called?"

I sighed. "Is Dad there?"

"No, he's at a deacons' meeting."

"Will you tell him I called and that I'm OK and I'll call next week?"

"I will relay your message."

"Hannah, I didn't mean to—"

"Any other messages? Perhaps a pointer on handling grief for Heidi when she comes home. Or would you rather just talk to her directly?"

"Just tell her to read your diary." I heard the phone click before the words faded.

I dialed the number for Merle Bruce and waited while Lori was paged. She knew more about what was going on, having received the letters mailed from Dallas, Hot Springs, and Little Rock. I told her about my new destination. She was relieved to hear I was taking the bus.

"But why are you hunting down this guy, M? What do you think he's going to do for you?"

"Nothing. I told you in the letters. I had to get out. I felt like I was suffocating. As soon as I made the decision I felt like I could breathe again. And it's been great since. I've seen Hot Springs. Have you been there? They have these old bathhouses that are great. Looks like something out of an Agatha Christie movie. And did you know that in Nashville there is a replica of the Parthenon? You should see the pictures I got."

"I can't wait."

"Are you upset about something?"

"You're just running around all over the country. Why should I be upset?"

"That's what I want to know."

"So, after Chicago, then what? New York, L.A., Paris? Maybe you'll run away and join the circus."

"Lori, what are you talking about?"

"If you had to go somewhere, why didn't you come here? How do I fit into this wandering?"

"Oh." I hadn't thought about that. Now I was thinking about why I hadn't thought about it. Was it another indicator of my lack of suitability as a mate? If I did love her, wouldn't my first thought have been of her, how what I was doing would affect her, or even a desire to go to her instead of away from Fred?

Lori broke the silence. "I see. I don't fit in."

"No, no, you fit in. I mean–"

"How long are you going to be in Chicago?"

"I don't know how long it will take me to find M."

"When you find M, what will you do next?"

"I'm not sure."

"Somehow I missed the part where I fit in. Could you go over that again?"

"Lori, I'm not going to be doing this the rest of my life. It's just something I have to do right now. I don't know why. I can't explain it, and I don't blame you for thinking I'm crazy."

"I don't think you're crazy; I think you're a jerk."

"I'm not sure that's an improvement."

"Then let me fill you in. It's not."

"Does this mean you're not going to wear my ring anymore?"

"You didn't give me a ring."

"I could send you one."

"OK, you send me a ring; I'll promise not to wear it anymore."

"Lori, it's not like we were going to see each other much until next fall anyway. How does this make a difference?"

"You had a choice. You're there. I'm here. Do you see the difference?"

I looked around the kitchen, searching for a clue. How could I explain it to her if I didn't understand it myself? I looked at the table where M and I sat ten years ago.

"You ever had chitlins?"

"What?"

"Chitlins. Chitterlings. Hog intestines."

"Mark, what—"

"Yes or no?"

"No!"

"Then you should know it's nothing like boudin, which is made from pork liver."

"What?"

"Did you know that new techniques in manufactured housing make it one of the best values for first-time home buyers?"

"What are you talking about?"

"I don't know. Lori, I don't know what I'm talking about; I don't know what I'm doing; I don't know who, what, why, when, or where. I don't even know how. But I do know I love you and I'm coming back."

There was a silence, then a sniff. "I knew you would do this."

"Do what?"

"Use mushy words to distract me."

"Mushy words? Lori, it's true."

"I know you're having a hard time. I was there last week. I saw you. But how can I help if you run away and I can't even call or write you?" I didn't have an answer. "People who love each other help each other and come to each other for help. If you won't come to me for help, do you really love me?"

"I do," was all I could whisper.

"I wish I knew it was true. Mark, I don't think we're going to settle this. You just go do this thing you have to do, and I'll do what I have to do."

"What does that mean?"

"I don't know. I don't know how to explain it. You should understand that. Bye."

The phone clicked before I could say anything. I set the receiver back on the hook and stared at nothing in particular for awhile. Then I left $5 on the counter and went to watch *Good Times*.

---

The stop in Indianapolis pulled me out of my reverie. A girl in her twenties with a haircut like Rod Stewart took the seat to my right. The smell of freshly smoked cigarette cloaked her. I nodded, smiled, and opened my book.

A few miles out of town, she spoke. "You like Greene, huh?"

"This is the first thing I've read by him. It's good."

"You should read *The Power and the Glory*." She took the book and flipped to the front. "There, it's listed in the front. Somebody has already circled it."

"I'll check it out."

She opened a mirror and inspected her left ear. An opal trapped in a silver sling hung from the lobe. Three holes ascended the curve, the first two filled with small rings that rested against the skin. The third held a stud that was surrounded by red flesh. While she inspected the stud I took a larger look.

She was wearing a blouse of some thin clinging material with a busy floral pattern. The sleeves were little more than short ruffles hanging over her shoulders. The front made a deep V, and a silver crucifix rested in the valley between her breasts. The wooden buttons down the front barely reached to her jeans.

She was the kind of girl that made me nervous. Attractive in an aggressive way, not like Lori, who was actually prettier, but somehow less obvious about it. Guys fluttered around these girls like moths around the porch light, all desperate to possess the light and all getting burned.

I ignored girls like this because I didn't want to be lumped with all the others, the pathetic losers and wannabes. I tried to concentrate on the book and keep my gaze from straying to the crucifix. With marginal success.

She spun the stud around and pushed her ear forward for a better view. "I don't like the looks of that. I'll give it another day." She snapped the mirror shut and dropped it back into her purse. "You sound like you're from the South."

"Texas. How about you?"

"Chicago. I'm Suzi."

"Mark."

"I was visiting my grandmother. Probably won't get many more chances to do that. Where are you headed?"

"Chicago. Looking up a buddy."

"Where does he live?"

"Don't know."

"That's going to make it hard to find him."

"Probably. All I know is that he joined the Nation of Islam two years ago."

"So why are you looking him up?"

"Haven't seen him in eight years. Thought it would be cool to see what he's up to."

"What do you know about the Nation of Islam?"

"Not much. Malcolm X. Muhammad Ali. That's about it."

"Did you read his autobiography?" I shook my head. "Did you realize you were a white devil?"

"That's what my girlfriend calls me."

"I bet." She laughed.

I was ashamed to admit to myself that I wanted to make Suzi laugh. I wanted to be charming and desirable. At the same time, I wanted to take my proper place outside the circle of those who pursued her. I wanted her to pursue me. I excused this mental infidelity to Lori by acknowledging the futility of my illicit desires. I was invisible to girls like Suzi for any purpose other than conversation and friendship. If there was no possibility that anything would come of it, what did it matter what I thought? She continued, unaware of my internal struggle.

"Just don't be surprised if he's not as happy to see you as you are to see him."

"We were pretty good friends."

"When you were how old?"

"Twelve."

"Yeah. A lot has happened since then."

I thought of Elrick. A lot had happened just in the last two years.

Suzi and I talked on and off for the three-hour drive into Chicago. She pointed out various landmarks as we entered town. The sheer size of the place daunted me. I'd been to Dallas, but mainly on the freeways. We didn't have a reason to venture downtown among the skyscrapers, the one exception being our trip to the book depository and the grassy knoll.

We hit Chicago on the tail end of rush hour. We crept through block after block, mile after mile of buildings. Tall, short, new, old, ugly, charming, stylish, modern, demolished. And cars. Everybody going somewhere with a purpose. I imagined myself out there, standing on the street corner. Where would I go; what would I do? Get run over most likely.

Suzi must have sensed my mounting terror. When we debarked, she made me wait while she got her suitcase. Then we walked together a block to the Clinton station and took the subway downtown. She walked me over to the Howard–Dan Ryan line and showed me the map. She pointed out the Chicago station a few miles north, only half a block from the Victor Lawson YMCA. She also showed me where she was taking the same line south to a transfer point to the Jackson Park line, which would take her to the university. When the northbound train arrived, she gave me her phone number and wished me luck. I shoved the paper into my pocket with a sense of hope and guilt.

I walked from the subway with my pack and my reshaped cowboy hat, feeling like Grizzly Adams come to town. The few people on the street looked pretty rough. I assumed a determined expression just short of a scowl and walked with purpose, only glancing to the side to check the street signs. The Y turned out to be an old art deco building more than twenty stories tall. The guy inside stared at me for several seconds while I wriggled out of the pack and leaned it against the counter.

"Got any spare rooms?"

"Spay-ur rooms? You just fall off the truck, John Boy?"

I narrowed my eyes at him. Scrawny, white T-shirt, and a fake blond crew cut greased down with something. Give him an inch and I'd regret it. I turned my head so the red scars were clearly visible.

"You got a room or not?"

"OK, OK. No need to get huffy. Yeah, we have rooms. Ten dollars a night, fifty dollars a week. Bathroom at the end of the hall."

I pushed fifty dollars across the counter. He counted it, took a key from a big board, and dropped it on the counter.

"Tenth floor. Elevator." He pointed.

I nodded, grabbed my pack, and punched the elevator button. While I was waiting, a tall guy in tight jeans joined me. His tank top revealed a well-developed physique. I nodded at him.

He smiled. "Nice hat."

I inspected the smile for signs of sarcasm, but it seemed genuine. "Thanks. Stetson." This was a lie, but I figured he wouldn't know the difference.

The door opened and we stepped in. I hit ten; he hit seven. At the third floor the elevator stopped and the door opened, but nobody got on. I looked at the guy as the door closed.

"Victor Lawson getting off."

"Who?"

"The guy in the picture in the lobby. Old Vic died in 1925. His ghost gets off here." The elevator doors opened on seven. "See you around. I'm Danny, first door on the right." He flexed his muscles. They rippled under the tank top. "Come by if you get bored. The door's always unlocked."

He stepped off. I nodded as the doors closed. I didn't figure on getting that lonely. I found my room. It was an eight-by-fourteen-foot whitewashed cell with single bed, a dresser, a sink, and a desk with a chair. I stepped to the window. I could see the lights of the city. A huge cathedral loomed across the street. I tossed my sleeping bag on the bed, emptied my clothes into the dresser, and ate a couple of sandwiches at the desk. I thought about Lori. The paper with Suzi's number seemed to burn in my pocket. I pulled it out, looked at it, and shoved it in my pack. To assuage my conscience, I wrote a letter to Lori. Then I snapped off the light and lay back in the bed. Tomorrow the hunt for M would begin.

# CHAPTER TWENTY-THREE The next

morning I loitered in the lobby until it was deserted and dropped some change into the pay phone. A male voice answered.

"Do this be the temple number two?" I asked in my best brother accent.

"Yes."

"Right on. I jus got into town and I be lookin' for my brother, Marcus Marshall. He come down here to hang wit the brothers in Chicago."

I felt like I wasn't getting it right. I started moving around, trying to get the feel of being one of the brothers. I dropped one shoulder lower than the other and bobbed my head and emphasized my phrases by jabbing my hand in the air.

"He told me to visit his crib and to call this number to get in touch wit' him." I winced in the long silence that followed.

"Do I understand you to say that you are asking for the whereabouts of one Marcus Marshall?"

"Bingo, man. You are right on." I hopped around a little.

"We do not give out personal information about members."

"That's cold, bro, cold." I tossed my head to one side like I'd been slapped. "Not even a phone number? He's not in the book."

"No."

"Whoa, cut me some slack, jack! How 'bout I groove on down there? I see you down on"—I consulted my notes—"Stoney Island Avenue. Do you be havin' church on Sundays or Saturdays or what?"

"Sir, I do not recommend you come down here. You will not find Marcus Marshall. He has not associated with us in over a year."

"What?" I was so startled I forgot my accent.

"And I recommend you learn to speak properly. You are a disgrace to your race." The phone went dead. I slowly replaced the receiver and turned around to see three black guys leaning against the counter watching me. They weren't smiling.

I smiled at them. "Yo, what up?" I attempted a stylized stroll, dipping low on my right leg and swinging my right arm. "What it is," I said as I pushed open the door. "Stay cool."

I disappeared around the corner, ran as fast as I could for three blocks, and ducked into a diner, watching the sidewalk. Nobody followed. The lady behind the counter was staring at me. I smiled, bought coffee and toast, and sat down at the window to plan my next move.

The news from the temple was a significant setback. It was my only lead. All I knew about M was that he was a Black Muslim and he played drums in high school. The search might take longer than I expected. A report from the accounting department indicated I had about two hundred dollars left. That wouldn't last long in Chicago. I was going to require some of the needful and in regular installments.

I blew a quarter on a paper and spent the next hour going through the want ads with a borrowed pen. My qualifications were limited. Not much demand for plywood mill workers or photographers. I skimmed the rest of the paper.

The Cubs weren't doing so hot. I had missed seeing Lynyrd Skynyrd by a month. Ford and Reagan were duking it out for the Republican nomination. Carter seemed to be doing OK in his run for the Democratic nomination. This Day in History told me that Chicago bass player and lead vocalist Peter Cetera was jumped at a Cubs-Dodgers game five years earlier, losing four teeth because some guys decided his hair was too long. I felt the scars on my left cheek. Maybe that haircut was a good idea after all.

———

After a few days of rustling through the newspapers in the library on the second floor, I bagged a minimum-wage job stocking groceries a mile from the Y. I did a little computing on my $2.30 an hour. That would get me about $360 a month before taxes. The Y would take two-thirds of it. It was time to get a real place.

I scanned the paper and monitored the bulletin board daily, but nothing promising showed up. Then I remembered Suzi. I dug the scrap of paper out of my pack.

"Funny you should call," she said. "Tammy rents the second bedroom, but she's leaving next week, going to California with her boyfriend. It's $100 a month and we split the utilities."

"Oh." My brain vapor-locked. I had considered sharing a place to save expenses, but assumed I would be sharing with a guy. I couldn't wrap my brain around the implications of sharing an apartment with a girl.

"So, this is two separate bedrooms? With doors?"

She chuckled. "Yes, with doors. And locks, even. You want to come see it?"

No harm in looking at it. It was a nice day, so I walked the ten blocks across the river and took the Jackson Park line to the university. It was a second-floor walkup. The neighborhood was better than the Y.

Suzi answered the door in shorts and a black T-shirt tied in a knot at her waist, a picture of Billie Holiday on the front. The place was small and sparsely decorated. I entered a kitchen with counters and cabinets on two walls and a third countertop separating the area from a living room with a couch, a chair, two large bean bags, and a coffee table. There were a few pictures on the wall–Suzi and a guy at various vacation spots. Funky, atmospheric music with no discernible melody oozed from the stereo on the opposite wall between two windows. A large LP collection dominated the wall opposite the couch, broken up by three doorways.

"That's my room." She pointed to the door closest to the stereo. "The one with the windows. You get the cell."

I followed her through the door in the middle. It was smaller than the room at the Y. It had a single bed that was a mess of sheets and shirts, a dresser with underwear cascading down the drawers, and a shallow closet bursting with shoes. The wall that bordered Suzi's room was a chaotic collage painted with skill, dolphins, mushrooms, marijuana leaves, Che Guerva, Jimi Hendrix, unicorns, rainbows, sunsets.

"Tammy's an art major. You can do whatever you want with the wall except put holes in it." She walked to the door, stopped and turned back. "So, what do you think?"

"It's an interesting mural."

"About the room. Do you want it?"

"Oh, the room." It was all I needed. Everything I owned I could fit in a backpack. I wouldn't even have to get sheets, just throw the sleeping bag on the bed.

On the other hand, what would Dad say if he heard I was rooming with a girl? What would Lori say? But how would they hear unless they were told? And who would tell them? Certainly not I.

"Too much money? Try to get something cheaper, and you'll end up living with rats and junkies."

"No, the price is right."

"OK. Then . . . ," She looked at me and laughed. "Oh, the locks. Here."

She closed the door and slapped the slide-bolt into place. Then she leaned against it, arched her back, spread her fingers out flat on the wood, and slid one foot up next to her knee. She lowered her chin against her chest and looked up at me from under her sculptured eyebrows.

"You will be safe from me in here," she said in a husky, mock-Russian accent.

I wished I wasn't blushing, but I knew I was. Even though she was joking, my pulse raced to see her looking at me like that. I noticed the stud in her left ear was gone, replaced by a small ring like the two below it.

"No . . . uh . . . I just wanted to make sure you had your privacy," I stammered.

She laughed at me and rattled the lock back and the door open. "The bathroom's over there." She pointed to the third door, the one nearest the kitchen. "You want some tea?" she called over her shoulder.

"Sure."

I browsed the LP collection, taking the opportunity to peek in Suzi's room. Twice the size of mine with a double bed, two windows, and a similar slide-bolt lock, neat and orderly. A bicycle hung from the ceiling in one corner. The record collection was extensive and eclectic, spanning five decades from Duke Ellington to Patti Smith. I didn't recognize half the names. I looked at the stereo. The album jacket lying on the turntable said Weather Report.

I sat down at the kitchen table where Suzi was smoking a cigarette, thumping the ashes into a porcelain skull. She held a pack of Winston's out to me. I shook my head, and she dropped them on the table. "Smart. Ray is always on me to quit. Maybe next year."

A kettle started whistling and she got up.

"Ray?"

"My boyfriend. He's in Europe, getting ready for the Tour de France." She set a mug in front of me. "Where you from, Tex?"

"Fred." I expected iced tea, but took the mug without comment. "Texas. Fred, Texas."

"There's a town named Fred?" She pulled her teabag out and dropped it on the saucer between us.

"Texas has a thing for names. Alice, Uncertain, Cut and Shoot."

"Those are all towns?"

"Yep."

"And how big is Fred?" She propped her elbows on the table and sipped from her mug.

I looked around the apartment. "Oh, I'd say about the size of my room."

"So you're going to take the room."

"Yeah, I think so."

She smiled over her mug, steam rising in front of her face. Her eyelids flared up. "Daring Mark Cloud from Fred, Texas. Living on the edge."

"You're talking to a man who has ridden down Roller Coaster Road with Darnell Ray. I laugh in the face of death."

"Who is Darnell Ray?"

"Well, it's a bit of a story . . ."

---

The morning of June first I called home from the pay phone in the lobby on the way from the Y to my new home. My fingers brushed the scars on my cheek out of habit while the phone rang. They were just narrow red lines by now.

"Hey, Dad."

"Mark?"

"Speaking."

"Where are you?"

"Mrs. Marshall sends her regards."

"You're in Middletown?"

"Not anymore. I'm on the road. Pay phone."

"When are you coming home?"

"Did Hannah give you my message?"

"Yes. Mark, I know–"

"Dad, I just want you to know I'm safe, I'm OK. Don't worry about me."

"Is there some reason you won't give me any information?"

"I don't want you to do something crazy like come after me. I'm OK. There's nothing wrong with me."

"Mark, you're an adult. You make your own choices. I'm not going to come hunt you down like a runaway teenager."

I was relieved to hear it. "I'm in Chicago. M moved here two years ago. I thought as long as I'm on the road I might as well look him up."

"Where are you staying?"

"I have a job. I got a room. Not much, but I don't need much. No worse than my dorm room."

"Do you have an address?"

"I'm getting a P. O. box."

There was silence on the line for awhile. "Can you tell me why you left?" He sounded thinner, like his skin hung loose on his bones.

I thought for awhile. "I'm not sure. Maybe because I realized I could."

"Does it have anything to do with our last conversation?"

"Probably."

"I remember we talked about Job. You're not going to get any answers by running. If you want to ask hard questions, you should have the guts to wait around for the answers like Job did. Otherwise you're just a hit-and-run scoffer."

"I don't think I have enough quarters for this topic. I'll talk to you later. Bye."

I hung up the phone, grabbed my pack, and hoofed it to the El, deciding against calling Lori. I would write her as soon as I got an address. I didn't want to use the address of the apartment in case somebody decided to hunt me down.

Over the next few days I started looking for work closer to the apartment. Suzi was working on a master's in geriatrics. She checked at the university and found a spot on the grounds crew. I got the job and was bagging grass the next day. There was plenty of daylight after I got off work, and I spent much of it roaming the streets getting a feel for the neighborhood.

One day I came across a photographer's studio, Geltman Photography, John Geltman, owner. A sign in front advertised darkroom rental–time plus paper. I went inside to check it out. The receptionist called to the back, and a guy with a gray pony-tail escorted me down the hall. We passed viewing rooms and a couple of studios and turned left into a passageway blocked by a series of heavy black curtains far enough apart that each fell back in place before the next was pulled aside.

It was a large room lit with a dim red bulb in the center. A set of six carrels occupied the middle, two to a side and one on each end. Each held an enlarger and a timer. Around the walls were six sets of trays interspersed with sinks. Drying lines crossed the room and lined the walls above the trays.

"This is the black-and-white room. The color is next door."

It was beautiful. I could see most of my paycheck ending up in this room. "Would you consider a barter?"

"Of what?"

"I could do prints for you in exchange for use of the darkroom after hours." He looked doubtful. "I could bring in some stuff I've done if you'd like to see it."

"Color?"

"Haven't done color, but I'm a quick study."

He looked even more doubtful. "Color is much more difficult. And it must be done in complete darkness."

"OK. How about I pay for darkroom time while you're training me? Once I'm doing work you will accept, I log the time I work for you. I get the same number of hours free for my own work plus free paper."

"You pay for time and materials you use while I'm training you. If you are good enough, I'll give time one-for-one during business hours, unlimited time after hours, and you pay for your own paper."

"Works for me. When do we start?"

"What are you doing right now?"

"Taking my first lesson."

# CHAPTER TWENTY-FOUR

My concerns about the apartment being a steamy nest of temptation were unfounded. Although I still found her as alluring, we operated almost as strangers. I usually left before Suzi got up. By the time I got home, she was buried in studies. I would make myself a sandwich or macaroni and cheese and read a book, occasionally glancing at Suzi, who was always on the couch in shorts and a halter-top or tube top or something else that failed to disguise her more compelling features. I would rinse my plate in the sink and escape the lust of the flesh by disappearing into my cell to write letters or read. Dad answered my letters; Lori didn't.

We had more time together on weekends, but even then she was studying. I would troll through the music collection and experiment. Sometimes she would look up from the table and smile at something I put on. She treated me like a clever junior high kid. I treated her like a black widow spider: fascinating but dangerous.

I bagged grass by day and learned color developing and printing in the evenings, experimenting with the shots I took on my trip. By July I was able to do the smaller prints in quantity by following the settings John printed with each job. John still did the larger portraits himself.

I was so engrossed in my projects that I barely noticed when the bicentennial arrived. Sunday afternoon, July fourth, Suzi declared an enforced holiday. We took a picnic to Grant Park and staked out a space for watching the fireworks. We ate supper and sipped Filbert's root beer, engaging in desultory conversation like an old married couple. I looked around at the crowd and wondered what they thought of us as a pair. Did they think we were lovers? I decided they probably thought I was her kid brother. I grabbed another sandwich.

Suzi asked if I was still looking for M. I told her I didn't know where to look as my only lead was the Nation of Islam. She interrogated me. I told her everything I knew about him from the sixties and the few facts Mrs. Marshall told me about the last eight years. Suzi picked up on one point.

"He played drums in the jazz band in high school. Maybe he's doing that here. Playing drums in clubs. Maybe jazz, even."

"Are there jazz clubs in Chicago?"

"Where have you been?"

"Fred."

"Yes, Fred, there is a jazz scene in Chicago. Segal's Jazz Showcase has great bands. Andy's is about a mile from here, just across the river on State Street. Rick's is even closer. And if you want some real excitement you can go to BJ's. There's more, but that should do for starters."

The fireworks took my attention. They were spectacular. I shot several rolls of film using a tripod I borrowed from John and the cable attachment that came with the C-3. Since the studio was closed on Monday for the holiday, I took the time to work on the fireworks pictures, making 11x14 prints of the best three. Tuesday evening I showed them to John. He looked them over for a long time, then looked me over for a long time.

"How much are you making at the university?"

"Minimum wage."

"I'll give you a dollar more, guarantee a minimum of thirty hours a week, most likely over forty hours, and unlimited use of the darkroom when you're off the clock. You buy your own paper for your projects." I looked at him in shock. "The less time I spend in the darkroom, the more time I can book in the studio."

That night I took the El downtown and walked to Andy's Jazz Club. It was unassuming from the outside. The sign in front said, "Tonight: The Bruce Wayne Trio." Perhaps they would open with the theme from Batman.

I took a deep breath and stepped in. It was the first time I had been inside a club. Just inside the door a few guys leaned on the polished wood of a circular bar that took up the near end of the room. Metal columns ran through the circle and down the middle of the room every eight feet. In the other half of the room, white tablecloths marked the location of a couple dozen small tables in a dark room, all empty. I was early. In the middle of the back wall, the trio was setting up on the bandstand: upright bass, drums, baby grand piano. All white. One band down.

"One for dinner?"

I turned to see a man about my height with short curly hair. He reminded me of Tony Bennett. I held out the press card I had made at the studio with my picture and "The Porkpie Hat" in large letters.

"I'm here with a music magazine out of Dallas. We're doing a series on the Chicago music scene." I patted the camera bag slung over my shoulder, courtesy of John. "Do you have a table near the stage I could work from?"

He looked at the press card and at me. I could tell he was trying to calculate my age. I nervously stroked the thin white lines on my left cheek that were all that was left of the scars Shane put there six weeks earlier.

"The regular guy got food poisoning in the hotel. Bad oysters. Months with an R and all that, you know." I smiled. "What time does the music start?"

"Seven." He looked me over again. "If you want a drink, I'll have to see some ID."

"Better stick to ginger ale. It's my big break. Don't want to blow the pictures for the old man, or he'll kill me."

Tony gestured to the dining area, and I took the table at the corner of the bandstand, giving me a nice side view of the stage. The musicians glanced at me. I nodded and loaded the camera with very fast black-and-white film. I planned to shoot in existing light.

I still had half an hour before the band started. I scanned the menu. Dinner would cost me a day's wages. I asked the band if they knew of a black drummer named Marcus Marshall. They didn't. I asked them if they minded if I took pictures. They didn't. I asked which one was Bruce. The drummer and bassist nodded at the piano player, who ignored me.

I listened to a few tunes before I started shooting. In keeping with my magazine persona, I pulled out a notepad and pen. Bruce called out, "My Funny Valentine" and started off dark, moody, and introspective. The others joined in, and they rolled through the song, the piano improvising in the middle. It was nice, but too much like elevator music for me. If I was going to listen to piano music, I'd like to hear Elton John. Better yet, Billy Joel. At least Jackson Browne.

They followed it with another slow tune that I didn't recognize and didn't care to. I closed the notepad and picked up the camera as they started the next song. It was a peppy number, kind of bluesy. They did the melody through twice very solid and soulful, then Bruce took off into a series of octaves which seemed to weaken the groove for a few measures, but came back in with some flashes on his right hand and settled into a stride that the rhythm section picked up. I set the camera back down on the table.

Bruce dropped his left hand to his side and played with the right for awhile with a deliberate pace, gradually introducing the left hand for staccato chords to buttress the melody. He kept building until he was steamrolling into a full, striding solo that swept me along with it. He faded into a blur of chaotic chords, and the bass player erupted with a frenetic, flight-of-the-bumble-bee beginning. The piano introduced a slow triplet to alternate with the bass, the drummer joining with ride cymbal. The bass gradually worked out of his frenzy to some lyrical double-stops, and then built the energy back up. They all tumbled into the melody with the cumulative energy of the entire song.

I was out of breath just listening. I never knew music like this existed. It wasn't a song; it was a conversation. Each player interacted with the others, adjusting as the others played, adding something that supported what he heard, or maybe contrasted. Ideas brought up by one person might be echoed and modified by another and passed along until it become something entirely different, yet still recognizable as the original.

I looked around. The place was still empty. Two guys at the bar were talking, one pointing to a TV where a baseball game was playing. I couldn't believe something so astounding was taking place and nobody even noticed. Were they deaf?

"Wow." I flipped the notepad open. "What was the name of that one?"

"Blues by Five," the bassist said.

"Miles," the drummer said.

"Take Five," Bruce said.

I thought, *They're taking a break already?* But Bruce started playing a choppy, awkward set of chords. After a few bars I realized why it sounded so awkward. It was in 5/4 time. I wrote "Take Five" in the notepad and picked up the camera. I wandered around in front of the stage, taking my time to frame shots. The light was so dim I was forced to shoot at F2.8 for 1/8 and 1/16 of a second. Careful focus and a rock-steady hand were required. I sat backward on a chair and used the back to anchor my hand.

I got some nice shots of Bruce from the side of the piano, the keys leading to his hands, his face floating above, his body invisible due to the black shirt and jacket. The drummer was more problematic, since he never stopped moving. I resolved myself to blurred pictures. The bass player was a little easier to shoot, being closer to the front where the lights hit the stage. I worked to the end of "Take Five." They immediately started another. I caught the title from the fake book on the bass player's stand: "Softly As in a Morning Sunrise."

It didn't start out softly, but rather with a strongly syncopated rhythm section that Bruce overlaid with a lyrical Latin theme. The bass player rose to his feet and moved with the beat. After the head, Bruce wended smoothly through the rhythms with a slight variation on the theme and then broke into a syncopated riff that gave way to a blinding explosion of notes. He kept his right hand going in flourishes nonstop for an entire verse. He followed with interplay between left and right hands and then took a funky segue into the bridge.

The bassist picked it up with his characteristic flashes, slid into a funky backbeat groove without losing the flash, and melded the two into a marriage of funk and jazz. Then Bruce and the bass dropped out and the drummer stepped in, sounding like he was stirring a stew with bones in it. He set down a foundation of Latin rhythms with two toms, a cowbell, the high hat, and the kick. Then he added a second layer: riffs on the snare. While I was still trying to figure out how he was doing it with only four limbs, he added a third layer of descant on the ride and crash cymbals. The bassist just smiled and tapped his foot. Bruce had his eyes closed, his head nodding with the beat.

Just when I thought he was asleep, Bruce stepped in and played four bars of blistering licks. The drummer answered with four bars of equally stunning riffs. Then the bassist took four bars, answered by the drummer. They kept this up for some time and boiled into the theme, taking it twice and then to the end.

When the silence settled, I took a deep breath and shook my head. I sat down at the table and gave up any pretense of taking pictures. I spent the rest of the night there as the place gradually filled up. A couple shared my table, but after smiling at them, I ignored them, mesmerized by the music until midnight. They ended with the Batman theme.

Suzi was still up studying when I got back. I gushed on about the music, reading song titles from my notepad. She finally silenced me by going to the wall of LPs and pulling out albums covering the entire list.

She tousled my hair and said, "Welcome to Chicago."

The next day after printing wedding pictures for ten hours, I moved to the black-and-white room, developed the film, ran a contact sheet, and selected five shots that stood out. I printed 8x10s and left them drying. I showed them to John the next day. He looked at them closely.

"You did this with existing light?" I nodded. "At Andy's?" I nodded. He nodded and returned to his studio.

I returned to Andy's for a week and a half. I abandoned the magazine cover story. Instead I took some prints to Tony and suggested that he might like to use some of them on the Wall of Fame. All I asked was that my card be displayed, something I threw together to give a name to my new enterprise.

After satisfying myself that M was not among the regulars at Andy's, I tried Rick's in the Holiday Inn. It was a classy joint, done up in the style of the café in *Casablanca*. I saw some faces I knew and some new ones, but no M. I did my photo thing there with some success and moved on to the Jazz Showcase with similar results.

# CHAPTER TWENTY-FIVE The second

week of August I cased BJ's on a Saturday afternoon. It was only a few blocks from the Lawson Y and exuded a seedy atmosphere in keeping with its location. That night I got there in time for the lady mud wrestlers, who evidently kept the crowd from getting fidgety between sets. From the looks of the place, I figured it might be dangerous to order ginger ale. I asked for the manager, gave him my card, and told him I was there to photograph the band. He shrugged and tossed my card in the trash.

I got a table as near the bandstand and as far from the mud wrestlers as possible, ordered a beer, and loaded the camera. I tried the beer and found it as odious as I remembered it to be on the camping trip years back. I kept it at my side to ward off waitresses and watched the backs of the crowd around the mud-wrestling pit.

A noise climbing from a low growl to a pinched-off screech turned me back around. A large, round white guy with short black hair was warming up on trumpet. A pale slender guy sprinkled a few arpeggios across a set of vibes and peered at the pit through Buddy Holly glasses. A guy who looked like a short-order cook at a greasy spoon tuned a standup bass. The drums were empty.

After more random noise, the horn player looked at his watch and glared at the two who were already there. The vibes player shrugged. The bass player grinned. The trumpet player stared at the back door for a few seconds, stuffed a mute in, and played a B for a long time. He played a few notes around the B, and the vibes player seemed to figure out what he was playing.

He began to play a set of three chords that climbed up and back down, the middle chord short, the top and bottom long. The bass player nodded his head and joined in. I recognized it as *All Blues* from a Miles Davis album.

As the trumpet player stepped into the melody of the song, the back door opened and a pale woman in a black dress walked in, followed by a black guy in black shades wearing black. The woman walked in front of the stage and past me to the bar, but I didn't bother with her. I was checking out the guy. His head turned briefly in my direction as he followed her to the edge of the stage and stepped up on the bandstand behind the bass player, who looked at him and rolled his eyes at the trumpet player. The black guy nodded at the trumpet player's back and smiled at the bass player. He unrolled a pouch, pulled out a set of brushes, and picked up the rhythm. When the trumpet shifted from melody to improvisation, he worked in a stick in his right hand for ride cymbal, keeping the brush going with the left. Then, as the trumpet became more aggressive, he swapped to a stick in the left hand and stepped up the feel.

My pulse quickened. I pulled out the telephoto lens for a better look. It was hard to tell with the sunglasses on. He was dark chocolate, but not pudgy as I remembered M. This guy was thick, more like a Marine. No gut. Then he turned his head, and I saw the elongated shape I remembered. It had to be him. Maybe. Maybe not.

I watched him play. He was quite good, accomplished without being flashy. He kept the feel going, but sometimes pushed it a bit, nudging a solo in a different direction, increasing the intensity. They followed with "Take Five." I had heard it several times by now, always with the sense that something was missing. In a world of four beats to the bar, a song that has five beats usually ends up sounding like a measure of three and a measure of two slapped together, and this song was no exception. Even the drum solo was three beats with two tacked on. I found myself wishing I could hear the song as if it had been written on a planet where people naturally counted five beats instead of four.

And then, as I heard the drum solo, I realized that I was hearing it. A seamless rhythm as natural as rainwater, accents that laid down a groove as primal as Motown, but in five beats. It was the perfect blend of the obvious and the unexpected that marks genius. I could see the others felt it as well. The trenchant set of the trumpet player's face relaxed to the point that you could sense a smile hovering just under the surface. When the solo ended, I could see the reluctance of the rest of the band to come back in and obliterate the feel with Brubeck's melody.

As the song finished, the woman stepped on stage, handed a glass of water to the drummer, and stepped to the mike. She nodded to the trumpet player. He glared at her and counted to four fast. The drums came in with a riff on the four, and they all came in on the one. She began singing, "Cigarette holder, which wigs me, over her shoulder she digs me. Out cattin' that satin doll."

Her voice was solid with a slight edge to it, Joe Cocker with estrogen. The dress had a sheen that could have been satin. Her long straight hair was white and her skin was almost as white. Even her eyebrows were white. Something about her seemed familiar. With the telephoto lens I saw that her eyes were a pale blue, like ice. I switched to a faster lens and started taking pictures of the band.

I worked my way around the front and side of the stage, getting group shots, close-ups, and unusual angles. I had been photographing bands in low light for more than a month and had developed some techniques for interesting results. The bass player mugged for the camera, making for some amusing shots. I got several shots of the trumpet player glaring. I couldn't tell where the drummer was looking, but he seemed to ignore me.

As I shot the second roll, I considered and reconsidered my conclusion about the drummer. I wasn't completely sure. And even if I was right, I was having second thoughts about approaching him. What if Suzi was right? He might not want to see me at all. I had read Suzi's copy of *The Autobiography of Malcolm X,* and it introduced doubt.

Then, in the pause between "The Nearness of You" and "Old Devil Moon," the woman turned and said, "Barton, why don't you sing a tune?"

The bass player smirked at her and looked at the trumpet player. "Drucker would rather French kiss a dog than hear me sing."

Drucker snorted and nodded his head slowly, his trumpet resting on the incline of his large stomach. The vibes player smiled. But the drummer said, "Bingo!" and followed it with a rim shot and a cymbal crash. Then he let out a laugh that sounded like the cat sirens in the old Mickey Mouse cartoons, the ones where they crank the tail and the cat lets out a wail. All doubt was slain in that moment. I had found M.

In the first break, the band stepped down and scattered. Barton made a beeline to the bar. The vibes player wandered over to the pit. Drucker disappeared down a hallway that I assumed led to a greenroom. M and the woman took a table to the side of the stage. The time had come.

I grabbed my camera bag and left the warm beer behind. M had his back to me, talking intently to the woman. She looked up without expression as I approached.

I cleared my throat. "M."

He stopped in midword and turned slowly. He inspected me from behind the shades. The woman shifted her gaze from me to him, surprise on her face. M's eyebrows crept up above the sunglasses. He stood slowly.

"Mark?"

"Yep." I held out my hand.

M ignored my hand. "Mark Cloud?"

"Yep."

He began laughing, the same laugh that annoyed and amazed me the first time I saw him, a sound like a bobcat eating barbed wire. He shook with laughter and grabbed my arms. The tremors transferred to me like electricity. He leaned his head on his left hand, which was on my shoulder, and pawed at my chest with his right hand, still laughing like a siren. As always happened around M, the hilarity spread. I began chuckling. The woman was already laughing, her face still suffused with surprise.

It took a few minutes for M to descend. He circled several times and did a few touch-and-go attempts before he finally landed. Then he pushed me down into a chair.

"Can you dig this cat?" he said to the woman.

She held out her hand. "Hi, Mark. I'm January."

I took her hand. "January?" I looked at M.

"I didn't name her. Just call her Jan."

"Hi, Jan. I'm Mark Cloud. M used to live in the house behind mine many years ago."

"M?" She looked at M. "M?"

"My sister used to call me M."

I set the camera on the table. "Everybody used to call him M."

She put her hand on his arm. "I like it."

"What do you go by these days?"

"Marcus. So, what are you doing in Chicago?"

"Looking for you."

They both looked at me in silence for a second.

"Looking for me?"

"That's it. It's the only reason I came to Chicago. It took me two months to track you down. First I called Temple Number Two, but they weren't any help."

"You did what?"

"Your mother said you joined the Nation of Islam and moved here, so I figured they would know how to get in touch with you."

"You talked to Mama?" I nodded. "What did she tell you?"

"Not much. I get the impression she doesn't know much."

Jan and I watched M. He looked away. "No, I haven't exactly kept in touch." He turned back to me. "It's a long story, man. Where you staying?"

I stayed for all four sets and helped tear down. They had an early gig on Sunday, a brunch buffet at the Hilton. M invited me to dinner at his place Sunday night. We exchanged information, and I rode the El home. Suzi was in bed when I crept into the apartment.

# CHAPTER TWENTY-SIX

Suzi wasn't busy Sunday night, so I brought her along for dinner. We took the Dan Ryan line to the end and walked to M's place near Chicago State University. Jan answered the door. She was wearing a black caftan with silver filigree, her pale arms and white hair visible in the half-light as we followed her into the dimly lit apartment.

Incense burned on a table in the corner. A chaotic frenzy of saxophone, drums, piano, and bass murmured from a stereo. There were no chairs. Cushions were strewn around the edges of a Turkish rug. In the center a low table held a bowl of a beige pasty substance and what appeared to be very thick flour tortillas.

M came in from a back room. He wore a brightly colored caftan shirt and white linen pants. This was not the M of the sixties fast-forwarded ten years. He was a very different person.

"Mark, I still can't believe you're in Chicago. And is this your girlfriend?"

Suzi held out her hand to shake his. "No, I'm his landlady."

M lifted her hand to his lips and kissed it. "How nice for Mark."

Suzi flushed and smiled at M. "'A Love Supreme' is my favorite Coltrane."

"It's a good thing for my wife that I met her first. You are a woman after my own heart. This is Jan."

My shock at seeing M become an African-American James Bond was overwhelmed by the word *wife*. I noticed for the first time that they both wore plain silver bands on their ring fingers. Jan and Suzi exchanged greetings, and we sat down on the floor around the table.

"Oh! I love hummus," Suzi said.

I said nothing, unwilling to be identified as the only person in the room who had no idea what hummus was. I already felt self-conscious that M seemed to have graduated to another plane while I felt like the same kid who used to slam nails in his basement in the hope of seeing sparks.

I looked at M. The shades were gone. Now that he was only a few feet away, I could see that his left eye was closed and a scar ran from the edge of his eye to his ear. It wasn't visible the night before under the shades.

"Marcus only drinks water," Jan said, pouring water from a carafe, "but I must have a glass of wine with my meals. Suzi, would you like some?"

"I'd love some," Suzi said.

"Mark?"

"If it's good enough for M, it's good enough for me."

Jan poured the wine. "To the reuniting of old friends and the making of new ones." We clinked our glasses. Jan turned to me. "Marcus told me so much about you last night. How did you get from Fred to Chicago?"

"I think M should go first. After all, I went through all the effort to track him down. I should get to call the toss. I elect to receive."

Jan looked at Suzi. She nodded. Jan tore off a piece of the pita on her plate and dipped it in the hummus. "Marcus, you want to go first?"

"Do I have a choice?"

"No." She popped the pita in her mouth and smiled.

"Didn't think so. What do you want to hear?"

I held the plate to Suzi, who took some pita bread. I took one for myself. "Everything. How did you join the Nation of Islam? How did you get to Chicago? How did you end up married at age twenty?"

"Twenty-one."

"OK." I dipped the pita in the hummus. "And how did you end up playing drums for a living?"

"Anything else?"

"That will do for starters." I chewed the pita and hummus. It had less flavor than I expected. Sort of like a bean dip with no kick. I tore off another piece.

"It could take the whole night."

"I'm not busy. How about you?" Suzi shook her head. "That's your cue. Roll the first reel."

M closed his right eye and rocked back in his cushion. "Hmm. Where shall I start?" He opened his eye. "You left in January of 1968. That fall I went to junior high school and joined the band. The director was a bebop freak, but he played trombone."

"Like Bennie Green," Suzi said.

M looked her over before replying. "Yes, like Bennie Green. He turned me on to bebop, and I was a goner from the first bar. It was 1969, and all the kids at school were heartbroken because the Beatles broke up. I was ecstatic because I had discovered Miles Davis. I spent every cent I could hoard the next two years on bebop records. I sold pop bottles, cut yards, washed cars. Then 1970."

"High school," I said.

"You remember the place?"

"How could I forget? It was only two blocks away. I walked past it just two months ago."

"You remember Terri?"

I jumped in my Wayback Machine and scanned the years in Ohio.

"Moses' wife!" I said in a flash of memory, then immediately wished I hadn't. It was the one moment I had always regretted. The one time that race became an issue between us. I glanced at M self-consciously and looked away.

"Moses had a wife named Terri?" Suzi asked, but she was

drowned out by M's cry of "Bingo" and the trademark laugh. When the cacophony settled, she asked again.

I was smiling from the overflow of M's good-natured humor that spanned the years and erased the awkwardness from the memory. I looked at him with gratitude. He looked back with his one eye and something passed between us that surely was lost to the women. In that moment I knew I had found M again. Or rather let myself be found. I let go of the self-consciousness I was nursing in the presence of the sophistication M had acquired. The awkwardness fell away, and I knew that M had been and always would be my brother.

I blinked back the sudden tears and held up my glass of water. "To the wife of Moses." M took his glass and clinked it against mine. We drank. Suzi looked on in confusion. Jan smiled.

M turned to Suzi. "Terri was a girl in the same class with Mark and me back in grade school. She went to a different junior high. But we went to the same high school. She was my first true love. And she was a white girl."

"What's the Moses thing?"

"Moses married a black woman. His family did not approve."

Suzi looked at Jan, who nodded. "Ah."

"Yes, ah." M looked around. "I think we're ready for the main course. Is roast lamb agreeable with everyone?"

Suzi said, "Oh, yes!" and I nodded, having no idea what roast lamb tasted like.

Jan rose from the table. "You tell the story, I'll take care of dinner."

M nodded and looked at Suzi. "You must understand that in elementary school I harbored a secret passion for Terri, known only to Mark." Suzi nodded gravely. "I knew the risks. I broached the subject with Mark to test the waters. His reaction confirmed my assessment. It was too dangerous. I said nothing to anyone else. The school year ended, and I thought I would never see her again. I buried myself in bebop. Then, two years later, she was sitting next to me in my algebra class."

Jan returned with a platter of lamb shanks and a bowl of yellow granules.

"Couscous!" Suzi said. "You guys are the best." We arranged the dishes on the table. "I'm sorry, Marcus. You were telling us about Terri."

I waited, watching the others as they served themselves and ate this completely foreign meal and then followed suit. M talked as he served us. Jan refilled the glasses.

"The proximity effect drove me crazy. Terri loomed in front of me, filling my field of vision. It seemed that everywhere I went, Terri was there. I spent the fall semester just watching her. By the spring I got enough nerve to talk to her in class and when we chanced to meet, which was often. She was friendly. I spent the summer obsessing about Terri and bebop."

I tried the lamb. It tasted moist and dark. The couscous had a mixture of subtle flavors that I couldn't identify but that balanced out the lamb. Very nice. I looked at Suzi and nodded as I took another bite.

"The next fall I asked Terri to a dance. I knew immediately I made a mistake. She became flustered, said she already had a date, and walked away. The next day I met her older brother.

"I was walking home from school on Girard. As I passed the alley between Young and Curtis, I heard a voice say, 'Hey, Sambo.'"

Suzi stopped eating and looked up.

"Three older guys leaned against the fence, seniors. I turned and walked away quickly. It's the scenario every black kid has nightmares about. Run and you trigger the predator pursuit response. Walk away and you might survive it.

"And I might have survived it if they were just casual punks in search of a thrill. But they had a plan. A very simple plan: make the colored boy regret the day he ever looked at the sister of a white man."

There was no trace of bitterness in his voice. He was merely stating a fact.

"Most of the effects of that meeting were temporary. There was blood in my urine for two days. The bruises took a few weeks to fade. The cracked ribs took longer to heal. But this was permanent." He gestured to his left eye. "They came prepared with a baseball bat. I was unconscious after the first swing. Merciful Allah be praised, I didn't feel the pain of the rest of the blows until I regained consciousness much later.

"Two disciples of Elijah Muhammad came to the hospital. They read about the attack in the paper. They talked to me about the state of things in the school and left copies of *Muhammad Speaks*. They didn't ask what prompted the attacks, and I didn't volunteer that information. When I got out of the hospital, I started going to the temple in Dayton. That was where I first learned of the white devils." He smiled. "First learned the name, that is. I experienced it firsthand in that alley."

I looked around the room. The food was cooling on the plates, forgotten. Suzi leaned on the table, wineglass in hand, transfixed.

"You're probably unaware that for six trillion years there was only one race. Then six thousand years ago Yacub, an evil scientist who studied genetics, sought to destroy the black race. He began with sixty thousand people and a six-hundred-year program to breed color, humanity, and morality out of black men. Darker offspring were killed, lighter were bred, creating races of progressively lighter skin and greater evil, from black to brown to red to yellow, until the final result was a race of white devils. A race without a soul, unredeemably evil."

"Elrick told me I had no soul, but I think he meant something else."

"He was probably right."

"You're no longer in the Nation, right?" Suzi asked.

"That's right."

"I've always wondered how somebody could believe that bizarre story." Suzi caught herself. "I mean, you don't believe it, do you?"

M smiled and allowed a nice, embarrassing pause before he answered. "No, I don't, but I did back then. Yes, it's a bizarre story, but not so hard to believe when you're recovering from a beating that could have cost your life, not just an eye."

Jan refilled the wine glasses. "People believe what resonates with their immediate experience. Especially after a traumatic event. Past experiences that contradict the belief are drowned in a wave of emotion."

M nodded. "Mama wasn't happy about it. She tried to make us regulars at the AME church, but for Pa and me it didn't take. Harriet started going after the twins were born. Mama didn't like the hate talk and me calling Christianity a white man's religion. But even she had to admit the successes. For all her efforts, her church was mainly an old ladies club. It couldn't get black men to take responsibility for their own families, something the Nation of Islam was very successful at.

"Men would come out of prison, men like Malcolm X, drug pushers, burglars, murderers, and become respectable, law-abiding, contributing members to society. Thousands of lives were turned around. I started seeing that blacks did stupid things like beating their women and children and staying drunk and high and worse because they were brainwashed by whites to think they were worthless. It made them easier to control. But when they came under the teachings of the Prophet, they cast off the lies they believed about themselves and began to take control of their own destiny. I could see that whites feared this most of all, which is why they hated the Nation and tried to destroy it.

"I became frustrated with the house Negroes who let themselves be controlled by whites so they could share in the spoils of their own exploitation. I became angry with those who continued to act in self-destructive ways and thereby perpetuate a system of control over our race. By my junior year I was very involved in the temple and aspired to membership in the Fruit of Islam."

"The fruit?"

"The security force. They provide paramilitary training. The young boys in the Nation all aspired to membership in that elite group. At least the ones I knew did." M fell silent.

I wasn't satisfied. "So how did you end up here?"

M looked at me and then off into the middle distance. "The deeper I got in the Nation, the more angry I became. My senior year I refused to play with whites in the school jazz band. I started a black-only jazz band, even though some of the white players were better than the guys I could get in my band. I picked fights with whites. I was suspended multiple times. The minister at the temple told me I was making things worse, but I couldn't bury my anger.

"Then something happened at home that made it impossible for me to stay there." He paused, started to speak, then stopped.

"Your mom told me your dad was in prison."

"Yeah, I was the one who called the cops. But they had to take him to the hospital before they took him to jail. He was one of those who made me angry, those who wouldn't cast off the lies. When I found out that it hadn't stopped, that he was still . . ."

He looked at me. The moisture in his eye did nothing to quench the fire that burned behind. "Let's just say I gave him good reasons to stop, reasons he won't forget for a long time."

I nodded in the silence that followed. M finally broke the silence.

"Of course, after that I couldn't stay in the house. The police were looking for me. Mark, you remember the old witch?"

Jan and Suzi looked at me in surprise.

"She wasn't a witch."

"I see you remember her. I did, too, and her hideout. I used it for awhile. I spent the days roaming the town, the nights holed up in an old refrigerator carton.

"Then one night I ran into Terri's brother. He was drunk, coming out of a bar downtown. He didn't recognize me, probably wouldn't have even if he were sober. I approached him as he fumbled with his keys. When he got the car door open, I came up and told him his tire was flat. He was suspicious, but he bent down to look. I brought up my knee and broke his nose. I broke a few other things too. I learned a few tricks from the Fruit. It only took a few seconds. I shoved him in his car and walked away.

"After that I had to get out of town. Mama fronted me some cash, and I took the bus to Chicago. I got a letter of recommendation to Temple Number Two, got some work and a place to stay. I entered the training program for the Fruit.

"One day I decided to actually read *The Autobiography of Malcolm X*. I knew that he was devoted to the Prophet, but then betrayed him somehow and was assassinated, but I didn't know the details. When I learned the reason he left the Nation, I was astounded. He didn't betray the Prophet. The Prophet betrayed him. The account of his last year was a revelation.

"As I read about his Hajj and the thousands of Muslims of all colors worshipping Allah together in Mecca, I thought back to the hospital and the day the two brothers opened my eyes to the Nation. I now saw that they planted a seed of poison and my anger watered it. I carefully tended my garden of hate until it consumed me and spilled over into the lives of others. I decided to follow the path Coltrane took, in pursuit of a love supreme." He smiled at Suzi, who nodded back.

"I met Jan at a gig. She was in the crowd, and Drucker asked her to come up and sing a few numbers. Things progressed as these things do over time. I avoided the temple for several months. I couldn't follow the party line anymore, but I didn't know how to start the discussion. Then I asked if Jan and I could get married there. That pretty much settled things. They took it pretty well, but my combat training came in handy at the end of at least one conversation."

Jan laughed. "See, that's one thing to thank the Nation for. You're in great shape. If you hadn't joined, you'd probably still be a pudgy little teddy bear."

M said "Bingo" and unleashed an abbreviated laugh. "Elijah Muhammad died more than a year ago. I hear Warith is taking things in a new direction, more like real Islam. He even changed the name of the organization." He turned to me. "The end. Your turn."

"I fell in love with a twirler. And I got beat up by a black guy. But it's too late to start another life story. Suzi has some finals coming up for the summer quarter."

Jan held up the wine bottle. "Surely there's time for a last glass of wine. There's only a little left."

"Sure." Suzi held out her glass.

M refilled the water glasses. "Mark, is your father still preaching?"

"Of course."

"Your dad's a preacher?" Suzi asked.

"And how's your mother?"

"She's dead," I said flatly. Glasses stopped in midair.

"What?" M blurted out.

"She died four months ago. Cancer."

"Mark, I'm so sorry," Jan said.

"Man. That's too bad," M said.

"Mark, you never said anything about it," Suzi said.

"It never came up."

The conversation was subdued after that. We left a few minutes later.

# CHAPTER TWENTY-SEVEN The El

was deserted on the return ride. Suzi was sleepy. She leaned against me as we swayed with the car. We didn't talk. I thought about M. We still had the connection. I didn't imagine it or invent it in my isolation in the wilderness. In fact, it felt stronger than before. Back then it was unacknowledged and unchallenged. But the unspoken communication that passed between us this night showed that the bond had survived eight years of drought. The bud was inching open, at the cusp of blooming.

Even so, it was also apparent that M was changed. Much more than I was. I wasn't sure I had come very far since those days. I remembered M in the attic, his face in shadow, fiercely insistent that things happened for a reason, and my dubious reply.

I had struggled with faith and the seeming indifference of the universe until I was confronted with the hand of God thrust into its fabric, a spike nailed through the open palm, a gory refutation of indifference. The response was inescapable. Does the condemned prisoner embrace the hand that signed the stay of execution? I could do no less.

But then I was faced with the realization that my life was no longer my own. Gratitude compelled me to live in service to the one who had spared my life. Figuring out what that meant turned out to be more difficult than I expected. The council of many yielded confusion, not wisdom. I chose to take my own path, walking out the implications of my decision as I understood them, to the dismay of those around me.

But now I found myself back where I started. Did things

really happen for a reason, or did they just happen? I didn't want to believe they happened for a reason because that meant God killed Mom on purpose, for some divinely perverse reason that I could not fathom. I wasn't grateful to a God who could spare my life only to take my mother's life, prematurely and painfully. There could be no just reason for doing that. So what was I to conclude? That God is not just?

Or maybe God is not. Not there, not anywhere. Maybe The Rack was right. Maybe an ancient tribe of unsophisticated nomads just invented Him, cobbling together pieces of superstitions they picked up along the way into a crazy quilt deity. And then by accident one of them got educated by the Egyptians and wrote it all down. Voila! The Torah!

The train jostled, and Suzi's head fell against my shoulder. I extracted my arm from between us and put it around her shoulders, holding her steady in the swaying of the train. She smiled and nestled against me, eyes closed.

I found myself thinking there are worse things than riding on the El with your arm around a beautiful woman. I thought of Lori with a twinge of guilt but shook it off. What did she expect? I wrote her at least once a week, had done for three months. Not one reply. That message seemed pretty clear to me. She had moved on. I was no longer in the picture.

We got off at the Garfield station. It was almost a mile to the apartment. The walk woke Suzi up, and she talked on about M and Jan and how remarkable it was that I found him after all these years. It was a warm, humid August night, and we were both sweating by the time we climbed the stairs. The phone was ringing as Suzi unlocked the door. She left the keys hanging in the deadbolt and rushed to answer it. I listened to her half of the conversation as I locked the door and sat down at the table.

"Hello? Dad? Boy, you're calling late." She checked the clock on the stove. "What about Gamaw? What? Oh no!" She turned to me with panic in her eyes. I stood up. "When? How?" She put a hand on the counter to steady herself. "OK. Yeah. I can leave tomorrow afternoon." She wiped a tear from her cheek with the back of her hand. "OK. I'll check at the airport in the morning. OK. Bye. I love you. Bye."

I came around the table. She hung up the phone and turned to me. "My grandmother. She died just an hour ago. Heart failure."

Her attempt at a calm exterior crumbled, and she fell against me. I put my arms around her. We were about the same height. She laid her head on my shoulder and began to cry. Her arms were folded up against her, her hands grasping my shoulder blades. She twisted the fabric of my shirt in her fingers and shook against me as the sobs came out. I squeezed her tighter, holding her close to contain the shaking.

I could see the second hand of the clock on the stove creeping around. She cried with sobs for more than five minutes, then calmed down. I loosened my hold some and rubbed my hand against her back. The shirt clung to her, damp with sweat. She nestled her head deeper into the hollow below my jaw. Her cheek pressed against my neck, our sweat mingling. I could feel the three earrings against my jaw. I stroked her Rod Stewart hair and said nonsense like, "It's OK." I could feel her tears running down my neck and soaking my shirt. Her scent filled my nostrils, a mix of perfume, cigarettes, and sweat.

After another five minutes the tears slowed. She squirmed her arms out from between us, wrapped them around my lower back, and squeezed me tighter, pressing her body against mine. She slid her face against my neck, kissed it, and whispered, "Thank you."

I squeezed her in response. She pulled her head back and kissed me on the lips. Her hands moved up to the back of my head; fingers dug into my hair. My hands moved to her hair. I kissed back. Slow, lingering kisses. Then she pushed her fingers against the back of my head and kissed me hard, almost pushing my lips away from my teeth. I could taste the wine on her lips.

She laid her head back down on my shoulder and sighed. Then she ran her hands down my back, pressing my shirt into the sweat that trickled down, and leaned closer against me. She pulled her head back without releasing her hold on me and looked in my eyes.

"Mark, I don't want to sleep alone tonight. I really don't want to sleep alone. I need someone to hold me."

I could feel the blood coursing through my body. I thought of lying next to Suzi, holding her through the night. I had no doubt what would happen if I joined her in the double bed and the room with the view. I'm sure she saw my hesitation. I don't know if she saw the desire that also raced through my veins. I doubted that it was completely hidden from her.

A smile flitted nervously across her face before she looked at me with more intensity. "Nothing has to happen. And even if it does, it doesn't mean anything. It won't change anything. But I can't be alone tonight."

I kissed her, a long, gentle kiss, then loosened my hold on her body slightly. "Suzi, I wish I could. I really wish I could. But I can't. I know it feels inevitable. But it wouldn't be right."

She shook her head. "You silly preacher's kid; don't try to be some white knight saving me from myself. I know what I'm doing. You wouldn't be taking advantage of me."

"Maybe you do know what you're doing. But maybe I'd be taking advantage of myself. As much as I want to, I know even more that I can't. I'm sorry."

Tears overflowed her eyes. She nodded, laid her head back down on my shoulder, and squeezed me softly. Then she walked to her room and closed the door. I heard the bolt slide into place.

Suzi left for Ohio the next day. Wednesday night I took the subway to Rick's American Café in the Holiday Inn. Jan had a solo gig during happy hour, mainly show tunes and standards. She was at the grand piano, wearing a silver-white dress the color of her hair, so that at first glance I didn't even realize it was there. I took a second look and noticed the shimmer of the cloth with some relief. I knew Chicago was the big city, but I didn't expect they were featuring nude pianists at the Holiday Inn. Yet.

I found M at a nearby table and ordered a tonic water with lime to match his. He was dressed in black like at BJ's, the shades covering his scars. Our conversation turned to Islam.

"No matter how much you want to believe something, it was hard work to swallow that Yacub story. And the further I got in school, the more science I took, the harder it got."

"How did you keep believing it even when it seemed crazy?"

"When you accept a religion, you're admitting that there are things you don't understand, things that are outside the realm of the senses. You choose to believe them. What would you do if your sister . . . what was her name?"

"You mean Heidi or Hannah?"

"Take your pick. What would you say if Hannah turned up pregnant but insisted she was still a virgin? You think your dad would believe it?"

"Watch it. You're talking about my sister."

"Cool your jets, man. It's just an example. We can pick Jan if you like. Let's say she's pregnant, insists she's a virgin, and says God magically got her pregnant. Would you buy it?"

"Only if God was her nickname for you."

"But you believe that about Mary. You choose to believe something that is physically impossible. So, if you suspend the laws of nature, where do you draw the line? Might as well be hung for a sheep as a lamb. If you're a true believer, you want to believe. You don't hold back."

"But that Yacub story isn't about what God did. It's about what some mad scientist did."

"Exactly. It felt funny from the start, but at the time I wasn't being picky. Once I read about Malcolm X, I realized that Fard took some liberties in his depiction of Islam."

"But you're still a Muslim."

"Yes, but not a Black Muslim, as some call them. Like Mama's preacher used to say, I ate the chicken but I spit out the bones. Islam has been around a lot longer than W. D. Fard and the so-called Nation of Islam. The Qur'an doesn't have any stories of evil scientists in it."

"Does it have Job in it?"

"He's mentioned in the book of Suad."

"Talk about a story that is hard to stomach. If I killed your entire family, would you curse me or praise me? 'The Lord giveth and the Lord taketh away. Blessed be the name of the Lord.' Give me a break."

"There's one minor detail you're missing. You're not Allah."

A laugh broke out behind me. "You have a God complex?" Jan sat down at our table.

I ignored her. "Why should God get away with something that any decent man would be ashamed to do?"

Jan signaled to a waiter and ordered a glass of wine. M looked at me in silence. I looked at him, daring him to answer the question.

"This wouldn't have anything to do with your mother, would it?" Jan asked.

"That's not the point. We can use Job as an example, or we can use Mom. Either way, God is killing innocent people who don't deserve it."

M shook his head. "Allah is not a man, that he must explain to us his actions."

"Job got an explanation."

"And it is recorded for your instruction. Are you not satisfied with it?"

"No, I'm not," I said, perhaps too loudly. Several people looked in our direction. I lowered my voice. "It wasn't an explanation. It was a 'who are you to ask in the first place' answer, which is like a parent saying 'because I said so.' It's a nonanswer."

"Do you think God owes you one?"

"Yes. Mom was a true servant, like Job. She didn't deserve to die like that, in pain, being eaten away from the inside."

"So she was a good person, and God owed her one?"

"If you want to put it that way."

"I did put it that way ten years ago. You don't remember? I saved your life so you could save the witch's life so she could save the guy's life. So I thought God owed me one."

"She wasn't a witch," I said automatically, but I wasn't thinking about her. I remembered. Two kids in a gloomy attic, one desperate for an edge, a marker he could use to get a favor from God.

"Mark, you were the one who told me God doesn't work that way. God doesn't bargain; He doesn't have to. He's holding all the cards. He doesn't have to cut a deal to get what He wants. Now, if you want to bargain, I hear Satan is always offering some kind of deal."

Jan cut in. "Those aren't exactly words of comfort, Marcus. Mark doesn't need logic, he needs reassurance."

"Actually, I'd like some logic that would make sense of it all."

"Mark, reality is a paradox," Jan said. "Logic is fine for working out puzzles or building highways, but it's no good for living. We are spiritual beings with a physical manifestation, and the spirit world doesn't work by logic."

I looked at M. He shrugged.

Jan ignored him. "God, whom we do not see, is real; and the world, which we do see, is unreal. In experience, what exists for us does not really exist; and what does not exist for us, really exists."

"Huh?"

"We must become completely void inside to be completely possessed by God. Complete emptiness means absolute fullness. We must become nothing, so as to be absorbed in the infinity of God. Nothing means everything."

"This is supposed to be comforting?"

"It's all from the Bible. The first will be last. He who would be leader must be the servant of all. If you seek to save your life, you will lose it. But he who loses his life shall find it. Unless a seed fall into the ground and die, it cannot live. The spirit world doesn't run on logic. It works through paradox."

"I'm not saying any of this makes sense, but just for the sake of argument, how does any of this apply?"

"You say your mother was a true servant. What was she like in her last days?"

"Same as she always was. Thinking of others, trusting that God is good."

"See? She knew what I'm talking about. If you grasp at life, it will slip through your fingers, and you will end up with nothing. All is empty except the open hand."

I jerked as if I'd been slapped. "What did you say?"

"Your mother understood the paradox of life."

"No, no, the last thing."

"All is empty except the open hand." She held her hand out, palm up. I stared at her, my mind reeling. "The open hand is the symbol of both giving and receiving. It brings fullness. The closed hand is the symbol of possessiveness. It brings emptiness."

I wasn't listening to her anymore. I was lost in a fog where a woman with translucent skin and white hair loosed a single drop of water from her finger onto my forehead. She was the woman in my dream, clothed in shimmering silver hair. I recognized her face. I had seen Jan in a park in Hot Springs.

What did that mean? Was she some kind of multicultural messenger from God, a Zen-Buddhist married to a Muslim quoting the Bible? I stared in her direction, but my eyes were unfocused as I searched for something to explain this inexplicable coincidence.

"It can't be," I whispered. In the periphery of my mind, I saw Jan and M exchange glances. I tried to shake it off as a fantastic story, but I couldn't escape the fact that I knew it had happened. I was there in the park. I was here now. And so was Jan.

"How did you . . ." I looked around. Jan was gone. She had returned to the piano. I looked at M. "I saw her two months ago. In Little Rock. I heard her say those exact same words."

"What?"

"In a dream. It was Jan. She held out her hand and said, 'Everything is empty except the open hand.' Then I woke up."

M looked at me for awhile, and we sipped our tonic water. After a few songs, M broke the silence.

"Mark, I don't think you came here looking for me."

"What was I looking for?"

"I don't think you're looking. I think you're running. And Allah is pursuing." I grunted and sipped my drink. "You got a job, you got a room, but you're just marking time here. There might be a future for you in Chicago, but you won't find it until you settle what you're trying to leave behind and can't."

I flushed. "You seem to have suddenly become the expert on my life and what I should do. Kind of outspoken for a guy who hasn't talked to his mother in two years."

An awkward silence descended. We listened to Jan sing *Lush Life*. I looked around for the waiter. I wanted some whiskey. Instead, I looked at M.

"Look, I'm sorry. I shouldn't have said that."

M cleared his throat. "No, you're right, man. I can't tell you what to do. I have my own problems. Don't listen to me."

I fought back the moisture in my eyes. "Maybe we should listen to each other."

M laughed quietly and fell silent. Then he took off the shades and looked me in the eye.

"You may find this hard to believe, but in the eight years since you moved to Texas, I never found anyone who could take your place."

I looked at him. He waited.

"Me neither," I finally whispered.

"When you walked up to our table at BJ's, I refused to believe it was you at first. A long time ago I gave up on finding the lost brother and buried those longings deep enough so they couldn't torture me anymore. Then you showed up again."

He looked in Jan's general direction. "The past few days, I've been reliving a lot of memories. I don't want to have to bury them again. I don't want to close off that part of myself as protection from the melancholy of emptiness."

He looked back into my eyes, and I saw the tear brimming. "But I wouldn't be a true friend if I didn't tell you what I see, what I'm still fighting myself. We both have unfinished business. Maybe we have to quit trying to cut deals or trying to cut and run. I think Allah is saying we have to hold out the open hand. Maybe we have to accept."

He couldn't be right. I didn't want him to be right. "But how can I accept the unacceptable?"

My voice broke and I fell silent. Worse yet, how could I accept the emptiness? The void that I had begun to suspect lay beyond the curtain of belief we hang up to hide the ugly truth.

"I don't understand it either," M said. "But do you really think it's a coincidence you came looking for me and found Jan? I hope you come back to Chicago, but I know you have to go back to Texas."

# CHAPTER TWENTY-EIGHT He an-

swered on the third ring.

"Are you busy Friday night?"

"Mark?"

"Hi, Dad."

"What's this about Friday night?"

"Are you busy around six-thirty?"

"Why?"

"That's what time the bus gets to Beaumont, and I'm going to
need a ride."

---

I left before Suzi got back from Ohio. I left the September
rent with a note telling her if I didn't come back by October, to
rent the room out. I boxed up all my negatives and prints suit-
able for mailing if I didn't return. I packed what clothes I could
fit into the backpack, leaving the rest in the dresser. I brought the
camera.

On the bus I read through Job. At first when it got tedious, I
skipped over the interminable speeches of his useless friends and
cut to God's speech. When that failed to answer my questions,
I went back and read the whole thing. It still made no sense. I
shoved the Gideon Bible in my pack and stared out the window
through East Texas.

Dad was standing outside the door of the terminal when the
bus pulled up. I walked up to him awkwardly. He smiled and
gave me a side hug. I squeezed his shoulder gratefully and said

nothing. During the hour drive to Fred, the conversation stayed on safe topics—the thirty-hour trip, M, my job at the studio. Heidi was completing a summer-session course to finish off her degree. Hannah was preparing to attend Baylor University.

I spent the weekend recovering from the trip. Saturday night Dad was in his study, finishing up his sermon for the next day. I was on the couch in the den, listening to Presti and Lagoya do magical things with Bach on two guitars and reading Job again. Hannah walked in with two root beer floats, set one on the coffee table, and took the other. She settled into the armchair next to the couch and tucked her feet under her.

"Thanks." I set the book aside. We ate in silence for awhile. Then I looked at her. "Hey, about that phone call back in May—"

"Yeah, yeah," she said.

"I shouldn't have said those things."

"You were right, you know."

"Yeah, so were you. But I think we both already knew that. No need to actually say it."

"Probably not."

We ate our floats and listened to the album.

"Hey, what's with the little white lines down the side of your face?"

I stroked the scars. "Did you ever wonder what would happen if you dragged a green pinecone across your face?"

She gasped. "No."

"Me, neither. But a couple of hicks in Arkansas did."

On Sunday they had dinner on the grounds after church. I never heard the reason, but I suspected my presence had something to do with it. Mac rolled up in his wheelchair and shook my hand. Scooter and Brenda were there. She told me they were moving to Ft. Worth the next week so Scooter could start at the seminary. I feigned surprise. Even Parker showed up, flashed a rare smile, and told me to come visit him in the next few days. I promised I would. I didn't see Sonia. Deacon Fry nodded in my general direction. I took the lack of a scowl as a sign of improvement. Vernon rolled up in his green Pontiac Bonneville and smoked Lucky Strikes in the gravel parking lot.

Jolene told me she was pregnant. Buddy smiled, shook my hand, and slapped my back like he was congratulating me. I looked at Bubba. He shook his head. I shuddered, imagining the offspring of dueling pranksters. I just knew I didn't want my kids going to school with it. Ralph was there with Squeaky. They were engaged. To my surprise, Darnell showed up for the lunch, parking his rig under the pines near the creek. He quizzed me on the various rides I caught and the route I took to find M. He was disappointed when he heard I completed the trip on the bus. Of course Jimbo didn't show up. Nothing would convince a Perkins to come near a church.

Monday morning Dad woke me up at sunrise. "Put on some work clothes."

I found him at the table finishing a cup of coffee. He was wearing Grandpa's old work coveralls, a Texaco logo stitched above the breast pocket.

He shoved a cup at me. "Got a heavy schedule today?"

"Wide open."

"Good. You can come help me."

That was all the explanation he provided. We took the Falcon down past Vernon's place all the way to the river bottom and stopped at Uncle Herbert's camp house. It was deserted.

"What's the occasion?"

"Time to work the trot lines." He got out and opened the trunk. I met him behind the car.

"What?"

"Check them for fish, bait them." He opened an ice chest and pulled out a bucket of fish chunks.

"I know what it means. I'm just wondering why you're doing it." He had always been the professorial type. The only thing missing was the pipe and the tweed jacket with the elbow patches. "Since when did you become interested in fishing?"

He handed me a net and collapsible wire basket. "Lot of people getting new interests these days. Traveling, jazz, photography."

I followed him to the top of the bank, a steep twenty-foot drop to the water. "Where did these come from?" I indicated the wooden steps next to the slick trail that was the traditional route to the boat. The lumber was fresh. Traces of sawdust were still visible on the ground.

"Just something I helped Uncle Hub throw together. Neither one of us is getting more limber."

I followed him down the steps to the boat tied to the platform. "You've been busy."

He steadied himself in the back of the boat and looked up at me, pushing his glasses up on his nose. From the angle above I could see the full crescent of his receding hairline like a tonsure. "We can't just sit around waiting for you to come back. Things need doing, we do them."

"We?"

"Hannah is my usual helper. She's taking a break to give you the seat of honor." He motioned to the front seat.

"Hannah."

"Yes, Hannah. Now untie that line and grab an oar."

"Are we talking the social butterfly, society maven, Baylor sorority wannabe Hannah?"

"That's the one."

I grunted as I pushed us away from the dock. "Somehow I don't see Hannah as the *Field and Stream* type."

"She wasn't crazy about it at first. I had to threaten to hide the car keys before she came along. Now she loves it. Here, head up that way."

I looked at the brown water rippling past the boat. The smell of mud and rotting fish wafted by.

"What's to love?" I asked through my teeth as I pulled against the current. "Did you ever consider investing in a motor?"

"There's much to love. Out here, alone on the water this time of morning, just you and God and a bunch of critters. Hear that?" I looked back. He pointed a dripping oar at a mockingbird that seemed to be dialing through all the channels on his radio. Traces of a morning mist drifted past, hugging the chocolate current. I brought us in close to the bank to avoid a branch. A frog yelped in surprise and splashed next to my oar. "You run a motor, you'll miss most of what's worth coming out here for. Over there."

He pointed to a spot where a rope jutted out of the water, tied to a tree hanging over the bank. We angled for it, pulled alongside, and shipped the oars. Dad worked his way hand-over-hand down the line, grunting as he leaned over to add bait where it was stripped. He found a couple of catfish and tossed them to me. I dropped them into the wire basket hanging over the side of the boat, being careful of the spines.

When we got to the end he pushed his glasses up with the back of his hand and nodded upstream. "There's another up in that branch. On the right."

I rinsed my hands in the river and began paddling. The branch was vaulted with trees. We nudged the boat up this woodland cathedral.

"You find what you were looking for?" Dad asked from behind me in the gloom. "In Chicago?"

"I found M."

"Was that what you were looking for?"

"No, not really."

"Why did you come back?"

"M told me to."

"How long are you staying?"

"Don't know."

"You are just a fountain of information. Here it is." The branch was only fifteen feet across. Dad worked through the hooks. "Nothing. Uncle Hub told me I wouldn't get anything up here, but I wanted to try it. Sometimes you just have to find things out for yourself, no matter what folks tell you." He rinsed his hands and picked up the oar. "There's one more farther up the main river."

We rowed in silence out of the branch and up the river.

"All is empty except the open hand," I said. "What do you think that means?"

"I was afraid you might start smoking marijuana up there."

"Dad, I'm serious."

"All is empty except the open hand. Sounds Buddhist."

"Do you think reality is a paradox?"

He was silent for awhile. "I will go so far as to say that sometimes truth is nonintuitive."

We found the last trotline and got a few more catfish. I added them to the basket, and we drifted back down the river.

"Do you ever have doubts?" I asked.

"About what?" Dad paddled a few strokes to keep us in the center of the current.

"If what you believe is really true."

"Sure."

I pulled my oar from the water and twisted around in my seat. "You do?"

"Don't look so shocked. I would say anyone who doesn't have doubts hasn't thought about what he believes. If you don't question the answers, you haven't really answered the questions."

"What about the whole 'Let him who asks do so without doubting' thing?"

"You mean James?"

"Probably."

"That verse is specifically about asking God for wisdom."

"A double-minded man is unstable in all he does."

Dad set his oar across his legs and leaned against the back of the boat. "Let's say you're on some farm-to-market highway without a map. You come to a fork, and you're not sure which road to take. You have to pick one, so you do. You could have doubts all the way down the road, but if you stick with your choice, eventually you will get to a place where you can find out if you are right or not. A double-minded man would keep going back to the fork and going for a few miles down one road, deciding he was wrong and trying the other for a few miles, then switching back. He would probably run out of gas before he ever found out which road was the right one.

"You can have doubts about the road, but if you keep going you will see signs that tell you if you've made the right choice or not. Or at least give you an idea that you're headed in the right direction. You might have to change roads a few times before you reach your destination."

I dropped my oar in the bottom of the boat and turned all the way around. "But I thought the Bible is supposed to be our map. So we shouldn't have any doubts."

"Perhaps we shouldn't, but we do. We always do. But God isn't gasping and saying, 'Oh my goodness, Mark has some doubts. How did this happen?' He knows we will have doubts. Look at the Israelites. They saw miracles happen right in front of them, but as soon as the food supplies got low, they went from doubts to open rebellion. Our doubts don't surprise God."

"The day before I left, you said you believed even when it didn't seem real."

"We're talking about faith, not knowledge. Believing isn't the same as knowing. 'Faith is the substance of things hoped for, the evidence of things not seen.' If you hope for something, you don't have it yet. We don't know now. We can't know. And anything you can't know about, you will have cause to doubt. Paul said, 'For now we see through a glass, darkly; but then face to face: now I know in part; but then shall I know even as also I am known.' We only know in part. That's why we must have faith."

"So I can doubt and still have faith?"

"You can't live constantly with doubt and have an effective faith. You will become that double-minded man. But even a man of faith can have doubts. John the Baptist had doubts. He sent his disciples to ask Jesus if He was the messiah. Jesus wasn't outraged that the man who baptized Him and told the crowds He was the messiah now doubted Him. He sent them back with a message to calm his doubts and restore his faith.

"Doubt is not fatal. In fact, I would say a man who never doubts is either incredibly blessed or appallingly devoid of curiosity."

The platform was in sight. We rowed to it, tied up the boat, and carried the fish and gear up to the camp house. Dad put all but two of the fish on ice and then set me to getting things ready in the kitchen while he cleaned the fish. He battered and pan-fried them with some potatoes, and we sat down to a river-bottom brunch.

I poured some ketchup on my plate. "So how do you move from doubting to knowing?"

"You asked the wrong question. How can you move from doubt to faith? That's the proper question. You follow John's example. You ask the one you doubt to either confirm your doubts or restore your faith. That's why I said what I did when you called."

I frowned, trying to remember the conversation.

"If you want to ask hard questions like Job, you must have the guts to stick around for the answers. Job had doubts about God's fairness. And he trusted God to answer his questions. He said, 'Though he slay me, yet will I trust him.' I think you have some of the same questions. God answered Job's questions, and didn't kill him doing it. Although it was a long answer. It goes on for four chapters."

"I read it. I don't get it. What does it mean?"

"I think you need to get the answers yourself. Read Job again. Ask God. Wait for His answer."

# CHAPTER TWENTY-NINE

Tuesday afternoon I talked Dad out of the Galaxy and pointed her nose north. On the drive, I thought about Job. I had read the book through a few times and wasn't any closer to finding sense in it. All the action happened in the thin veneer of the first and last chapters, with forty chapters of complaining and rebuking sandwiched in between. Job seemed to be schizophrenic, sometimes demanding a chance to plead his righteousness before God, other times exclaiming that nobody can stand blameless before God. Then God shows up and says as soon as Job can explain all the mysteries of the universe He will answer Job's questions. What kind of deal was that?

Around five I rolled into Stanley, Louisiana, and asked around for the Street house, the one with six boys. Five minutes later I stopped in front of a rambling, two-story frame farmhouse surrounded by oaks and pecans on the edge of town. A small crowd of young boys played football in the waning afternoon sun. Dragonflies darted through a cloud of gnats above the overgrown field that formed their western boundary. Smoke drifted from behind the house. I caught the scent of a barbecue grill.

Lori sat on a bench swing under an oak thirty yards off. She was reading something and didn't look up. I left the car door open and walked across the yard to the swing. As I approached, I saw a shoebox in her lap. Her hair was longer. It hung in a curtain on either side of her face, her head bowed over the paper she was reading. She was wearing a softball jersey, shorts, and cleats. The pangs of longing I felt the first time I saw her returned, intensified by the thought that I had driven her away by my own stupidity. An earthquake shook my foundations, a yawning rift split open inside my chest, sucking my heart into its depths.

She didn't hear me until I was ten feet away. She was smiling as she looked up, her eyes misted over. Then her mouth opened in a silent exclamation and her eyes flared open. She jumped up, leaving the swing quivering behind her. The shoebox tumbled to the ground amid a cascade of envelopes. She ran to me and pinned my arms to my side with hers, burying her face against my chest.

This was not the greeting I expected. Based on our last conversation and the complete radio silence, I wasn't sure if I would even be allowed on the premises, an uncertainty that suggested the surprise visit as the best approach. I wiggled my arms out of her clutch and wrapped them around her. We stood there for several minutes. The football game continued, oblivious to the emotional reunion by the swing.

Lori eventually relaxed her hold on me, gave me a single kiss, and stepped back. I knelt down to retrieve the box and discovered that it had been full of my letters from Chicago, half of them still unopened.

Lori knelt down next to me and began stuffing the envelopes back into the box. "I can get it."

I held the box and she filled it. Then we sat on the swing. Lori nestled under my arm, sorting the letters by postmark date.

"I'm back," I said.

She snuggled closer. "I can see that."

"What made you decide to open my letters all of a sudden after three months of ignoring me?"

"There's a lot you don't know, buddy boy."

"That's true."

"I didn't open the first two or three because I was still mad. Actually, I threw them away. Plus, I figured after a few weeks you would get tired and give up and the whole problem would go away.

Then I went on a ten-week mission trip with my church to Mexico. I just got back Sunday. I found this shoebox on my dresser. When your letters came, Daddy threw them away with the junk mail. But Mama sneaked them out of the trash and put them in this box. She even rescued the ones I threw away myself."

"She is a very wise woman. You should learn from her example." Lori slugged me in the ribs. It hurt. I had seen her hit home runs over the fence. "Ow!"

"Don't whine. You deserve worse." I didn't bother to contradict her. "So I came out here on the swing to read your letters. I couldn't believe you kept writing for three months."

"That's only because you didn't think I would remember what you said when we were dancing." She lifted up her head and squinted at me. "You told me to remember that I was lucky to have you. And I did."

"That's right," she said, leaning back against me. "You don't deserve me."

"Nope."

"There's lots of guys who come by here courting me who wouldn't get kicked out of school and go running off all over the country."

"I shall vanquish them all, singly or en masse. Bring them forth."

"Quit talking like The Captain and tell me why you came back."

"For you."

"That's not all."

"It's enough."

I told her about meeting M and his advice. I told her about Jan and the dream. I didn't tell her about Suzi. It didn't come up. She noticed the scars, so I told her the whole hitchhiking trip, from Beaumont to Middletown. By that time, somebody noticed the car and me on the swing. I was invited to dinner.

Mrs. Street was a short, billowy woman with a perpetual smile. Mr. Street was large and imposing and sat at the head of a monstrous table that could accommodate a dozen people in a pinch. He insisted I be seated next to him, with Lori across from me. One of the older brothers sat next to her and said nothing, giving me intense stares as he chewed the half-chicken on his plate, blackened on the grill out back. There was no evidence of the oldest brother. The three younger brothers in high school glared at me openly. The youngest, only four years old, made goofy faces at me and showed off, ignoring Mrs. Street's admonitions to behave as she scurried back and forth from kitchen to dining room.

Mr. Street asked me many pointed questions about my family and plans. I told him about my work in photography and the increasing responsibility John had given me. He asked me about the studio and its financial success. I told him John drove a BMW. He relaxed a bit after that and switched his focus.

"Thanks to you and your wanderlust, you've infected Lorraine. She's taking a year off school and traipsing all over Europe."

"What?" I set down a chicken thigh and looked at Lori.

She blushed. "I didn't have time to tell you. I met a couple on the mission trip. They're spending a year in Europe and are looking for an au pair to help them out. She's expecting in January."

"A what?"

"An au pair. Don't tell me I've stumped Dr. Dictionary." I waited as she gloated. "An au pair is a young person, usually a woman, who does light housework for a family in exchange for room and board. If things work out, I might become the nanny when the baby comes."

"You're going to Europe?"

"For a year. And they will teach me French. We're spending the first six months in France in the country."

"When do you leave?"

"October."

"Wow," I said. "That's nice."

The older brother smiled for the first time. The four-year-old put his napkin on his head and pulled his ears.

After the meal I told everyone good-bye. I had to get back to Fred so Dad could use the car for hospital visitation. Lori walked me to the car.

"Europe, huh?"

"Mark, I was going to tell you all about it, but we got dragged into supper."

"I guess I was lucky to have you. Too lucky, it turns out."

"Mark, there's another side. I found out how lucky I am to have you." She pointed to the box of letters on the swing.

"Then why are you running off to Europe? At least I only went to Chicago. And it was only for a few months."

"I made the commitment while I was in Mexico. Before I came home and found these. But I have an idea. You can come with us."

I laughed. "Yeah, I've got the cash to tour Europe for a year."

"You don't need it. They're looking for a driver. They know someone in France who could do it, but he can't do the road trip through Italy, Switzerland, Austria, Germany, and the Netherlands. You could come and do the whole thing."

"A driver?"

"And I bet when I show them some of these pictures you sent and remind them how nice it would be to have memories of the baby's first trip, well . . ."

"They can afford to pay their way and two other people?"

"Oh yeah. They have a house in San Francisco, New York, and southern France."

"Sheesh."

"Think plop, plop, fizz, fizz."

"Oh what a relief it is?"

"That's it. But you'll have to get your passport right away."

It was a crazy idea. Lori gave me a few kisses to remind me to come back, and I spent the next three hours rolling it around in my head. I got home at midnight, full of confusion and hope.

---

The house was deserted when I got up the next morning. I dusted off the bicycle and headed down the highway a mile, turning off to the right at Frank's Branch Cemetery. I left the bike by the old church, pulled a book from my pack, and walked between the headstones to a grave not four months old, in the shadow of the pine trees that lined the highway. The center was still high. I sat down cross-legged at the foot of the mound and looked at the headstone.

*Elizabeth Thomas Cloud, Beloved Wife and Mother, Born June 12, 1927–Died May 2, 1976*

"Hey. How about some Twain?" I opened *Roughing It* to chapter LXVII, "Life in San Francisco," and read it through. I looked up at the headstone when I read about the "curiosities" of the earthquake, remembering how Mom laughed at the crazy stories of prominent citizens caught by the tremors and the dog that climbed the ladder to the roof of the stables.

I set the book down and stared at nothing for awhile.

"I've been gone, but I guess you know all about it. I've been kind of angry." I cleared my throat. "No, that's not right. I've been very angry. I tried to hide it from you, but I think you guessed it. I'm sorry. I'm still angry though."

I looked around the cemetery self-consciously. Nobody there on a Wednesday morning. Everybody off living their lives, staying busy.

"I didn't cry at the funeral. I'm sorry. I didn't cry when you died. I didn't cry when I found out you were going to die. I'm sorry about it, but I can't seem to do anything about it. I think I'm defective somewhere. It's not that you don't deserve it. It's me.

"But I'm worried about Lori. She probably deserves better. Shouldn't I warn her? Oh, I didn't tell you about Lori. You'd like her. She'd like you. She's going to France."

The sun edged up over the trees, the shadow inching down the headstone like a thermometer when a northerner comes through. "Like I said, I've been angry. It's not fair. You deserve better too. You deserve a son who would cry at your funeral. I know life isn't fair, but even Squeaky said God should be fair, and what's wrong with that? Seems right to me."

I gestured to the headstone. "But what I don't get is, why weren't you angry? Wasn't life good enough that you felt cheated to leave it behind? Did you really want to go to San Francisco that badly? Were you really that miserable in Fred that death was a nice alternative?"

I laughed. "I mean, I know I've complained about Fred enough, but I don't think I'd go so far as to say 'Better dead than Fred.' That seems a bit extreme."

I looked down at the grass for awhile. The light crept down the marble to the mound. "Didn't you love us enough to be angry about leaving us?" I asked in a softer voice. I looked down at my hands lying limp in my lap. "Didn't you love me enough?" I whispered. "To be angry?"

Then something happened. I felt it down deep, in the same place that broke open when I saw Lori on the swing—smiling, misty-eyed—reading my letters. Something pushed up, almost like a retching. I tried to push it back down, but it resisted. It rose like bile in my chest. My throat felt thick, like my tonsils had suddenly closed it shut. My eyes burned and felt swollen. A tear dropped into my open hand, followed by another.

"I'm sorry," I whispered over and over. I shook my head back and forth. Tears ran down my cheeks and dripped off my nose and chin.

"I should have loved you more. I should have noticed you more."

Images flashed through my mind: Mom on vacation reading us jokes from the *Reader's Digest,* Mom telling Dad she'd rather learn patience in the air conditioning, Mom creeping between the auto shop and the liquor store to see if I was back there with the Creature, Mom fixing up my Lil' Abner costume for Sadie Hawkins Day, Mom upset that I was going out to shoot Bambi, Mom playing Christmas carols as we all tried to remember the third verse, Mom bringing ice for Sonia's black eye after Parker hit her, Mom bringing ice for my black eye after Elrick hit me. Mom.

The light crawled down the mound until I could see my shadow on it. My back was warm. The back of my neck glowed. My face was wet. I grabbed the book and clambered to my feet. My right leg was asleep. I limped past the headstones to the bike.

As I neared the church, I suddenly felt a heaviness, like the air pressure had increased. I took shallow breaths. The sky seemed to press the weight of several atmospheres onto my shoulders. I looked up. High above the earth, cirrus clouds were shredded across a flawless blue background. The steeple of the old church at Frank's Branch bisected the sky. It careened and I swayed, collapsing on the red clay and gravel of the drive. The Twain book rolled end-over-end down the hill and fell open a few feet away.

I was suddenly aware of every sensation over my entire body. I could feel the imprint of every speck of gravel on the stripes of my left cheek, the dust mingling with the tears. I felt the threads of the chambray work shirt against my chest and stomach and the ripples in the denim of my jeans against my thighs and calves. I felt the seams around the pockets placing more pressure against my buttocks than the rest of the fabric. I felt the elastic of my socks hugging my ankles and the shoelaces threaded through the eyelets pressing against the bones in my feet.

My pulse thundered in my ears. I felt the blood pumping

through my veins in spurts like the squishing of waterlogged tennis shoes. I felt the electrical impulses crackling along my nerves to my brain.

And in my brain I felt a thought.

*Me.*

At that moment I knew every aspect of my existence, down to the electrons whirling around in my innermost parts. It was all laid out before me like a blueprint.

*I.*

It echoed again in the empty chambers of my brain. My vision pulled back to see my body lying on the red dirt. The scene whirled backward, and I saw my body rise from the dirt like a marionette, limp backward to the grave. I saw tears climb up my face and squeeze themselves into my eyes. The speed increased as I backed to the bike and it rose to greet my outstretched hand. I flashed backward down the hill and the highway. Faster I slept through the night and backed to Stanley, Louisiana. My view rose higher as I saw my life recede through all the experiences I could remember and many I couldn't, but all were as individual and distinct as the threads in my shirt.

*I am.*

I saw the ripples flowing out of my life into others, bouncing off M and Pauline and Vernon and Deacon Fry. I drew farther back until the whole world was a web of ripples and the earth a coruscating globe of interconnectedness.

*I am that I am.*

And I knew. I knew as I was known. I was broken open and poured out like water. All my bones were out of joint. My heart turned to wax and melted within me. My strength was dried up like the cracked clay drive under my ribs. My tongue stuck to the roof of my mouth. I saw all my desires, both pure and profane, laid out like keys on a piano, playing a chaotic bebop of pain and ecstasy.

*I am that I am.*

Then, as I thought my chest would explode and my head with it, I heard another tune. A subtle descant that wove through the strident cacophony. Alone, the music of my desires made no sense. But as the single, pure notes of the alternate melody pulsed through the noise, I began to hear the joy and grief pulled together into a higher music of a form I had never guessed. It was like hearing M play "Take Five." A foreign beat, a deep form that called to a forgotten melody deep within the fabric of the ripples.

*I am.*

Out of the chaos and the pure melody, I felt something stroke the scars on my cheek. A calm spread from its touch through my body. My mind, as tight as a fist, relaxed. I felt an enduring love surround me, invade me. The images of Mom were a distant echo of this love. There was no reason, no explanation, no excuse. Just love. A love that stretched out a hand to accept death like a spike through the flesh. A hand scarred by love, yet open, accepting all that came.

*I.*

Love.

I struggled to respond to the deluge.

"Surely I spoke of things I did not understand, things too wonderful for me to know," I whispered into the dirt.

*You will doubt again. I already know it. Do not despair.*

"I know it," I gasped. Indeed, I already knew it. I was already wondering if this experience was the last gasping hallucination of a brain destroyed by aneurism.

But my head didn't explode. I didn't die. I got up and dusted my pants and shirt off. I squeegeed the mud from my tongue with my teeth and wiped it off with my hands, wiping my hands on my jeans. I found a faucet behind the church and washed my face. Then I dropped Twain into the backpack, jumped on the bike, and pedaled home.

# CHAPTER THIRTY

The black notebook fell from my lap and startled me into consciousness. Dawn had crept into the room, flushing everything in its peach glow. Dad's desk seemed ancient and fuzzy, the Selectric an angular anachronism squatting on top like an old Buick. It took me a few seconds to realize which decade I was in.

The fading image of the old church and graveyard reminded me there was a funeral to attend. In a few hours I would be back at Mom's grave. A decorative tarp from the funeral home would cover a pile of fresh earth. A canopy would shelter me from the threat of rain as I sat between Heidi and Hannah and gazed into the rectangular hole gouged out of red, raw East Texas clay.

Was Dad disappointed in the choices I had made? He never said so, but I sometimes wondered if he would have preferred me to follow in his footsteps. His was a pilgrimage of perseverance and devotion, of promises made and kept. Mine was less certain—tentative steps on an erratic path conjured piecemeal from the reticent ghosts of the future. Sense could be made of it in retrospect, if at all. Perhaps it was an illusion, but Dad always seemed sure of the next step. But maybe he hadn't seen it mapped out before him with the clarity of prophecy as I supposed. Maybe he wasn't sure of himself, but instead was sure of the one who held the next step.

I was avoiding answering my own question. I gazed through the morning gloom at the bookshelf I found yesterday, hundreds of magazines of various titles, neatly arranged chronologically on the shelves. Any magazine that included my photos, from stock prints in an advertisement or a column to photo-essays in *National Geographic,* all were there. Along with the inevitable index in a black notebook on the top shelf, kept current with the Selectric and penciled notes. That was the best answer I could hope for, probably the only answer I would get. Unless there was another black notebook I hadn't found yet.

I sighed with fatigue, grief, and jetlag and pulled my weary bones from grandmother's chair. I sampled my underarms, pressed my shirt against my nose, and decided a shower was in everyone's best interest. By the time I was dressed, Heidi would be starting breakfast and Hannah would want hot water.

I twisted the water on. The mirror was fogged before I was undressed. I left my clothes in a pile on the floor and stepped into the shower, water as hot as I could stand it. I thought of Dad and the lives he had shaped in his three-score and ten. I thought of Mom and her quiet infusion into the lives of those around her. I thought of M. I smiled sadly as the water streamed over my head.

The shower curtain quivered, sucked out by the opening of the bathroom door. I heard a familiar clinking sound. The curtain was pulled aside, and Lori peered through the steam in a flannel nightgown. She didn't ask why I never made it to bed last night. Instead, she held up the pitcher in her right hand.

"Jolene called this morning. She asked me to give you a message," she said, deadpan.

"No," I said.

"Yep," she said.

The water was very cold. I reached some notes that would have made the castrati of Italy flush with jealousy.

As she closed the shower curtain, I caught the glimpse of a smirk. "Your clothes are on the bed. I'll get the kids up."

I thanked God for His mercies and turned up the hot water. I knew Dad was smiling.

# ACKNOWLEDGMENTS

Thanks first to you, the readers who have stuck with Mark Cloud on his journey to enlightenment. If somehow you missed the earlier legs of the journey, you owe it to yourself to start at the beginning.

Thanks to The Woman for the excellent input and for not complaining once that it took three books to get a dedication; Mark Spyrison for invaluable assistance at all stages of the manuscript, making this book significantly better than it would have been without his input—all readers should be grateful; Merle Bobzien for proofreading; Rob and Robin and the gang at Common Groundz in Hawaii Kai, where this book was written with the aid of high-test coffee and free wireless internet access; Lanny Hall for a few law enforcement pointers; Mike Favazza for a few medical pointers; jazz expert George Spink for information on Chicago jazz clubs in the '70s even if he didn't like Mark's viewpoint of them; Margaret Hoyt, YMCA VP in Chicago, for information on the Victor Lawson YMCA in the '70s; Robert Gontarz for giving me a tour when I dropped in at the Lawson Y with no advance notice one Monday afternoon; Gary Terashita for enduring me through three novels and for a few well-placed suggestions that took it to the next level; Leonard Goss for great advice and assistance; Lisa Parnell for once again making up for my grammatical and typographical deficiencies; Gordon Atkinson for continually pouring himself out at reallivepreacher. com and providing the quote for this book in his inimitable self-effacing style; FredNotes subscribers for picking the right cover; and all the Rudies, wherever you may find yourself, for providing the foundation for many experiences that will never make it into a book—Hug a Rudy today!

All three *Fred* books were fueled by large doses of classic rock played at bone-jarring volumes with moderate infusions of jazz, string quartets, and black gospel. I greatly relied on biblegateway. com, allmusic.com, dictionary.com, google.com, and various Web sites documenting highway systems, bus and subway systems, and other details of urban life in places where I don't live. The Internet is a beautiful thing.

Thanks to all of you who have dropped by the Web site, sent me e-mails (those always make my day), and signed up for FredNotes. Also thanks to Phillip Freeman for being a great friend. And if you are *that* Phillip, then yes, I am *that* Brad and you need to contact me immediately.